SHE'S SECRETLY ROYAL.

The Heir and THE SPARE

HE'S SECRETLY LOYAL.

EMILY
ALBRIGHT

MeritPress

Published by
Merit Press
an imprint of F+W Media, Inc.
10151 Carver Road, Suite 200
Blue Ash, OH 45242. U.S.A.
www.meritpressbooks.com

ISBN 10: 1-4405-9010-9
ISBN 13: 978-1-4405-9010-8
eISBN 10: 1-4405-9011-7
eISBN 13: 978-1-4405-9011-5

Printed in the United States of America.

10 9 8 7 6 5 4 3 2 1

This is a work of fiction. Names, characters, corporations, institutions, organizations, events, or locales in this novel are either the product of the author's imagination or, if real, used fictitiously. The resemblance of any character to actual persons (living or dead) is entirely coincidental.

Many of the designations used by manufacturers and sellers to distinguish their products are claimed as trademarks. Where those designations appear in this book and F+W Media, Inc. was aware of a trademark claim, the designations have been printed with initial capital letters.

Cover design by Stephanie Hannus.
Cover images © stillfx/123RF, bytedust/123RF, Clipart.com.

This book is available at quantity discounts for bulk purchases.
For information, please call 1-800-289-0963.

Dedication

For Madie, who never ceases to amaze me.

Acknowledgments

A gigantic thank you goes to my critique partners. Without them, I can't imagine where I'd be. Victoria Van Tiem, you are a rock star plain and simple. Thank you for your fabulous eye, your kind words, and your brilliant catches. Amy Anhalt, you catch movement inconsistencies like no one else and ask questions that I never thought of, making the story much richer. Kaci, Nicola, Joy, and Shaneen, thank you for all your help in making Evie and Edmund shine. You ladies are truly wonderful.

To my amazing agent, Jessica Watterson, you took a chance on Evie and Edmund and I will always be eternally grateful. I feel truly blessed to have you in my corner. Thank you for being my champion.

Special thanks to my editor, Jacquelyn Mitchard, and all the wonderful people of Merit Press and F+W Media for getting this story out into the world and making it all polished and pretty.

For my parents, I don't think a thank you is quite big enough to cover it. Your unfailing love and support all my life has been invaluable. All I am today is because of you. Not to mention you two financed my serious reading addiction growing up. Love you always.

To my hubby and kidlet, the two loves of my life. You are the reason I even dared to dream I could do this. I can't imagine my life without you. Your love and unceasing belief in me are what motivate me. I love you both to the moon and beyond.

And to you, the readers, I hope you enjoy Evie and Edmund's story. Thank you for picking up my book and giving it a chance. I think each and every one of you is utterly fabulous.

Chapter One

My Brave New World

Hand on the knob, I closed my eyes and held my breath. *I can do this.* With a gentle shove, I opened the door. *Please, be nice.* I cracked an eyelid, peeking. My breath released in a rush as my eyes opened. *It's perfect.*

Look out Oxford! This year's so going to rock.

I tossed my new keycard on the desk and dropped my bags. Twirling, I scanned the room. Next to the minimalist workstation was a twin bed. On the opposite wall, a substantial floor-to-ceiling wardrobe stood. Large windows wrapped around the corner between the two. A black, L-shaped couch filled the space below.

The trunk that had once been my mom's sat by the wall. I'd been so nervous to ship it. *Thank God it made it.*

With a jump, I threw myself on the unmade bed and sighed. *I did it. I'm here.* Exactly where Mom had always dreamed I'd be.

Quest one, complete . . . finally. It had only taken three years.

Where's the second letter? I shot upright and peered around again; nothing.

How the new letters would find me, I hadn't a clue.

Every year on my birthday I'd get a new letter from Mom. It was tradition. Dad would wake me bright and early and hand me an envelope. My hands would tremble with excitement—it was the letter I'd been dying to get hold of since I'd ripped open the last one.

Together we'd read it. Together, we'd remember.

On my seventeenth birthday, things changed.

Oh, Dad still delivered my birthday letter. But a few days later a second one appeared, postmarked from London. In that moment my adventure with Mom began. She was sending me on a quest. One Dad had no clue about.

I'd expected my next quest letter to be here, waiting to welcome me to my new world.

Maybe it'll come in the mail again?

With a disappointed sigh, I dragged a suitcase onto the bed and unzipped it. Grabbing my toiletry bag, I headed for the bathroom. Unlike in the States, everyone here got her own room. There'd be no dealing with a snoring roommate or listening to someone doing the mattress polka.

But, the best part, I'd managed to snag a room with a private loo. That word still made me giggle.

I tossed the bag in the sink and went back to work on my suitcase. My clothes fit in the wardrobe—barely. I fluffed my aqua coverlet over the bed and, exhausted, I nearly crawled in. Instead, I reached for a stack of photos to put up and continued my unpacking.

Above the bed I Sticky Tacked my favorite picture of Dad and me. I was in my cap and gown, Dad in his suit, his arm slung over my shoulder, a proud smile on his face. We each held a light pink peony in memory of Mom—peonies were her favorite flower.

God, I miss her.

Next came a picture of Abby and me. We were fifteen and at a slumber party. Our fingernails freshly painted, red lips perfectly puckered, and two large balloons stuffed down each of our shirts. I laughed, remembering the silliness of the night.

"Oh, Abs, who's gonna make me try new things?" I said to my empty room.

Tears stung my eyes as I looked at the pictures. It'd only been a day, but I already missed home so much it hurt. The pile of pictures dwindled and soon I had a collage of the faces I loved splashed across my wall. Standing back, I smiled at my handiwork then glanced at the shelf above the bed.

What a perfect place for my treasures.

I pulled out the stuffed cat Mom had given me and placed it up there. Its name was Pinky, and for the first seven years of my life I didn't go anywhere without it. Next to Pinky came my books—I loved anything by Jane Austen, L.M. Montgomery, or Louisa May Alcott.

I smiled. My little room was feeling more and more like home.

"Now, a place for my letters."

Pulling them from my bag, I sat on the bed. My hand ran along the top of the pile. The cream ribbon holding the stack together untied with a gentle tug. I always figured Mom chose the heavyweight paper because she knew the letters would have to stand the test of time.

At the top was the first quest letter. I opened it and scanned down the page to the bottom paragraphs.

And so, my darling Evie, I'm setting you off on a life-altering adventure. For years I've kept a secret; one your father doesn't even know about. It's time you know who I was and discover who you really are. I've designed a series of quests for you to complete. You need to understand why I chose the path I did. And to know your options, before you, too, must choose. Bear with me, it'll be worth it in the end, I promise.

Task one: graduate high school and gain acceptance to my alma mater, Oxford. Another letter will find its way to you there.

How will it find me?

I sighed, refolded it, and carefully tied the letters back together before slipping them into my desk drawer.

I went to my trunk and popped it open. On top of the books, shoes, and favorite munchies from home sat a wrapped photo. Inside, I knew I'd find the picture of my parents the day they graduated from Oxford. It was my favorite. They looked so young and happy.

Picking it up, I pulled the edge of its pillowcase wrapper back. I stopped when I saw the corner of a plain white envelope peeking out from behind the frame.

Here it is.

Tearing off the protective layer, I sat the photo on my desk and looked at the letter left in my hands.

What did she have in store for me next? And why was I suddenly so nervous?

"Hi. You must be new," a voice chirped from my open doorway.

I turned, facing a girl with long blond hair who looked like she'd just come from riding at her country estate.

"I'm Suzy Rees," she said and smiled.

"Evangeline Gray." I tossed the letter on the desk and went to shake her hand.

The first thing I noticed was her height. Or lack of. She was tiny. Granted, I considered myself quite tall at five-eight. But she looked like she was barely squeaking in at five feet.

"Evangeline, that's quite a mouthful, isn't it?" Her accent curled around the syllables of my name. "Do you have a nickname?"

"Everyone calls me Evie." I glanced at the snarled ponytail of strawberry curls draped over my shoulder and envied her smooth golden perfection. "Are you on this floor?"

"I am, just a few doors down. Caroline's your neighbor." She pointed to the wall behind the wardrobe. "She's fabulous; you'll love her. She's on a date at the moment, but you'll meet her soon, I'm sure."

"Great." I smiled as she sat on the couch.

Suzy gave me a quick once-over and arched an eyebrow. "You should meet the rest of the gang."

"The gang?"

The corner of her mouth turned up. "My group of friends. There's Caroline." She pointed back toward the wall. "And Marissa, Preston, and Edmund. They're really top drawer. You'll love them."

"I hope I get to meet them."

"You will," she said with a grin. "I should probably go finish unpacking, but I'm absolutely famished. Want to grab a bite to eat?"

"Love to." I grabbed my sweater and followed her. Closing my door, I bit my lip and stole a glance at the unopened letter.

"So, are you a first year?" Suzy asked as we walked down the hall.

I scrunched my nose. "Yes and no. I did a year in Seattle, but Oxford won't let me transfer my credits. So, technically, yes, I'm a first year."

"What made you come all the way to Oxford?"

"My mom. She went here."

"She must be very proud of you."

"Thanks." I smiled. I didn't know her well enough to delve into my tragic little family history. "So, what's your major?"

"Maths."

"Math? Really? I had you pegged for an English major."

She curled her long blond hair around a thin finger and laughed. "I get that a lot. Mathematics has always just come naturally to me, I don't know why."

"You're lucky, it definitely doesn't for me. I wish it did."

We stepped into the dining hall. Shiny wood floors and huge windows looking out onto the campus greeted us. Scattered around the room were long tables filled with students. Above us dark wood chandeliers hung from the ceiling.

Suzy and I grabbed trays and got in line. With a plate of spaghetti, I followed as she wove her way to a table by a window.

"What are you studying?" She glanced up as she popped open a can of Coke.

"Art history."

"Oh, you'll get along great with Edmund then. He's studying history and loves old artifacts and all that crap. Math I get, history, not so much. It's all so boring."

"Really? I love learning about the people who came before us. I find it fascinating." I laughed. "It's a good thing it takes all kinds."

"Too true."

"There you are." A tall girl with beautiful mocha skin and a chic dark bob came up behind Suzy and leaned on the table. "I've been looking for you all over."

"Caroline, what are you doing here? I thought you had a date," Suzy said.

"I did, but he was an absolute arse, so I cut it short."

"Bummer." Suzy looked up and waggled a finger between this new girl and me. "Evie, this is Caroline; she's your neighbor."

I smiled and held out a hand. "Nice to meet you."

She gave me a firm handshake and said, "Lovely to meet you. I'm going to grab some food quick-like and then we can all chat."

Once Caroline was out of earshot, Suzy filled me in. "She finds the majority of the men she dates to be arseholes."

"Why doesn't she date a guy that's not her usual type then?"

"Oh, she has. She's dated nearly every type." Suzy smiled when Caroline returned carrying an enormous salad.

Caroline sat next to me, and entertained us with the story of her date from hell. Girls really are pretty much the same everywhere you go.

I wonder if the boys are, too?

Chapter Two

Circle of Friends

Snuggled under the covers, I tapped the flashlight app icon on my phone, illuminating the darkness. The page slid smoothly from the envelope and my vision blurred at Mom's curly script. Her hands were the last hands to touch this paper. I loved that mine were the next.

My Darling Evie,

An Oxford girl! I knew you could do it. I couldn't be more proud. Now that your first assignment is complete, this next one is easy—sightseeing. I want you to go into London, visit Big Ben and the Houses of Parliament at Westminster Palace. Have fun, take in the ambience, and enjoy your English side.

Before you leave London, I have someone I'd like you to meet: Anton LeClerc. He's expecting your call and should prove quite useful on this journey.

Always remember, anything's possible.

Love you,
Mom
xoxo

Anton's number was scribbled across the bottom. *Who is he and what does he have to do with Mom?* I folded the letter and tucked it away.

How on earth would sightseeing help me discover her and myself? I lay back on my pillow and held the envelope over my head. Staring at the large number two scrawled on the back.

Checking out London? Fine by me; in fact, I was excited to go back and see something other than the airport.

Kissing the envelope, I slipped it under my pillow, not quite ready to part with it. Curled on my side and completely wiped out, I don't remember trying to fall asleep.

With less than a week until school started, I'd spent the day exploring campus. I'd mapped out all my classes and practiced my route. I'm a dork like that.

"Evie, you in there?" Suzy asked as she knocked on my door.

Walking over, I swung it open. "Hey, what's up?"

"There's a party in the commons and everyone's there. You have to come meet the rest of the gang."

"Sure." I slipped on my black ballet flats and grabbed the pale blue cardigan off my desk chair. A quick glimpse in the mirror confirmed I wasn't a total mess. I slid my keycard into my jeans pocket and followed, glad she'd come by. My plan had been to hole up in my room all night, eating pizza and watching *Doctor Who* reruns. Which honestly is a pretty good way to spend an evening.

Downstairs, the common room was packed with people. I kept my eye on the magenta flower of Suzy's headband as it wove through the crowd. Straight ahead people waved at us; Caroline, my new neighbor, was with them. Suzy returned the gesture. *They must be her gang.* I smiled at the idea of Miss-Country-Estate-Suzy having a gang.

Suzy bumped her way through the crowd as a blond-haired boy, sitting with the group on the far end of the couch, snagged my attention. Long denim-clad legs stretched out in front of him. His broad shoulders perfectly filled his gray sweater.

Holy hotness. Boys shouldn't be allowed to be so good-looking.

I dragged my gaze up, and the blond cutie smiled at me. *Shit. He totally just caught me checking him out.* My face warmed as I nervously returned his grin.

"Everyone, this is Evie, the new girl we told you about," Caroline said. Next to her sat an athletic girl sporting a pixie cut. "Evie, this is Marissa." She indicated the impish girl. "That's Preston, and *of course*, Edmund."

"Nice to meet you all." Something in the way she introduced Edmund, Mr. Blond-Hottie, made me think I should know who he was. But I didn't.

Edmund scooted closer to Preston and gestured me to the free spot. Suzy looked like she wished he'd made the spot for her.

"Thanks." I tucked a wayward curl behind my ear and sat.

"Are you liking England?" Edmund asked, his voice deeper than I'd expected.

Nodding, I said, "So far it's been great. Granted, I haven't really seen much of it."

"Well, there's lots of great places we can show you. What do you like to do?" His blue eyes met mine.

"Honestly?" I scrunched my face.

He nodded, looking confused.

"I should warn you first, I'm a bit of a geek."

"Okay." He laughed.

My words spilled out. "Museums. I love to go to museums."

"Museums? Really?" One of his eyebrows arched.

Great, Mr. HottieMcHotDude thinks I'm a giant dork.

I shrugged. "My dad and I go all the time," I started to explain. "My mom was an art conservationist, so maybe it's in my blood. I just like imagining the artists and what they were like, what inspired them. It's lame, I know." My face now an inferno, I turned the subject away from me. "So, what do you do for fun?"

Edmund cocked his head to the side and looked at me. *Really* looked at me. A fluttery heat settled low in my belly. I glanced around the room as a warm wave of nerves crashed over me.

"You enjoy museums? Is that true?" He persisted, not following my redirection.

I scrunched my brow. "Um, why would I lie about that?"

He shook his head. "It's just . . . if that's the case, I don't think I've ever met a girl like you before."

"A girl like me? What does that mean?" I eyed him closely, a glimmer of recognition fizzed through me. *Hmm, maybe I have seen him somewhere.*

"Well, one who's attractive, modern, and well . . . American." He angled himself toward me.

Laughter bubbled up inside my throat. "So because I'm American I shouldn't be interested in history? By that same logic, shouldn't you have bad teeth?"

Wait, did he call me attractive?

"That's not exactly what I meant." He laughed and ran a hand through his mop of wavy hair. "Of course Americans can be interested in history. It's just not what initially comes to mind when I think of a charming American girl such as yourself."

I'm charming now?

"Most people find museums boring. They go because they think they should. I've yet to find someone who *really* enjoys them," Edmund finished.

"He's right, you know. He's been dragging me to them for years and it's painful." Preston turned from his conversation with

Marissa and chimed in, his lip quirking mischievously. "It's like being in a lecture hall on my off days."

Suzy and Caroline nodded emphatically in agreement.

"Secretly, you know you love it, you git." Edmund grinned and elbowed Preston.

"Riiiight, sorry, must've forgotten." Preston rolled his brown eyes.

"I take it you must like museums, too." I eyed Edmund.

"Absolutely, I love going."

He's a geek like me! "Well, if you ever want someone who won't be miserable, I'm your girl. Any museum, any time." *Oh. My. God. Why did I say that?* I fought the urge to bury my face in my hands.

"Deal." He chuckled. "What are you specializing in?" He leaned closer.

Lordy, he smells delicious. "Um, history of art."

"Brilliant, we'll probably have classes together. I'm specializing in history, so I tend to take a lot of the art history courses as well."

"That's great; it'll be nice to see a friendly face in the crowd." I glanced over at Suzy, who was turned around, talking to a guy on the couch next to ours.

"Well, technically I'm a history and economics major, but I really only enjoy the history."

"Then why not just major in history?"

"I would, but economics comes in handy with the family business," he said with a dry laugh.

"What's your family business?"

Edmund's brows drew together and he leaned back to study me.

My heart fluttered nervously in my chest. *Was that a stupid question?*

His face softened and the corner of his mouth curled up. "Well—"

"Edmund! You're looking gorgeous, as always. How was your summer?" A blond girl rushed him.

It looked like she was going to plop onto his lap. Instead, she stopped a few steps short and bent over so they were eye-to-eye. Well, nearly. She positioned herself to give him a direct view down her filmy white tank top. So, really, they were eye-to-boob.

Edmund smiled tensely, his gaze focused on the girl's face. "It was good, Chloe. How was yours?"

"Splendid." She ignored everyone but Edmund as she described her summer. I zoned out, listening to the music thumping in the background.

Suzy sat behind Chloe, imitating her. I stifled my laughter.

Next to me, Edmund squirmed as Chloe placed her hand on his arm. When she reached out to brush hair off his forehead, he moved away, eyebrows raised.

"Hi, I don't think we've been introduced." I smiled and extended my hand. "I'm Evangeline Gray; most people call me Evie." I wanted to give Edmund a breather by claiming her attention.

The blond straightened and gave me a slow head-to-toe once-over. "Oh yay." She sneered, ignoring my hand. "Another little *American*. Chloe Saunders." She scoffed at me before focusing back on Edmund.

Wow, rude much? Clearly Miss BitchyBoobsInYourFace wasn't going to join my fan club any time soon.

"Pleasure to meet you, too." The words rolled in a sarcastic tumble from my tongue.

Chloe turned on me with a glacial stare. "Do you have a problem?"

"No, but I can see you sure do."

Chloe narrowed her eyes. "Americans are all the same. Arrogant, self-entitled trash. *You* are evidently no exception." She looked away.

"Huh, and here I assumed you had the corner on self-entitlement. Then again, I guess it compliments that elitist attitude you've got going on."

"How dare you," she snapped at me.

"You know what?" I stood and checked the time on my phone. "I have zero tolerance for small-minded bigots. I'm going to call it a night. Catch you all later."

I waved and walked off. At the stairs I looked back, wanting one last glimpse of Edmund. My shoulders slumped. Chloe now sat in my vacated spot, blocking my view.

Sure screwed that one up, Gray.

Tonight had turned into a disaster. In my room, I flopped onto the bed and buried my face in a pillow. *Why do I always let my temper get the better of me?* I may have told Chloe off, but I'd also proved her point. I'd be a social pariah now. She looked the type to exact revenge.

This meant I'd probably have to make friends from scratch. *Damn my big mouth.*

I inhaled a shaky breath. I needed Mom. My hand slid under the pillow, searching for my new letter. A knock on my door brought me up short.

When I opened it, Suzy rushed me, nearly bowling me over with a hug.

"Oh my God, Evie, that was brilliant. You have no idea how many times I've wanted to tell her off, and you just went and did it." She grasped my shoulders and looked heavenward, beaming. "That was perfection."

I laughed. "Um . . . glad you enjoyed it, I guess." *They don't hate me?*

One by one the rest of the group filed into my room. Perhaps I hadn't screwed anything up after all. My shoulders relaxed as I sat on my bed.

"You should've seen her." Caroline mimicked Chloe's disdainful look. "See, typical American."

"Did you see her face when we all got up and left?" Marissa asked, eliciting laughter from Caroline and Suzy.

Edmund came and sat next to me, which secretly thrilled me. I'd met the guy a minute ago, and here I was, completely crushing on him. This was so not like me.

"So, who are all the pictures of?" Edmund asked as he leaned back on my pillow to get a better view. Mom's letter crunched and crumpled beneath him.

"Um, that's my dad and my best friend, Abby." I pointed to a few pictures of us at graduation. "These are my girlfriends back home and that's Grant."

Edmund studied Grant's picture. "I'm guessing he's not your brother."

"No, he's my boyfriend back home." I shook my head. "Sorry, ex-boyfriend. We broke up just before I left. We're still friends, though."

Marissa leaned in to get a better look. "That's one good-looking guy. Why'd you break up?"

"I didn't want to do the long-distance thing. If he's the one, he'll still be the one after I graduate."

"Oh, he *is* rather dashing, isn't he?" Caroline leaned between us to check out the photo. "For your sake I hope he's the one."

I smiled. "We'll see what happens. Three years is a long time."

A phone rang and Edmund leaned back, sliding his cell from his pocket. "It's Jax. I'll be right back."

"Who's Jax?" I asked once he was out the door.

"His social-climbing wannabe girlfriend, Lady Jacqueline," Suzy said.

Marissa groaned. "Is she still sniffing around? I thought she'd finally backed off."

"Nope, still hoping to snag him," Suzy said. No one looked happy at the news. "You know how badly their families want them together."

"Why don't you guys like her?" Sighs and eye rolls met my question.

Caroline tucked her feet up underneath her on the couch. "It's not that we don't like her per se—"

"She's mean, bitchy, stuck-up, and treats everyone like shit, even Edmund." Preston spat the words out. "Caroline might be too nice to admit it, but I'm not. He's my best mate and I hate that he'll probably end up married to her. She's a really horrible, vile person."

Married to her?

"Hmm, maybe if I'm really lucky, I'll get to meet her," I said wryly.

Caroline studied her manicured nails. "I wouldn't count on it. She's not up here much. She has Edmund go into London."

"Is she a student?" I asked.

"She graduated from London College of Fashion a year ago. She's been working for some hoity-toity fashion label—can't remember which one. She thinks she's the cat's meow. It's revolting, actually." Suzy scowled.

Edmund returned to my side on the bed. Everyone stared at him, waiting.

Caroline finally spoke. "So, Jax, was it? We thought she'd gotten a clue. What happened?"

He ran a hand over his face, looking worn out. "It's a long, boring story, but she's still very much around. She'll actually be up here next Monday with a friend and wants to get dinner with us."

"Us? She can't stand us." Preston scrutinized him.

"She wants to set up one of her single friends with Preston—"

"Oh, hell, no!" Preston stood, his mouth in a tight line.

Edmund gestured toward him. "And *that's* why I want you all to come."

No one spoke.

"Look, it's not my ideal evening, either, but you know what her friends are like. I need an idiocy buffer. Please say yes." Edmund looked around the room, stopping on me with a crooked grin.

I returned his smile. *He's so going to be a problem.*

"Fine," Preston groaned. "But you're paying."

"Deal." Edmund clapped his hands and pointed at Preston.

As the gang groaned about having to go, I watched Edmund. Maybe I should ask him to come into London with me when I do Mom's next task, Big Ben and Parliament. I closed my eyes and shook my head. I probably *shouldn't* ask him. This Jax chick certainly wouldn't appreciate it.

We'd be going just as friends, I rationalized. *It's not like he's interested in me.* Plus it sounds like he practically has a girlfriend. I kicked off my shoes and tucked my feet underneath me. *I'm totally asking him.*

Chapter Three

New Discoveries

I tapped a nervous beat on the table as I ate my breakfast. Today was the start of term. When I stepped into my first class, I'd officially be an Oxford girl. My bag sat beside me, filled with new pens and notebooks. Mom's letters were tucked inside the front flap. I wanted her close today.

The early morning light streamed through the windows into the nearly empty dining hall. The quiet was nice. I jumped as my phone buzzed on the wooden tabletop.

Dad.

"Shouldn't you be in bed?" I answered. It was well after one in the morning, Seattle time.

"Well, I wasn't about to let you start school without wishing you luck." He laughed. "Now that I have, I'm going to crawl into bed. I love you, Peaches."

We chatted only for a minute more, but it was enough to give me a shot of courage to get through the day.

I nibbled on my chocolate croissant, trying not to drip any on my hunter green summer dress. Students slowly filtered in, fueling up for the day. Pulling my book from my bag, I opened it to the first chapter. Losing myself in a book always helped calm my nerves.

"*Anne of Green Gables*? My grandmother liked that book. She read it to us as children."

I jumped. It was Edmund. His deep voice alone was enough to get the butterflies stirred up in my stomach. "Did she really?"

He sat on my left and leaned close, reading over my shoulder. "Yeah, Gram always read to my brother and me. She loved Anne Shirley. Well, she just loved to read, really."

I took a sip of my tea and laid the book down, turning to face him. *Does he ever not look good?*

"Sounds like she was a wonderful woman."

"She was." The corners of his lips curled into a wistful smile.

This boy, and his crooked grin, had spent far too much time in the forefront of my thoughts. I was glad he was here. It gave me a chance to see if he really was as awesome as my brain kept telling me he was. So far, he was.

"Morning." A chipper Suzy sat across from me.

"Morning, Suze," Edmund said as I waved.

She tossed her hair over her shoulder. "So, Evie, you ready for this?"

I nodded. "I suppose so. Can't be all that different from back home."

"You'll do great," Edmund said, his voice low and soft. "What's your first class?"

With him so near, I suddenly couldn't remember. I pulled my schedule from my pocket and smoothed it on the tabletop. "Um, European Art with Professor Sawyer."

Suzy looked at Edmund. "You like Professor Sawyer, don't you?"

"I do; he's quite entertaining. That's why I'm taking the class as well." He raised his cup of tea to his mouth.

I get to spend the morning with him? My pulse quickened. This day was off to a fantabulous start.

"Morning, everyone." Caroline sat beside Suzy, eating an apple. "So, Edmund, where are the bodyguards?"

I glanced at her. Bodyguards? *What is she talking about?*

"Oh, they're around here somewhere." Edmund did a brief survey of the room.

Were they talking about Preston and some other friends? Brit slang was so different from American. I mean, if plaster meant Band-Aid, maybe bodyguards was the equivalent of buds.

Edmund checked the time and turned to me. "We should get going."

I nodded, finished my croissant, and looped my bag across my body.

"You heading our way, Suze? Caroline?" Edmund asked.

Caroline shook her head as she took another bite.

"Nope. Opposite direction, actually," Suzy answered, looking disappointed.

"See you later then." I waved, my thin leather sandals clapping against the wooden flooring.

"Later," Edmund called as we walked away, his warm hand settling into the small of my back.

My breath caught in my throat. The butterflies in my stomach were now fully awake and flapping all over the place. I knew his touch was innocent, just guiding me to the doors. But it was still sexy as hell.

A crowd of students passed, headed in for breakfast. His hand fell away. *No . . . put it back.*

"We've got a bit of a walk." He slipped his sunglasses on. The warm autumn sun filtered through the colored leaves above us.

"Yeah, but it's a gorgeous day. Doesn't it feel perfect? Like it was made for new beginnings." *Ugh, how cheesy.* I rolled my eyes at myself.

"How poetic." He chuckled. "So, do you have any brothers or sisters?"

"Nope, I'm an only."

He watched me as we walked. "That must've been lonely."

I shook my head. "Why does everyone always think that? I always had friends around and pets. It was far from lonely. I found plenty of ways to get in trouble and keep my dad busy." I laughed.

"Did you like being an only?"

"Loved it. What about you? How many brothers and sisters do you have?"

He looked perplexed. "Um, just one, an older brother."

Silence enveloped us. I had the sinking suspicion I'd said something wrong. *What is he thinking?*

Edmund abruptly stopped walking and turned to face me. "Do you really not recognize me?"

"Oh God, should I?"

Shit! I knew he looked familiar. Why the hell hadn't Suzy or Caroline said something? I was going to feel like such an idiot when he clued me in.

"No, not necessarily, I suppose," he answered slowly. "It's just . . . I'm not used to people *not* knowing who I am."

He started walking and I stood there, confused, trying to sort out who the hell he was. With a little jog, I swerved around a bicyclist and caught up to him. "That first night I met you I thought you looked familiar. I just couldn't put my finger on why."

"Really?" A hint of a smile played on his lips.

I waited for him to enlighten me, but he didn't. "So?"

"So what?" he asked, a playful glint in his eye.

"Care to tell me *why* I should recognize you?"

"Not really, no." He laughed. I liked the sound of it.

"No, no, no, you brought this up. You have to tell me." My eyes widened.

With an adorable grin he shook his head. "No, I don't."

"Mean! And *yes*, you do, or else I'm going to walk around looking like a moron," I said, laughter burbling up in my throat at the game he was playing.

He bumped his shoulder against mine. "You won't walk around looking like a moron. Quite the contrary, you look very smart."

"You're really not going to tell me?" I asked, stunned.

He turned to me. "Nope. This is a momentous occasion for me. I'm going to enjoy it. Plus, I have no doubt you'll quickly figure it out. No doubt whatsoever."

"You really suck." I smacked his arm playfully, making him laugh. "You have no idea all the names I'm calling you in my head right now."

"Oh, I can imagine. Trust me, you'll figure it out. I wouldn't be surprised if you had it figured out by dinner."

"Are you an actor?"

"Nope."

"Athlete?"

"Sorry, no." He grinned down at me and chuckled.

"Oh this is going to drive me insane." I flipped around and walked backwards so I could get a better look. I studied him: shaggy blond hair, blue eyes, strong jaw, and broad shoulders. The sleeves of his white button-down were rolled up, hinting at the musculature underneath. He gave me a big cheesy grin. Nope, nothing was coming to me. I bit my lip in frustration.

He's lucky he's so cute.

Down the path behind us were two guys, keeping their distance but their eyes stayed on us. They looked like regular students, but something was off. They didn't look . . . *right.*

"Careful," Edmund said and pulled me against him. "You were about to bang into that pole just there."

Once I remembered to breathe, I glanced behind me and saw the lamppost Edmund had rescued me from. "Thanks."

With an embarrassed sigh, I spun around and fell into step beside him.

"And here we are." He pointed at a large, weathered gray stone building on the left.

Inside the lecture hall were rows of seats with retractable flip-top desks. Edmund gestured to a pair of seats near the front of the classroom. We sat just as Professor Sawyer dimmed the lights.

"I still can't believe you won't tell me," I murmured, pulling out a notebook.

"Let me enjoy it while it lasts," he whispered.

"Good morning, students, and welcome to History of European Art." Sawyer took off his wire-rimmed spectacles and polished them against his tie.

The professor launched into lecture mode and I scribbled down notes. With Edmund so close, it was a struggle to concentrate. I had to fight the urge to just sit and stare.

When I rested my arm on the armrest, Edmund brushed against it, startling me. A tingle of energy raced through me at his touch. He looked over and cracked one of his adorable grins.

Oh my stars, I'm in trouble.

I leaned back and crossed my legs away from him. My mounting attraction to him was a problem. With this Jax chick lurking in the background it was bound to be a recipe for disaster. Getting my heart trampled was not something on my Oxford agenda.

When the lecture wrapped up I stood, stretched, and glanced at Edmund, who gave me a strained smile. I watched him roll his shoulders and tilt his head from side to side.

On the walk back neither of us said much. I was glad the tall maple trees offered us shade. I slipped my navy sweater off and slung it over my messenger bag.

It was killing me not knowing who he was. I couldn't take it anymore. "Singer?"

"What?" He looked at me, brows lowered.

"Are you a singer?"

He burst into laughter. "No. I absolutely cannot carry a tune."

"Any type of musician then?"

"No, good try though."

"Oh come on, won't you just tell me? I'm a Type A personality. I'm not going to be able to stop thinking about this until I figure it out."

"Ah," he said, his eyes lighting up. "So, you admit you'll be thinking about me nonstop then, will you?" He leaned close, his eyes on the same level as mine, and gave me an irresistible grin.

A flash of heat settled in my cheeks. "Oh yes, I freely admit it. Except I'll also be cursing you the whole time." I smirked and pushed against his shoulders, making him take a step back.

"I'm sure you will." He laughed, brushing up against me, hands in his pockets.

No matter how much I wanted to deny it, the more time I spent with Edmund, the more I liked him. *Really* liked him.

"Model?"

"Do you think I'm good-looking enough to be a model?"

"You're not too terribly bad on the eyes," I flirted back. "Is that it then? Am I right?"

"Despite my dashing looks—" He playfully posed. "I'm not a model."

"Rats. I'll get it, just you wait." Normally this sort of game would irritate the shit out of me, but with Edmund it was fun and flirty. I was enjoying myself.

"I never doubted you," he said and walked me to my next class.

Pulling out my phone, I snapped a picture of myself frowning in front of a Starbucks sign. It made me think of Dad. We were the Gray in *Gray's Coffee* back in Seattle. With a chuckle, I sent it to Dad as a text: *I think you have a franchise opportunity here.*

"What are you doing?" Edmund watched me curiously as we walked back from our last class, which we ended up having together.

"Just sending a picture to my dad."

"Of the Starbucks logo?" He looked puzzled.

"No, well, yes. I was just telling him about a business opportunity." I put my phone away.

He shook his head. "That makes no sense, but okay."

"We own a coffee chain in Seattle. Starbucks is our main competitor." I gestured to the circular logo on the wall. "You could really use a Gray's Coffee here."

"Ah, now I see." He nodded.

Walking on, Edmund told me about his classical history course. His baritone voice was borderline hypnotic. If he wanted to talk all day, I wouldn't complain.

We neared the residence hall, and needing my key, I reached in my bag to dig for it. My fingers brushed against the packet of Mom's letters. They reminded me of my next task.

This is the perfect time. I should ask him now. My nerves sparked rapid-fire and an uneasiness encompassed me. I wasn't sure I could do this. My palms were sweaty and my head light.

"Um, I-I'm not sure what your plans are this weekend . . ." My hands motioned as I spoke. "But I was thinking of heading into London . . . do some touristy things, Big Ben, Parliament, and the like."

"That sounds like fun." He tucked his hands into the pockets of his jeans.

I cleared my throat. "Would you be interested in coming with me? I really don't want to go alone."

My heart stopped beating as Edmund stared at me. *Shit. What do I say if he says no?* I should've thought this through more.

Then he nodded. "While we're there we can catch a museum, too."

"Perfect. Maybe by then I'll have figured out who you are." My heart was doing somersaults and my cheeks were hurting from trying not to smile too big.

We stopped outside the dorms and he kicked at a loose pebble on the sidewalk. "Well, I'll see you later. I've got to round everyone up for this do tonight."

"Right, have fun. Later." I smiled and scampered up to my room.

Hot damn! He said yes. I threw myself on the bed and buried my squeals in my pillow. When I couldn't hold my breath any longer I flipped over and stared at the ceiling, grinning like a fool. *I love Oxford.*

With a dreamy sigh I went to my desk. My to-do pile was already overwhelming. At least there'll be study sessions with Edmund. Well, I sure hope there will be. My mind drifted. Us, alone, in a quiet room. *I wonder what his lips feel like?* I closed my eyes, imagining. Soft, full, and warm . . . mmm. I giggled and stood, abandoning my desk.

Remote in hand, I climbed onto the bed and flicked the TV on. I clearly needed to unwind before I could concentrate on homework. Mindlessly, I zipped through the channels.

Wait, was that Edmund?

I stopped and backtracked. Edmund's face flashed across the screen.

The female news anchor was mid-story. ". . . continuing his studies as classes resumed today . . ."

One after another, pictures of Edmund streamed over the TV. A photo of him from behind, walking with a girl popped up.

Is that . . . "No way!" *That's me.*

Chapter Four

The Dating Game

"Why aren't you ready?" Edmund stood in my now-open doorway in a dark suit, giving me a once over.

It was after seven and I had no intention of going out. The homework spread across my bed had been my evening activity. I definitely hadn't planned on seeing *him* tonight.

I knew exactly who he was.

He was the spare heir to the British throne.

That little shit. I wasn't sure how to behave. My discovery shouldn't change things, but it did. Honestly, I didn't know what to think. Staring at him, I wished I'd phoned Abby earlier. I could use some advice.

But it was too late for that. Here he was, *Prince* Edmund Stuart, standing in front of me. Staring.

"Evie?"

I shook my head. "Sorry, what did you say?"

"You should be ready to go."

My eyebrows lowered in confusion. "Where am I going?"

"To dinner with us, of course."

"Oh." I stepped back. *Dinner with royalty? Me?* "I didn't realize I was invited."

Edmund entered my room and leaned down, leveling our faces. "Of course you're invited. You're part of the group now."

He was so close. I inhaled deeply. *Mmm, clean soap and sunshine.* My knees wobbled, as if they'd been replaced with JELL-O. "Oh."

That's right, Evie. Keep it eloquent.

Edmund's eyes softened. "You, um . . ." He reached out, brushing a long curl over my shoulder. "There's a fuzzy in your hair."

Warm fingers lightly grazed my neck, making me dizzy. I leaned against the wall, trying to stay standing. *Breathe. Need to breathe.*

He pulled his hand back, cleared his throat, and looked away. "Everyone's downstairs. Um, how much time do you think you'll need to get ready?" He stepped away, putting some space between us.

"Ten or fifteen minutes, I suppose."

"Great, see you in a bit." He raked a hand through his hair and excused himself.

With a squeal of delight, I sprinted to my wardrobe and pulled out my little black dress. Edmund looked incredible in his suit, so dressing up was essential.

I slipped into my dress and spun around, struggling to reach the zipper. Once on, it fell snugly below my knees.

At the mirror, I powdered my shiny spots, perked up my eye shadow to enhance the green of my eyes, and slapped on some lip gloss. I only had time to run a brush through my hair and tie it in a low, messy bun.

Brimming with excitement, I beamed at myself. Then I remembered: Jax, the girl everyone hated. The girl who wanted Edmund for herself. The girl with his parents' stamp of approval. *If they want them together there has to be something special about her.* Self-consciousness seeped into the crevices my excitement had just dribbled out of.

I stuck my tongue out at my reflection. "He's totally off-limits and way out of your league." The news anchor only confirmed it. I turned away, stepped into my nude heels, and grabbed my silver clutch. Time to join the gang.

Pushing the stairwell door open, I immediately saw Edmund. He stood by the front exit, the light of the sunset streaming in behind him.

"Evie, you look smashing. How did you get ready so quick?" Suzy left the group by the double doors and joined me.

I tore my gaze from Edmund and shrugged. "I just threw on whatever."

"Well, you look great."

"Thanks, so do you," I said. She wore a short crimson dress and, aside from her scowl, she looked gorgeous.

"Can we go already? I just want to get this night over with," Caroline huffed as she walked outside with Marissa following.

"Let's go." Suzy went to the doors, staring at Edmund on her way out. I wasn't certain, but I suspected she had a thing for him, too. Nothing but trouble can come when two girls like the same guy.

Still standing by the stairs, I glanced at Edmund. He abruptly averted his eyes from me and said something to Preston.

Nodding, Preston blew out a resigned breath and jogged to catch up to the girls. "Tally ho."

Edmund walked toward me, a small smile playing on his lips. "Evie, you look beautiful."

"Thank you." Warmth spread up my neck and settled into my cheeks. "You look very handsome, yourself."

"Shall we?" He gestured toward the door.

Outside, a sleek black Town Car was parked at the curb. A chauffeur stood holding the door. *Holy cow.* This was so out of my realm of experience. The last time I'd ridden in a chauffeured car I was ten and I'd been forced into an ugly orange flower girl dress for my uncle's wedding. I still hated those pictures. Orange on a redhead, so not okay.

I stopped walking, glancing at him. *This is his normal.* Our worlds couldn't be further apart. *How the hell did I get here?*

"You okay?" He paused beside me.

"Yeah, sorry." I shook my head and went to the car.

Offering his hand, Edmund helped me in, then sat beside me.
"No, Christopher Eccleston was the best Doctor." Preston
shook his head at Suzy.

She stood her ground. "Matt Smith is."

I sat back and watched them go back and forth before I
intervened. "You're both wrong. David Tennant was the best,
hands down."

Preston's eyes lit up when he looked at me. "You're a *Doctor Who* fan?"

I nodded with a grin.

"Trust me, don't get him started. You'll never get him to stop."
Edmund rolled his eyes and looked out the window. The car left
the dorm behind and merged onto the city streets.

Making a face at Edmund, Preston gave me a thumbs-up and
went back to his squabble with Suzy.

I noticed Marissa and Caroline deep in conversation. I couldn't
make out what they were talking about, but Marissa's hand rested
on Caroline's knee; she didn't seem to mind.

Edmund remained silent, staring out his window. I leaned so I
could see his reflection in the glass; he didn't look happy. His eyes
snapped up and met mine.

"You seem deep in thought," I said as I leaned back.

"Not that deep." Edmund turned, a hint of a smile on his lips.
"I was just thinking how much I'm going to owe Preston."

"Because he's stuck with Jax's friend?" I glanced at Preston,
who winked at me.

Edmund nodded. "He's never met Kelsey. He has no clue what
he's in for."

"What's so horrible about her?"

"It's not one thing, really. Jax and her friends are . . . difficult.
They all have ti—" He stopped and looked at me. With a smile,
he shook his head. "Let's just say they consider themselves better
than everyone else."

"So they're *titled*, then? Like you, *Prince* Edmund." I don't know how I didn't recognize him. I'd seen him and his brother on magazine covers all my life. He must think I'm an idiot.

His eyes widened and he laughed. "You figured it out. I knew you would."

"With the help of the evening news anchor." Pictures of us as we'd walked around campus had peppered the screen. "Only my second week in England and I've already wound up on the news."

The gravelly voiced anchor had questioned who I was and planted the seed that I was possibly the prince's new love interest. *Don't I wish.*

Edmund looked sheepish. "I should probably tell you, those around me tend to spend some time in the press."

"Yeah, kinda figured that out." I chuckled.

"I'm sorry. I should've warned you." The light in his eyes faded and he yanked at his tie with a finger.

"Don't worry about it."

With a sigh, he turned to the window again.

"Why do you hang out with them?" I asked, hoping to pull him back to our original conversation.

"Who?" he asked as he angled himself to me again.

"Jax and her friends."

Edmund studied the palm of his hand. "You could say we're forced together because of our families. I'm obligated to maintain a friendly . . . relationship with them."

He buttoned his top two coat buttons as the car slowed. Falling silent, he wouldn't meet my eyes.

I placed my hand on his arm, wanting to connect with him. He looked where my hand rested.

Softly, so I wouldn't be overheard, I asked, "Obligation isn't the only reason you're her friend, right?"

Edmund's eyes blazed into mine. Leaning near my ear, he softly said, "Unfortunately, it is."

Before I could respond, the car came to a stop and the door flew open. Flashbulbs popped and the paparazzi lining the entrance shouted at us. Edmund's bodyguards led the way. He followed past the photogs, not stopping for pictures.

Spots blurred my vision as I followed the group toward a fancy restaurant. Every part of me wanted to shrink away from the blinding flashbulbs. I focused ahead on the shimmering crystal chandeliers visible through the large glass panel doors.

"Just lovely; Jax must've tipped them off. Daft cow, loves to see her face in the rag mags," Suzy whispered near the entrance.

The doors closed behind us, shutting out the shouts of the press. A pianist played a soft, slow tune to our left. It was pretty, but mournful, a strange choice for a restaurant.

Still seeing spots, I stopped with the group as the maître d' approached us. He bowed and fawned over Edmund.

I can't imagine people treating me like that. Just watching it felt weird. Then again, growing up with it, he must be used to it.

"Is the rest of our party here?" Edmund asked.

"Right this way, Your Highness." He led us to a table tucked in an alcove of floor-to-ceiling windows. It was a giant fishbowl. Outside, people surrounded the windows, snapping pictures.

I so don't belong here.

"Edmund, darling." A tall, lithe woman stood and walked around the table.

Is that Jax?

She had long, thin, blond hair and very white teeth. I never trusted people with overly bleached teeth. Everything about her exuded artificiality, from the warm greeting she gave Edmund to the color of her hair. She reminded me of a robot—just going through the motions.

"Everyone made it. *Fabulous.*" She smiled, but it looked far from sincere. Her eyes scanned our faces and paused when they fell on me, her mouth a thin line.

Oh boy, she already doesn't like me.

She came forward and extended a bony hand to me. "I don't think we've met. I'm *Lady* Jacqueline."

It's the title. Something in the way she said "lady" made things click together in my brain. *That's why they want them together.*

"Evangeline Gray." I took her cold, limp hand and attempted to shake it.

"Pleasure." She raised a perfectly plucked brow and gave me a thorough head-to-toe appraisal. "Shall we sit? We may need more chairs. I didn't expect you'd all want to come." Her laughter sounded hollow.

Edmund and Jax flanked Preston and Kelsey, who sat across from me. This Kelsey chick never smiled. Okay, that's not entirely true. She smiled at Edmund and Jax. The rest of us weren't on her radar.

Preston looked uncomfortable. He sat stiffly, his jaw set. Kelsey pursed her lips and scrutinized him. Raising her eyebrows, she gave Jax a look I interpreted to say: *Really? This is the best you can bring me?*

Caroline and Marissa separated Edmund and me. The few times I caught his eye he smiled, causing a churning sensation to spark inside me. I was grateful no one could read my thoughts or knew what I was feeling. Particularly his watchdog wannabe princess, whose eyes were on me nonstop. It seriously creeped me out.

The tension at the table was palpable. Even the staff seemed to feel it. Our waiter looked rattled. A thin sheen of sweat was noticeable on his upper lip, poor guy.

"I don't drink tap water." Jax scowled, pushing away the water glass our waiter had placed in front of her.

"It's Evian, ma'am," the waiter, whom I pegged around our age, answered.

"Take it away. *Now*," she ordered.

With a nod he picked up the glass and excused himself to check on our order.

"What a little prat," Jax huffed under her breath. But she was smiling, always smiling. She had to; there were cameras watching.

During dinner Preston kept looking at Caroline and me. Several times he mouthed, *save me*. Thank goodness his back was to the windows. His date spent the evening ignoring him. After the initial hello, they didn't speak at all.

Before the dessert course I excused myself to find the ladies' room. I giggled when I walked in. There were mini crystal chandeliers in the loo. *What am I doing here? This isn't me.* Shaking my head, I went into a stall.

When I finished, I opened my door and found myself staring at Jax's reflection. She was reapplying her lipstick but her eyes were fixed on me. She watched as I washed my hands, her face expressionless.

"So are you liking England? Making friends?" The lid of her lipstick went on with a snap.

"I am." I met her glaring eyes in the mirror as I rinsed off the soap bubbles.

"That's just great." She looked at me like I was a threat she needed to neutralize.

Am I a threat?

"Listen, Evangeline, before you get any ideas, here's some advice." She spun to face me, leaned over, and placed a hand on my arm. Her eyes narrowed to slits. "Stay away from Edmund. Is that clear? He's mine. *Mine*. And his family would *never* approve of you." Her fingernails dug into my arm.

"Are you serious?" *Is she really threatening me?* This felt like a scene from a bad '80s movie. I chuckled, which only infuriated her more.

"Just keep your hands off. Got it?" She punctuated every word by poking a finger into my shoulder.

Bitch.

"No. Get *your* hands off. Got it?" I wrenched my arm from her grasp. Grabbing a fluffy towel, I dried my hands, then shoved it at her. "Don't ever touch me again." With that, I left the bathroom.

I had no intention of staying away from Edmund. *If that's what she wants, she'll have to threaten him.*

I stopped before rounding the corner to our little display tank. Taking a deep breath, I attempted to compose myself. Jax had me frazzled.

Suzy gave me a questioning look as I sat beside her. Shaking my head, I mouthed *later.* She nodded, but I knew she was dying to hear what had just gone down.

The rest of the evening, any glance I gave Jax was met with a look that said, *I'd bitch slap you if Edmund weren't around.* Caroline and Suzy kept glancing back and forth from Jax to me. No doubt they were picking up on the hatred being sent my way, too.

I struggled to not look at Edmund. And I actually did pretty well, for a few minutes anyway. When I broke down and peeked in his direction he was already watching me. Having caught my eye, his eyebrows pulled down and I thought he might be trying to see if I was okay.

Unsure how to respond, I turned to Caroline. Avoidance was my only option.

A ripple of relief went around the table as dinner ended. Preston looked like he'd just gotten a reprieve from the electric chair. Edmund blew out a breath and tossed down a credit card. I didn't want to think what this miserable evening had cost.

On the way out, Jax pushed ahead of me so she could exit first. Just outside the doors she spun and said, "I'm so glad we had our talk. I do hope we're on the same page."

"Same page?" I laughed. "How can we be? We're in two different books."

The photographers still snapped away. I followed her cue and kept my face friendly.

Jax whipped around and huffed to Edmund's side. Leaning up on her tiptoes, she kissed him passionately on the mouth.

Edmund's eyes went wide as he grasped her shoulders. Before he could push her away, she pulled back, a satisfied smirk on her lips.

Marking your territory?

With a pointed look at me, she hopped into her little red sports car and tore away from the curb. The Wicked Witch's theme song played inside my head.

"I think she likes me," I said to Suzy and Marissa; both burst into laughter.

"What's so funny?" Edmund asked, wiping his sleeve across his lips and coming to stand by Preston.

I half-smiled. "Just girl stuff."

Jax was going to be livid when she found out Edmund and I were going to London together next weekend. *Good.*

Chapter Five

Family Heirlooms

"That's a big clock." I craned my head back, trying to take it all in.

Edmund laughed. "Yup, it sure is. It should chime in a few minutes," he said glancing at his watch.

I'm actually standing in front of Big Ben. How awesome is this? The scene from Peter Pan, where the kids soar through the night sky in front of it, flickered in my memory. Mom couldn't have sent me to a better place for my second quest. Well, having Edmund tagging along made it infinitely more amazing.

I pulled out my phone and snapped some pictures. A shot of Edmund looking up at the tower may have been added to my favorites file.

"I can actually see a bit of this from my room at the palace."

Laughter burst from my lips. "Must be rough." I leaned and nudged his shoulder. How strange, to think I had a friend who lived in a palace.

Edmund surveyed the surrounding area. We'd managed to make a run for it and lost the paparazzi on the Underground. He warned me they'd find us again.

His bodyguards were nearby. I turned my head and saw them, standing and watching . . . always watching. Here in the city, they didn't attempt to blend in.

I jumped as Big Ben sounded the hour.

"Told you." Edmund looked down at me.

A breeze ruffled his wavy hair. I was tempted to reach up and smooth it off his forehead. Instead, I met his eyes with a grin. "Awesome."

"I've got a bit of trivia you might not know." Edmund leaned against the railing with his back to the massive tower.

"Lay it on me." I looked into his face, loving that he knew these little tidbits.

He smiled, pointed up at the clock, and said, "This isn't Big Ben."

"It's not?" I looked up at the clock, skeptical. "Sure looks like all the photos I've ever seen of it."

"It's actually Elizabeth Tower."

I stared up, confused. "Then why is it called Big Ben?"

"Because Big Ben is the name of the largest bell of the five up there."

"Huh, that's pretty cool." The corners of my lips curled up. "Do they all have names?"

"No, it's just four quarter bells and Big Ben. I don't know how the nickname started or why it stuck, but it did."

I glanced up, smiling. "Well, I like it. Who knows, maybe it wouldn't be as famous if it didn't have the nickname."

"Big Ben does have a nice ring to it."

I rolled my eyes. "Good one."

He chuckled. "You ready to go check out the Houses of Parliament?"

"Let's go." I nodded as he pushed himself off the fence.

Around the corner and into Westminster Palace we went. Inside the large hall, I stopped to take it in. Stone walls, vaulted ceilings, marble floors, and statues everywhere. With the addition of paintings, this trend repeated in most of the rooms we visited.

"Beautiful, isn't it?" Edmund's voice echoed as he stood beside me and looked up to the coffered ceiling.

"Very."

We spent the morning wandering around, admiring the art and architecture. I jumped when Edmund grabbed my hand. "Let's go to the archives."

I looked down at our fingers threaded together as he guided me down a long hallway. *He's holding my hand.* It was warm and strong. I liked the way it felt in mine.

He released my hand at the door. I kept a smile plastered on my face so he wouldn't see my disappointment.

Victoria Tower was opposite the building from Big Ben. Inside was a room dedicated to all the bills and acts Parliament had passed. There were displays with lists of current titled aristocrats and their predecessors. Large signs detailed the historical facts of the building and England.

I walked around the room one way, Edmund the other. We met up at the list of nobles. I stood next to him. He was so close our shoulders touched. The warmth from his body seeped into mine. It felt wonderful. I looked through the list, lingering to stay near him.

Don't move away. Stay.

"Lawrence Prescott, that's Lauren's family." Edmund turned his head to look at me as he pointed.

"Lauren?"

"My sister-in-law, Philip's wife."

"Gotcha, that Lauren." My cheeks warmed. I turned back to the list. "Do you know most of these people?"

"A good deal of them, yes. Let's see." He used a finger to scan through the names. "The Chamberlains are good friends of my parents. And here's Jax's family, the Prices."

I continued scanning as he pointed out names. My eyes paused at Maxwell Elliot. Wasn't Elliot Mom's maiden name? *Or was it Elliott? I think it was double Ts.* Oh look, there's a Gray. And a Fitzgerald. I snapped a picture and sent it to Abby.

"The Bunburys are related to Preston." Edmund pointed at another name.

"Is Preston's family titled?"

"No, but they have a lot of money. *New* money."

Turning toward him, I asked, "As opposed to?"

"Old money," he said, chuckling.

I wasn't seeing why it mattered. "I take it there's some distinction between the two I should know."

"There's nothing worse to the Old Money set than New Money coming in; well . . . unless it's their own." He sniffed. "The Old come from generation after generation of family members passing down their familial legacy. They don't like to see the New waltz in. They think they're after their titles and land."

"Are they?"

"Occasionally, I suppose, but it's not common these days."

"So then why would Jax have wanted to set her friend up with Preston?"

He blew out a breath. "With her it could be just about anything. It's probably just an excuse to get together, or she's thinking she'll get closer to me if our best mates started dating. I've never understood her."

A door behind us slammed shut. Edmund and I both turned. A greasy-haired man leered and started snapping pictures.

Edmund gave me a look and I knew we were done. I followed as he walked outside and hailed a cab.

"Just drive," Edmund ordered through the window after we jumped in. The cab driver did a double take, then put the gas pedal to good use.

"What about your guards?" I asked, looking behind us.

"They'll grab another cab. I'll text them when we get to where we're going. What would you think about The National Gallery?" Edmund relaxed into his seat.

"Sounds great." I pulled out my phone and checked the time. "I need to make one stop first; I hope you don't mind."

Edmund pursed his bottom lip and shook his head.

I opened the window to the driver and said, "21 Fetter Lane, please." When he nodded I closed it again.

"What's on Fetter Lane?"

"My mother's lawyer." I shook my head. "I mean, solicitor." I'd set up an appointment with Anton LeClerc. Our meeting was in a half-hour.

"Why does your mum have a solicitor here and not America?"

I shook my head. "They do have one in Seattle . . . well, Dad does. But Mom was English. She only moved to America to marry my dad. She died when I was little."

"I'm so sorry; I didn't know." His eyes searched mine.

I looked away and studied my hands. "It's fine, really. I don't go around telling everyone."

"That must've been really hard, growing up without her." Edmund's voice was soft and low.

"We're here," the driver said as he pulled the cab to a stop in front of a tall brick building.

I sucked in a breath, wishing we'd had longer to talk.

Edmund paid the driver and we stepped out.

What can this Anton dude possibly tell me about Mom?

"You don't have to answer this, but I'm curious. If your mum's been gone for years, why are you visiting her solicitor now?"

"That's a great question." I grinned and checked the time on my phone. "It's a long story, and I have to be inside in ten minutes. Can I explain after?"

"Of course." Edmund reached out to open the door for me.

Inside, the receptionist sat behind a glass-and-metal desk, surveying the waiting area. Everything was sleek in white and black, so not what I'd been expecting from the outside. I checked in while Edmund sat.

"Mr. LeClerc will be with you momentarily."

"Thanks." I went and joined Edmund.

"You look nervous." He closed the magazine he was reading. His face was on the cover.

I sighed. "I am. I don't know why Mom wants me to see him."

His eyebrows drew together. "Wait, your mum wants you to?"

"Miss Gray, I've been expecting you for a very long time." An older, well-dressed man approached me, arms outstretched.

Is he going to hug me? I stood and froze, steeling myself for an embrace. Instead, his hands grabbed mine and held them tightly. The more he smiled, the more crinkles formed around his brown eyes. I guesstimated he was Dad's age.

"For a moment I thought you were Lily standing there. The resemblance is remarkable. Your hair is the exact same shade of red." He released my hands.

"You must be Anton LeClerc?"

"My apologies, I should have introduced myself." He shook his head and put a hand over his heart. "Anton LeClerc, your mother's solicitor and good friend."

"Thank you for seeing me on a Sunday."

"I'd make arrangements to see you any day of the week. I've been looking forward to this meeting for years. Shall we go to my office?"

"I'll wait out here." Edmund stood.

"I'm sorry, I . . ." Anton stopped and took a closer look. His eyes widened. "Your Highness, could I interest you in anything to eat or drink? We have a lounge you might find more comfortable. Jenna would be happy to see you settled. Unless of course you were joining Evie."

Edmund shook his head, not looking at me. "The lounge will do."

Anton guided me into his office. I turned back and caught Edmund's eye. He smiled before I disappeared around the corner.

"You must be wondering why your mother wanted you to come see me."

I nodded. His office matched the sleek motif of the waiting room. His personal photos gave it a coziness the lobby lacked.

"Maybe I should start from the beginning." He offered me a glass of water.

"The beginning's a fabulous place." I took the glass and sipped from it.

A warm smile filled his face. "Your mother and I grew up together. Up until university we were inseparable. Even away at school we kept in close contact. I quite fancied her, truth be told."

I wasn't sure how to respond to this dude telling me he had a thing for my mom. I squirmed in my seat.

"When she met Henry, your father, I knew I didn't stand a chance. It was love at first sight for her. Your dad's a very lucky man. And a very good man, too. After meeting him I knew he was perfect for Lily."

"If you're friends with my dad why haven't I heard about you before?"

Anton shook his head. "I was always Lily's friend. You father I knew, but we were never close."

"Were you at her funeral?"

He nodded. "I was. It was the worst day of my life. You were so little and confused. Your father was absolutely gutted." He closed his eyes and shook his head. "I remember when she told me about the cancer. Then when she passed . . ." Anton cleared his throat and looked at his desktop. He polished away a smudge on the glass surface with a fingertip.

My eyes burned and my vision blurred. *Keep it together, Evie. Don't cry.* I wouldn't be able to stop if I got started.

"And that's why you're here. When she was first diagnosed, she called me with a plan. I think she knew from the beginning she wasn't going to make it."

I flinched. *She knew she was going to die? From the start?*

"At first I didn't want to hear it. I couldn't imagine her not being around. Eventually, she persuaded me to listen and agree should the worst happen." He looked at me, his eyes watery. "And it did." Inhaling deeply, he continued. "She needed my help. Even though she wouldn't be here, she wanted to play a part in your life. That's how the birthday letters started. They were my suggestion. I assume your father has been seeing you get those."

I nodded. "What about the quest letters? What's your role in those?"

"It's my job to make sure you complete the tasks."

"You sent the first two letters, didn't you?"

His eyes glinted brightly. "I did."

"But how did you know I'd been accepted?"

"Your father. I called him concerning a sizable trust that your mother has set up for you. We were catching up and he told me your news. Which, I must admit, was the primary objective of my call."

"So why can't you just tell me what she wants me to discover?"

"She asked me not to." His mouth drew into a serious line. "Plus, it's not a simple secret. These tasks are to help you understand her and for you to know what to do when the time comes."

"What's that even supposed to mean? Mom's letter said something similar and I don't understand."

A funny smile curled his lips. "You've just explained why you need to follow her letters better than I ever could; you *need* to understand."

"Then I check in with you when I finish one of her tasks?"

He nodded.

"Well, I went to Big Ben and Parliament today. Task two, check." I made a check mark in the air with a finger.

He rolled back in his chair and pulled open a desk drawer. "Then you'll need your third letter." He stopped and eyed me with a suspicious smile. "Do you have proof?" *Is he serious? Okay, Sherlock.* "Would pictures work?"

When he nodded, I pulled up the photos on my phone and passed it to him.

"Ah, yes, Big Ben, Parliament, is this the archives?" He turned the phone to me.

I leaned in and looked. "Yup."

His eyebrows rose as he slid his finger across my screen. "Oh, that's a nice picture of Edmund."

Shit. I reached for my phone. "See, I was there."

"Indeed, here's your next letter." He passed the letter across the desk. "I'll wait for your call."

I stood and clasped the letter. "Thanks."

"Have a safe trip back to school."

"I will." I smiled as he stood and walked me to the door. My hand on the knob, I stopped. "One question: how did you get the letter into my trunk?"

"Ah, yes. I have something else for you." Anton went back to his desk and pulled a small item from the top drawer. "This is yours."

He dropped a small, but weighty, metal key into my palm. It matched mine exactly. "*You* put it in my trunk?"

"I did. You see, the trunk used to be mine. I gave it to your mum when she moved overseas with Henry. I couldn't find the extra key to give to her before she left."

"Why didn't you just send the letter to Dad? He could've slipped it in before we shipped it."

"I didn't want to involve your dad in the quest letters until I knew what you'd told him. I thought this was a clever way to get it to you." He scrunched up his nose. "I was counting on you wanting to haul that old trunk of hers over here."

My smile faltered. "Clever, and a little creepy."

Anton laughed. "Yes, now that I say it aloud, it does sound that way, doesn't it? I didn't think of that when I concocted the idea. To ease your mind, an advisor went with me and didn't let me out of her sight."

I opened the door with a nod, unsure how else to respond. "I guess I'll talk to you soon."

Anton waved as I approached the desk to ask after Edmund.

The letter hot in my hand, I wondered what Mom would have me do next. *And how much of this should I tell Edmund?*

Chapter Six

Confidants

Edmund and I slowly walked through The National Gallery, our footfalls echoing through the rooms. Paintings by fabulous artists dotted the walls: Titian, Rubens, and Michelangelo. *This is heaven. I love it here.* Really, I loved being here with *him*.

We followed his bodyguards into a room of Dutch paintings. From the corner of my eye, I noticed Edmund watching me. It wasn't the first time I'd caught him today.

When we left Anton's I wanted to tell him about my mom and the crazy adventure she was leading me on. It nearly burst from my lips. But I wasn't sure if I should trust him. I barely knew him. Did I want him to know this about me?

Edmund stopped and stared up at *The Guitar Player* by Johannes Vermeer. He sighed. "I've tried several times, but I've no idea how to start this conversation. So, I'm just going to come out with it. Do you want to tell me about your mum?" He turned to face me.

I studied him before nodding and sinking onto a worn wooden bench in the center of the room. "Her name was Lilliana, she was English, and she was . . . wonderful." Inhaling sharply, I looked at my boots. I'd tear up if I met his gaze. "Right after I turned six, she was diagnosed with breast cancer. The really aggressive, fast-moving kind. It metastasized throughout her body and she died three months later."

I pulled her letters from my bag.

Edmund straddled the bench and studied me, not saying a word. In my hands I rolled the bundle of letters end over end.

"Every year on my birthday I get a letter from her. They're just little snippets of her life, her dreams, the things she wished for me, and reminders of how much she loved me."

"And these are the letters?" He gestured to the packet in my hand.

I nodded.

"That's lovely. It must be nice to have a connection to her."

"It is. And I'm lucky. They help me remember." I smiled, my eyes watery.

"So, what did you mean earlier, when you said your mum wanted you to see her solicitor?"

Leaning toward him, I said, "Today . . . this, it was all about a letter."

I explained the quest letters and how our sightseeing was my second task, as was meeting Anton and getting the next letter from him.

"Do you have any idea what she's guiding you toward?"

I shrugged. "No, not a clue. I know nothing about her side of the family. I don't even know if I have any living relatives here. I mean, this could be some deep, dark family secret that I don't want to discover." I rolled my eyes, feeling a trifle overdramatic. "Then again, she could just want to tell me she really likes mangos."

Laughing, Edmund said, "Ah, mangos, such a sketchy fruit."

With a grin, I got up and tucked the letters away. When I glanced back at him, he was still watching me.

"So, what's your next quest?" He stood, his blue eyes locked on mine.

"I don't know." I looked away and noticed Edmund's bodyguards blocking the entrances to the room. *That's handy.*

"I thought you said Anton gave you the next letter."

"He did. I haven't opened it yet."

"What? Why not? If you need privacy, I can go explore on my own for a while."

We walked past one set of bodyguards into a new room. It was longer and bigger than the last. I recognized a few of the paintings as Rembrandt's. We were the only people in the room, so I guessed Edmund's security was going ahead of us, clearing the way.

"That's not it at all." My tall brown riding boots captured my attention again. Along the top seam, a thread had started to unravel. "I'm just . . . nervous." I peeked at him from the corner of my eye. "I have this idea of my mom in my mind. I've built it up from all of Dad's happy memories and from what little I remember. I'm terrified these letters will change that. I don't want to lose . . . *her.*"

With a hand on my arm he stopped me. Heat spiraled out from his fingertips and spread through my entire body, sending a shiver through me.

"Your mother, no matter what you discover, will always be your mum and she'll always love you. Nothing in those letters can change that. This is your chance to get to know her as an adult, not a child." He still hadn't moved his hand. "It's really quite brilliant. She found a way to give you memories of her that will be yours, and yours alone."

Mine alone? *I hadn't thought of it that way before.*

I stared at him, taking in his words as his hand dropped away. I blew out a breath. "You're right. But whatever it is she's guiding me toward, she never told my dad. Her keeping it a secret from him scares me. It has to be bigger than a forbidden love of mangos."

He shrugged and looked at me seriously. "Or maybe your dad just *really* hates mangos."

I chuckled. "Yeah, that's probably it."

"So, do you want me to get lost? Give you a moment to find out your next task?"

"No, you're fine." I reached in my bag and slid the unopened letter off the top of the bundle. Clutching it between my fingers, I went to a nearby bench.

My hands were steady as I opened the envelope and pulled out the single page. Edmund quietly stood at my side as I read it to myself.

Dearest Evie,

By now you've met Anton. I've always thought of him as family. The brother I never had. Can't say that label made him very happy, but he accepted it with his usual charm. Truth be told, if I'd fallen in love with Anton, life would've been considerably easier.

Your next task is Welsington Manor. It's a country estate in Brighton of which I have very fond memories. Go check it out and see what you can find. I so wish I could be there with you. I'd love to see it through your eyes. It's magnificent.

I'll be watching over you in Brighton, as always. Give Anton my love.

Love you,
Mom
xoxo

I turned my attention to Edmund. "Welsington Manor? Ever heard of it?"

He scrunched his brows together. "Do you know where it is?"

"Brighton."

"It sounds familiar, but I can't picture it." He shook his head. "Is that your next task?"

I nodded. "She wants me to check it out; apparently it's quite a sight."

"Think you might want some company on that task?"

"Are you offering?" I coyly looked up at him as I put the letter away.

A corner of his mouth lifted. He shifted his gaze to his hands. "I'd be happy to join you if you like. It's only about an hour south of London."

Another day alone with Edmund? Yes, please. "Cool, I'd love the company."

"Brilliant. How about next weekend?"

Edmund sat across from me in a little pub in Belgravia, holding a worn menu. Looking at him, I smiled. Thank God he'd suggested getting dinner before we drove back to campus. My stomach had started growling back at the museum.

I glanced around the room; it was warm and cozy. Honey-colored wood paneling covered the walls, and rusty metal signs added spots of color.

"Philip and I've been coming here for years. James and Grace are good people." Edmund's eyes softened as he spoke of the pair. He seemed at ease. It was nice to see him relax and let his guard down. "They always make sure Philip and I aren't bothered by the press when we're here."

"How do they manage that?" I ran a fingertip across the red carnations in the tiny vase on our table.

"They close off this back room for us, which is great. But mainly, I know they won't tip off the press. Many places consider us free publicity. Not here."

"That's pretty awesome."

"It is." Edmund smoothed the front of his blue button-down.

I glanced at the menu to stop the fantasy of running *my* hands down his chest from forming. "So what's good here?"

"Everything. I love their pot pies, best in London."

A dark-haired woman approached the table. "Your Highness, James said you were here. It's wonderful to see you again."

Edmund stood and grasped her hand. "Always a pleasure, Grace."

"Oh sit, sit, don't you be getting up for me." She swatted him away with a grin, her cheeks flushing. "What would you two like this evening?"

Edmund turned, waiting for me to go first.

"Um, could I get a bowl of stew and bread, please? Oh, and a glass of water."

"Of course." She took my menu and tucked it under her arm with a grin. Her hazel eyes switched to Edmund. "And will you be having your usual?"

"Yes, ma'am."

"I'll get this started." She turned on her heel and bustled out.

We sat quietly. *It's now or never.* If I wanted to ask about Jax, this was my chance. I folded my hands under the table and looked down at my lap. "I've been wanting to ask you something."

"What's that?" he asked.

My eyes followed the wood grain on the tabletop. "I'm curious about what you said in the car the other day. About Jax."

"Of course." He leaned over, trying to see around my cascade of curls. "You mean about her being an obligation?"

I forced my head up, even though I could feel the burn in my face. "It's just . . . you don't like her any more than the rest of the gang do, yet you still seem to consider her a friend. I don't get that."

Grace returned with our drinks and we fell silent.

"Thank you." I took a sip.

"You're welcome, Miss. I'll be back with your supper shortly."

Edmund watched Grace leave. "Everyone considers Jax and me friends. But I can't stand her. Never have been able to. We've known each other since we were children and she hasn't changed a bit." He took a drink from his pint. "Our parents are close friends and it's well hinted that they'd like nothing more than for us to marry. It's a good connection for the family, blah, blah, blah."

Face scrunched, I asked, "What about what you want?"

"With our very public lives, personal wants and happiness are seldom worried about."

"Does she love you?"

He paused. "No. We tolerate each other. We're both trying to please our families, and really, her interest only goes as far as my title."

Grace returned with dinner. "Here we go. Is there anything else I can get you?"

"This is perfect. Thank you." Edmund smiled.

"I'll leave you to it. Enjoy." She grinned.

"Thanks," I chimed as she left. "It smells delicious."

"It always is." Edmund took a bite.

I ripped a piece off my crusty roll, preparing to dunk it in my stew. "If she's not in love with you, she's certainly convincing at protecting her claim on you."

"Oh good Lord, I knew something happened. What did she do?" His voice was low.

"She just advised me to stay away from you. She made it *very* clear that you belong to her."

His lips tightened and a look of anger flashed across his face. "She's trying to head off any girl I might take a fancy to."

"Maybe she really does care for you and this is her way of showing you."

"She doesn't know how to care for someone other than herself." His gaze steady, he reached across the table and put his hand over mine. "Whatever she did and said, I apologize."

I shook my head, my gaze darting from his eyes to the large hand covering mine. "Don't worry about it."

"I am worried about it. She was wrong and I'm sorry."

"It's really okay. No harm done. Besides, I can handle myself against the likes of Jax." I chuckled. "I'm just curious how your parents could want you to be with her? Do they seriously like her?"

Edmund cleared his throat and pulled his hand back. "She makes things easier for them."

"Why? Is there some archaic law or something that makes who you date important?" I'd wanted this question answered since I'd found out who he was. *Is he even an option for me?*

"Yes and no. There's no law anymore." He cracked a smile. "But there are certain expectations. Of course, they were absolutes for Philip, being the heir and all, but I'm not entirely exempt. Girls we date must come from good families, preferably titled, and there can't be any skeletons lurking in their pasts. They must behave properly, dress modestly, and above all be respectful. Jax, believe it or not, fits all those. Of course my parents only see the perfect image she projects. They know nothing of the real Jax."

Three strikes, I'm definitely out. I wasn't titled, I wasn't from a good ol' British family, and I probably had a closet full of skeletons that these letters would reveal. *Shit.* I knew it was a long shot.

"Most people I know would rebel against their parents telling them who to date."

"Rebelling isn't an option for me. I tried it. I partied too hard, drank too much, and ended up on the cover of one too many magazines labeling me a bad boy."

"You know, I think I remember seeing some of those headlines."
I chuckled. "So, what? Are you a reformed bad boy now?"

"No, I was never truly a bad boy." His grin faltered. "I was just going along and doing what Jax and her friends expected of me. When I realized I didn't enjoy being around them or the attention they attracted, I cut them off. Jax is the only one I'm still in touch with."

"And you're really okay with all this? Your family dictating your love life? Sacrificing your own happiness?"

He shifted uncomfortably in his chair. "I didn't say that. At this point it's self-preservation. One day I may have to challenge them. But I haven't come across someone worth fighting for . . . yet." His eyes steadied on mine.

A fuzzy feeling spiraled up from my toes. I took a sip of my water and cleared my throat. "I don't think I could be as cool about it as you are."

"It's what's expected of me. I don't really know any different. Surely your father must want certain things for you. Your mum had to have planned it out with him before she . . ." His voice faded off.

"It's okay, you can say it, before she died." I smiled.

Nodding, he continued. "It's just, if she wrote all these letters for you, she had to have talked to him about your future and how to guide you. They have plans they expect you to fulfill, just like my parents. They wanted you to come to Oxford, right? I'm sure they have a particular type of guy in mind for you. Didn't you ever get the 'don't bring this type of boy home' speech?"

"I didn't, actually. Dad offered advice and guidance, but he never told me what type of boys I could and couldn't date. I suppose he trusts me. Then again, he knows nice guys are my weakness." I laughed. "Bad boys come with too much drama and heartache. I don't have time for that." I blew on a spoonful of stew.

Barely above a whisper, Edmund said, "It's a good thing I'm a nice guy then."

My head snapped up to look at him. *Did I hear that right?*

The Town Car dropped Edmund and me at the dorms. I could see the lights inside were dimmed and the commons looked deserted. *What time is it anyway?*

I listened to the crickets chirping while Edmund opened the door.

"Thanks." I slipped past him, my arm brushing across his chest. "And thanks for coming with me today."

"Of course." Smiling, he slid a hand in his pocket as we ambled to the stairwell and up to my floor. "I haven't had this much fun in a long time."

I pulled at my lightweight scarf, needing something to do with my hands.

He leaned closer. "I'm looking forward to next weekend."

Thank God it was dark, because my cheeks were molten-lava hot. I bit my lower lip, tingles shooting through me at his nearness. "Me too."

Is he going to kiss me?

"I should, um, probably let you go, it's late."

I nodded, not wanting the night to be over. "Night."

"See you tomorrow."

I slipped through the door to my hall. Turning, I peeked through the long rectangular window and watched him walk up to his floor. When he rounded the corner, I pulled my phone out. *I have to call Abby.*

"Hey, Eves." Her warm voice carried through the line. "What's up, chica?"

I opened my door in a haze and threw myself on the couch. "I was just working on one of Mom's letters with a friend." My bag fell to the floor with a soft thump.

"You realize I can hear the giddiness in your voice, right? What kind of *friend* was this to make you sound so dreamy?"

I draped an arm over my forehead. "I just spent the day with the most amazing guy. It was . . . incredible. Abby, I . . . I just . . . can't describe it."

"Sounds fabulous. Who is Mr. Amazing?"

"You'll never believe me."

"Try me."

I laughed. "Edmund Stuart. Prince Edmund."

"Right." She chuckled. "And I'm the President. Now, who was it really?"

"Abby, I'm not making this up. We have a couple classes together and I'm hanging out with him and his friends."

"Seriously? How in the hell did that happen?"

"Your guess is as good as mine."

"What's he like?" The springs of Abby's bed creaked through the phone.

"He's actually really cool and surprisingly normal. And holy moly, Abby, I can't begin to tell you how freaking hot he is."

She scoffed. "Well, duh. He's smoking on the covers of magazines and on TV; he's bound to be better in person. I can't believe this. You have all the luck."

I stood and unbuttoned my jeans, needing to get into bed. "I wish you could meet him."

"You really like this guy, don't you?"

"He's a prince."

"So what? So he's royalty. You can still like him. You can still *want* him."

"Abby, I . . . I can't."

She inhaled sharply. "You're majorly crushing on him."

With a frustrated growl, I said, "I just met him, yet all I can do is fantasize about him. About kissing him and running my fingers through his hair." I buried my face in my hands. "I'm in so much trouble."

"What's the big deal? You're a single lady. This is a good thing."

"He's got a titled chick his parents love who's essentially hunting him. Edmund's not an option for me."

"For now. That could change. Obviously if this girl chasing him hasn't caught him, there has to be a reason. As for the prince thing, don't be such a snob."

"What? How do you figure I'm the snob?"

"Well, it's actually a reverse snobbery thing. You're counting him out just because he's royalty, rich, and totally out of your league. Give the guy a chance if he wants one."

"Abs, dating a prince isn't in the cards for me. I don't meet any of his family's qualifications."

Abby sighed. "Yeah, well, that doesn't mean you can't have fun. Maybe you can't marry him and produce the next king of England, but you could still make out with him. Sample his crumpets and tea, if you know what I mean."

"Abby!" I scoffed. "You're awful."

"You know you want to." Her smile carried through the phone line.

"I'm hanging up now. I've got classes early in the morning."

"Good night, Princess Evie."

I laughed. "Morning, Princess Pain-In-The-Ass."

Viable option for him or not, my imagination didn't care. In fact, it'd just kicked into overdrive.

Chapter Seven

Hogwarts Abbey

"You need to spill," Caroline said as she, Suzy, and Marissa barreled into my room Monday after classes.

"I don't know what you mean." I smiled innocently and tucked my feet under myself in my desk chair. They wanted to hear about my trip into London. With my hands clasping the edge of my desk, I turned the chair away from them.

"How did the date go?" Suzy perched on the edge of the couch, straightening her blouse. Her smile didn't quite reach her eyes.

I shook my head. "It wasn't a date." I grabbed a pen; the nib danced in and out as I spastically clicked it. "We just went sightseeing. So *not* a big deal."

"The press certainly doesn't agree." Marissa tossed a paper at me from her spot next to Caroline on my bed.

I dropped the pen to catch the paper. Pictures of Edmund and me wandering around Big Ben were splattered on the front page. I didn't need to read it. I'd caught the story on the morning news. *Jax must be overjoyed.*

Handing the paper back, I said, "We're friends. Nothing more."

Edmund's words tripped through my head again, *it's a good thing I'm a nice guy then.* I'd been overanalyzing them all night. What had he meant? I knew what I wanted it to mean.

"Evie, Edmund's into you." Caroline fixed me with a stare, her black eyeliner giving her brown eyes a feline quality. "He doesn't just hang out with girls *alone*. Not even us. He's always careful.

Every move he makes is scrutinized and publicized. For him to just go off with you and not worry about the risks—you're special."

I shook my head. "Or he's just helping a clueless American friend navigate London." I wanted their words to be true, but I refused to believe it. I couldn't fall for him . . . well, at least not any more than I already had.

"Okay, you tell yourself that." Marissa winked at me.

Rolling my eyes, I said, "Oh my gosh, you guys, you're being ridiculous."

"I wish I could see Jax's reaction when she gets wind of this." Caroline rubbed her hands together gleefully.

"You thought she hated you before, just wait." Marissa's eyebrows rose. Lifting a hand to the window, she ran it through a stream of sunlight.

The sharp rapping sound of knuckles on the door stole my next words.

Caroline zipped over and opened it. With a giggle, she turned and wrinkled her nose up, winking at me. "Evening, handsome, we were just talking about you."

Oh my stars. He's here? I lifted a hand to my hair and tucked my curls behind my ears, nervous.

"Oh, hey, Caroline." Surprise tinged his words. "All good stuff, I hope."

"Naturally." Caroline smirked.

Edmund's eyes found mine. At his smile, my cheeks burst into flame. *Damn redhead genes.*

"So, anything going on I should be aware of?" He surveyed the four of us.

"Nope, just girlie gossip." Suzy smiled and patted the spot on the couch next to her.

Taking her offer, he sat beside her, which placed him directly across from me. He looked sexy in dark jeans and a blue sweater.

A silence descended over the room. Caroline leaned against the wall, grinning like a Cheshire Cat. I could almost see *told you so* flashing through her eyes.

"What'd you want with Evie?" Marissa asked, now sprawled on my bed.

"Oh, um . . ." He cleared his throat and ran a hand through his already tousled hair. "I was just coming to see if I could borrow Evie's notes from our last class. I can't read my handwriting in some bits."

"Sure." I leaned over and pulled out my Romanticism notebook from my bag. "Here you go."

"Thanks." His eyes glinted as his fingers grazed mine.

I shivered at the tingles that raced up my arm. *Did he feel that?*

"I'll give it back tomorrow at breakfast. That okay?"

"Sounds good." I folded my arms across my chest.

"I was going to head down for dinner. Any of you want to join me?" Edmund offered.

Suzy stood. "I'm starving; let's go."

Edmund looked at me, the corner of his mouth twitching up. I got the impression he wanted to say something, but he kept quiet. Standing, he followed Suzy and Marissa.

Caroline waited for me. "See, what did I tell you?" she whispered once we were alone.

"You're right. It must be love, he borrowed my class notes. That's the universal sign of passion, right? Catch me, I think I might swoon from all the romance." I giggled.

We entered the dining hall moments behind the others.

Preston sat at our normal table. He waved but didn't stop eating.

Hanging back, Edmund let all the girls go before him. Wanting to be near him, I went last and ignored the look Caroline shot me.

"Are you looking forward to Welsington Manor this weekend?" He grabbed his tray and sidled up next to me.

"I am. I looked on the map and realized it's on the coast." Excited, I met his eyes. "I can't wait to see a beach again. In Seattle we're right on the Puget Sound. I miss the water." I put a turkey sandwich and a small salad on my tray.

"It's been a while since I've been to Brighton. It's beautiful there; you'll love it."

I wondered if the press would be all over us in Brighton like they'd been in London. Brows drawn together, I spun around to face him. "Why aren't the press hounding you here like they were in London yesterday?"

"They're around; they just keep their distance."

"Why?" I glanced out the windows, expecting to see photographers, flashbulbs popping, and noses pressed to the glass. Instead, darkness had settled. The only visible thing I could make out was the sidewalk, lit by the glow of the street lamps.

"The palace requests they give me space and privacy at school. They don't fully comply, but they do stay back, and there's nowhere near as many of them here." Gesturing behind me, he said, "Line's moving."

My tray bumped along the counter as I caught up. One by one we paid and joined Preston.

"Edmund told me he had a nice time in London. Did you?" Preston asked as Edmund sat down across from him.

"Yeah, it was great. It was nice to see more than just the airport and train," I said, sitting beside Edmund.

"Just so you know, you could have invited the rest of us along, too." Preston winked at me.

A loud thud shook the table.

"Ouch!" Preston reached under, scowling at Edmund.

Did Edmund just kick him? I glanced at the two of them, but their faces gave nothing away.

Guilt curled inside my stomach. I didn't invite the gang because I wanted to keep my quest letters private. Plus, being alone with Edmund had been a definite motivator.

I had to invite everyone this weekend, didn't I? It would only be right. It would only *look* right. I glanced at Edmund, but he didn't notice.

"I'm actually heading to Brighton this weekend, to Welsington Manor. You should all come." *I don't have to tell them about the letters to check out the house.* In my peripheral I caught Edmund turn and stare at me. Stabbing at the green leaves of my salad, I looked at everyone but him.

"Beach weekend!" Marissa called out and gave Caroline a high five across the table.

Suzy looked up from her plate. "Why are you going there?"

Excuses raced through my brain. *What do I say?* Edmund being in on my secret was more than enough. I'm not even entirely positive I'd been thinking with my brain on that choice. Essentially I'd given him a front-row seat to the "Why Evie Would Be an Inappropriate Girlfriend" show. But we had a connection. I knew I could trust him.

"It's for one of our classes." Edmund jumped in, saving me. "Professor Sawyer was ranting about how so many of these old country estates have their own personal art galleries. He feels all art should be shared and for the public. So, we're supposed to visit some of these houses and view their collections."

"If we go, we wouldn't have to be there for all the artsy stuff, would we?" Suzy asked, her nose scrunched up.

Edmund shook his head. "No."

"Good." She grinned and turned to plan with Caroline.

I glanced at Edmund and mouthed, "Thank you."

He nodded with a smile and took a bite of steak.

A disappointed breath escaped my lips. It wouldn't be just the two of us after all. *Bummer.*

Then a realization hit me; Edmund and I now shared a secret. Granted, this secret would probably come back to bite me on the ass when my family's skeletons came rattling out of the closet. Still, a secret only Edmund and I shared kind of made it all worth it.

"Wow, this is beautiful." Suzy's eyes focused out the rainy window as we pulled into a long drive. We'd spent the morning on a train and were now all squished into the back of a taxi.

I leaned forward, out of my Edmund-and-Preston sandwich, to see what Suzy was talking about. I gasped. "Whoa, that's not a house; that's a castle."

The gray stone building loomed at the end of the drive. Hundreds of windows overlooked the green lawns and intricate landscaping. Turrets topped with waving crimson flags completed the massive structure. It looked like some fantastic amalgamation of Downton Abbey and Hogwarts.

"Whose estate?" Preston asked, glancing at Edmund.

"The Duchess of Westminster." He made an unpleasant face and shook his head. "Hopefully we won't run into her. She's one disagreeable old woman."

"Do you know her well?" Caroline asked, from one of the fold-down seats.

"Not very. My parents do, though. When I was a child she scared me to bits," Edmund admitted with a chuckle.

I wedged myself back between the boys, angling myself toward Edmund. *Why had Mom sent me here?* Sure it was stunning, but what was the purpose?

Preston reached across me to pat Edmund's knee. "Don't worry, we won't let her gobble you up."

Edmund gave Preston a less than amused look. I laughed.

The cab rolled to a stop under a covered entrance. Caroline clambered out after Marissa, letting it be known how grateful she was for space. Personally, I didn't mind the tight quarters. Being squished between two attractive men was just fine with me. *Maybe I can get the same seat on the way back.*

I stepped onto the gravel drive and spun around. A small sign advertised a cafe in the old carriage house. Umbrellas were available for those who chose to walk around and not take the tour.

"And that's where I'm heading, tea." Suzy pointed to the sign and trotted off with Caroline and Marissa on her heels.

"You doing the tour, Pres?" Edmund asked.

"Why not? I'll keep you two company."

The three of us went up a short flight of stairs and through the double doors.

"Good afternoon." A sharply dressed woman stood behind the mahogany desk. She did a double take at Edmund and his security guards. "Your Highness, a pleasure to have you with us," she said, coming over to us.

"Thank you." Edmund nodded, shaking her hand.

"Will you be taking the full tour today?" She gestured to a sign in a gilt picture frame. We had three options: tour the art gallery, tour the house, or do both—the full tour.

Edmund turned to me, wordlessly asking if that's what I wanted to do. I bobbed my head.

"Yes, please."

"Fabulous. I'll inform the docent you're here. Please, make yourselves comfortable."

Edmund turned to Preston and me. "Shall we?"

The entry was a large rotunda with a glass-domed ceiling. This place had to cost a fortune in upkeep. Velvet-covered couches and high-backed chairs were arranged in little vignettes. A fire blazed in the hearth at the back of the room.

Preston walked toward the heat source and I followed; it was chilly in here.

"Wow, that's a Constable." I gestured above the fireplace, my mouth hanging open.

"Sure looks like it." Edmund leaned closer.

"It's actually a reproduction, Your Highness," a stiff voice echoed through the room. We turned to see a short, stocky woman whose black hair was streaked with gray and tautly pulled off her face. Unsmiling, she added, "All the original artwork is in climate-controlled areas of the house."

"Ah, of course." Edmund smiled at her.

"Welcome to Welsington. I'm Ms. Hollingbrook, your guide for the afternoon." With her heels click-clacking on the marble floors, we set off.

Room after room was chock full of antique furniture. My fingers itched to touch, but we'd been reminded several times not to lay a finger on anything.

Though our guide used her words sparingly and mostly for reprimands, I did glean that the duchess rarely came to the manor. Years ago, when the duke died and the duchess was left to manage everything, she'd made a permanent move to London.

Maybe she left because it was too lonely here. As I went through the rooms I tried to picture it filled with a family, but I just couldn't. Everything was too formal and fancy.

"We are now entering the East Wing Gallery." Ms. Hollingbrook thrust open a pair of white doors into a room with paintings lining the walls and marble statues in two neat rows down the center. "I'll give you twenty-five minutes to look around. Personal portraiture is on the left, the private collection on the right. The plaques should answer most of your questions." Hands clasped behind her back, she set to pacing the long rectangular room.

"She's not intimidating at all," Preston whispered in my ear.

I snickered. "Nope, not even a smidgen."

Edmund veered to the left, studying a large painting of a formidable woman. Preston went toward the statues. I was tempted to head right, that way we'd cover the room and could compare notes later. But who am I kidding? I followed Edmund.

"Is that the duchess?" I murmured.

Leaning down, he whispered, "Yup, the old dragon herself."

The woman in the painting had soft green eyes and silver hair piled on top of her head in a severe bun. Arms crossed in front of her, there wasn't even a hint of a smile on her lips. She looked calculating and cold. Yet there was something about her eyes that caught my attention.

We walked down the row of paintings and the years appeared to peel off their elderly subject. She was quite an attractive woman when she was young. In a few of the pictures she stood next to her husband, a handsome and distinguished looking gentleman with a kind smile. At the very end of the line was one family portrait. A little girl, with curly red hair that matched her mother's, had her arms wrapped around the neck of small cocker spaniel. Behind the girl stood the duke and duchess.

"I'd forgotten they had a daughter," Edmund said, catching up with me. I hadn't realized I'd left him behind.

"Did something happen to her?"

"I'm not sure." He shook his head. "I seem to recall hearing she'd been disowned." His brow furrowed. "But I might be thinking of a different family. It's difficult to keep them all straight."

I stood, staring up at the large portrait. The little girl looked familiar. Uneasiness settled in my stomach. What was Mom trying to tell me? *Oh, God, this doesn't feel right.*

Hoping to see their names listed, I got a closer look at the plaque. *The Duke and Duchess of Westminster, at Welsington Manor with family, 1971.*

Why weren't there more family pictures?

"Excuse me, Ms. Hollingbrook?" I turned to see where she'd gotten off to.

"Yes?" Her heels cadenced her impending arrival.

"Is this the only family portrait?"

She stared me up and down before answering. "At the manor, yes. However, there are more at the London townhouse, with the duchess."

"What about the daughter?" Edmund eyed the happy family again.

Hollingbrook cleared her throat. "I'm not at liberty to discuss private family matters."

Preston came over and stared up with Edmund and me. "She's definitely less scary in this one than the first one."

Beside me our guide scoffed with a huff. She glared at Preston, her lips pressed into a thin line. "How disrespectful. The duchess is a pillar of society. You should learn to hold your tongue, young man."

Preston's mouth popped open. "Right. Okay. Sorry." He took a step back. "Um, which way to the cafe?"

"Through that door, down the stairs, and take the first pair of doors outside. You can't miss it." Hollingbrook's words were clipped and tightly enunciated.

I dared a glance at Edmund. He looked like he was holding back a grin. "You'll have to excuse our friend, Ms. Hollingbrook. He meant no disrespect."

She totally didn't buy it. She glanced at her watch. "Shall we finish with the tour? I'm on a tight schedule."

Edmund nodded and gestured for her to lead the way.

With Preston gone, Edmund stayed closer to me. No matter where we went he seemed to be touching me. A graze of his fingers on mine. His hand on the small of my back as we turned a corner. Our shoulders pressed together as we listened to Hollingbrook spout facts about the house.

"And this concludes our tour of Welsington Manor."

"Thank you," Edmund and I said together.

"The cafe and gift shop are just through these doors. Enjoy the rest of your day." She trotted back up the stairs.

Edmund leaned back on his heels and stuck his thumbs through his belt loops. "So, any clue why your mum sent you here?"

I shook my head. "I don't know, but something's . . . off."

"What do you mean?" His brows furrowed.

"It's probably silly, but I get an odd feeling being here."

We stood by the doors. His hand rested on the handle as he waited for me to continue.

"Those paintings, there was something in that old woman's eyes, they looked familiar. Is that weird?"

Edmund shrugged. "There's obviously a reason your mum wanted you to come here. Maybe the duchess has something to do with it." He reached out and brushed my hair over my shoulder.

I closed my eyes and shivered as his fingers softly brushed against my cheek. Such a simple touch from him and my thoughts completely derailed. With a shaky breath, I turned and headed out the door Edmund held open.

Stopping, I looked at him, my eyes squinted. "Then the little girl in the family picture . . ." I shook my head, not sure what I was saying. Maybe I just didn't want to give a voice to my suspicions.

What if the little girl in the painting was my mother?

That would explain why she sent me here. Does that mean I'm related to a duchess? I shook my head. Impossible, there had to be some other explanation. Some other reason.

I can't be related to the dragon duchess, can I?

Squeezed together with Edmund in the open doorway, his breath whispered across my face. "If you want, I'll try to help you figure this out." He reached up and cupped my cheek. "Just say the word and I'm there."

I managed to get out a nod. His hand was so warm and we were so close that if I leaned ever so slightly, my lips would find his.

If I am related to the duchess, can I have him?

Chapter Eight

Jane Austen Would Be Proud

Jaunty music filled our little corner of the commons. The girls and I were watching *You've Got Mail*. Every time I watched it, I wanted to pack up and move to New York. My laptop supported on my legs, I glanced from one screen to the other.

"So, the party's only two weeks away. What are your costumes?" Caroline plopped on the couch across from mine, making Marissa bounce.

"Not a clue." Suzy looked up from the rug. "What about you?"

Tuning out their conversation, I continued to multitask. Abby and I instant messaged as I struggled to finish my European Art paper. I was such a slacker, a fact Edmund had reminded me of just this morning. He'd finished his paper ages ago. *Overachiever.* My body exhausted and my brain on the verge of shutdown, I was frazzled.

My paper wasn't the only thing I'd been dragging my butt on. I still hadn't dealt with the fourth quest letter. I wasn't ready to. And it was a simple task: research the Elliot name. *Elliot, with one t.* Easy peasy. But I couldn't bring myself to do it. After Welsington, I was terrified of what I might uncover.

"Hello? Earth to Evie." Suzy waved her hand in front of my computer screen.

"Huh? Sorry." I smiled. "What's up?"

"Just wondering if you've figured out your costume?"

"Not yet. I was thinking maybe Rapunzel or Guinevere." I shrugged and closed my computer. "I'll figure it out when we get to the costume shop tomorrow."

"Oh, Rapunzel would be fun; I'd get tangled up in the hair, though." Marissa smiled as she stuffed a handful of popcorn into her mouth.

"What does Edmund want you guys to go as?" Caroline asked.

I looked at her, confused. "Um, we're not going together."

"Really? But you spend so much time together. I thought you guys had progressed to something more." Caroline's face scrunched.

"Hasn't Jax even backed off? I thought she was lying low because the two of you were secretly dating." Suzy pushed up her tortoiseshell glasses. She looked fabulous in them, but she didn't agree. She rarely wore them.

"No, we're still just friends." I traced the glossy white apple on my laptop.

"Wait, you mean to tell me the two of you have been going to museums and gallivanting all over England, but you haven't been on an actual date?" Caroline sat up straighter.

"That would be what I'm telling you," I said with a tight smile.

She scoffed. "Aside from Welsington, we haven't tagged along because we thought you two wanted to be alone."

I looked around the deserted commons and then at the television, avoiding her eyes. I *had* wanted to be alone with him.

"What bollocks. I was sure you two were dating. Has he tried to kiss you at least?" Marissa leaned in, elbows on her knees.

I adjusted myself on the couch, feeling hot and increasingly uncomfortable. "No, well, maybe. Oh, I don't know." I said it louder than I intended. I thought back to the doorway at Welsington and after our trip into London. Had he been thinking about kissing me either time? Or am I the only one with snogging on the brain? I took a deep breath. "I'm not sure where we stand. At times I think he might be interested, but then nothing comes of it. I know I don't meet his family's criteria. He knows it, too. I doubt we'll ever be anything more than friends."

Caroline sighed. "If he really wants you, his family wouldn't stop him."

I cocked my head to the side and scrunched my face. *Not helping.* "You know, that doesn't make me feel better. Now I *know* he doesn't want me."

"That's not what I meant. It's just I'm irritated for you. Bloody hell, just watching the two of you circle around each other and never hitting the mark is frustrating."

I laughed. "I feel for you, Caroline, really I do."

The four of us burst into giggles, just as the guys came in.

"What'd we miss?" Preston asked as he plunked down on the couch next to me.

"Nothing, Caroline's just feeling frustrated," I answered, bending my knees to make room for him.

Grabbing my legs, Preston pulled them across his lap. It wasn't the first time he'd been overly friendly, but it still surprised me. Edmund sat on the arm of our couch and shot a glare at Preston.

"What sort of 'frustration'?" Preston countered.

"Figuring out Halloween costumes," Caroline answered.

"Oh? That's not nearly as interesting as I thought this conversation was going to be. So, what are you girls going as?"

"You'll just have to be surprised." Suzy stood. "I'm off to bed. I'll see you guys in the morning."

"Night," we chorused.

I was surprised Suzy had gone up so early. Lately, whenever the guys were around, Suzy wasn't. *What's going on with her?*

Preston's warm fingers tickled the backs of my bare knees. I squealed. Laughing, I smacked his hands away and tucked my legs underneath me, then covered them with my dress.

When Abby logged off, I decided to skip the end of the movie. "I'm gonna follow Suzy's lead and head up to finish this stupid paper." I stuffed my books and laptop into my bag.

"I'll walk you." Edmund stood, shooting a glare at a hugely grinning Preston.

I waved to the group as I spun and left. "Let me guess, you want to rub it in some more that your paper's finished. Gloat that you didn't wait 'til the last minute, like me?"

He chuckled. "I promise not to crow. I just wanted to see if you needed any help." He walked at my side as we climbed the two flights of stairs to my room. "Mind if I come in for a tick?"

"Not at all. You okay?" I asked. He looked nervous. I leaned into him and caught his clean scent. It made my head reel.

"Yeah, I'm fine. I just wanted to talk to you away from the group. Is that all right?" He stopped at my door and studied me.

I beamed at him and nodded. "Come on in."

Looking back at the door we'd just come through, I noticed his bodyguards lingering there. With my door unlocked, I did a quick survey: bed was miraculously made, desk was tidy, and thankfully no underwear or bras were hanging about.

Edmund followed me in and sat on my couch. We were actually *alone*. A nervous energy thrummed through me. I sat on my bed, too on edge to sit next to him.

"So, how's your paper coming?"

"It's getting there." With my computer resting on my thighs, I ungracefully scooted toward my pillows. "I'll be happy when I'm done and it's turned in. Writing papers usually isn't hard for me, but this one's been a real booger."

"Who are they?" Edmund picked up the picture on my desk that sat beside a sparkly Eiffel Tower replica.

"That's my parents when they graduated from Oxford."

"Your mother was very beautiful."

"Thank you." I met his eyes and smiled.

"Anton was right, you do look just like her." Standing, he placed the photo back by the miniature Eiffel Tower, then came over and sat next me. "So, is there anything I can do to help?"

Under the pretense of adjusting my shirt, I maneuvered myself so our shoulders now touched. I loved how warm he always felt. That, and the fact I was close enough to feel it. "Um, I don't think so. I'm just trying to make sure I cover everything."

Our assignment was to pick a Renaissance artist and compare and contrast his portfolio of work. I picked Leonardo da Vinci—he'd always been a favorite. But his large and varied body of work made it tough to wrap everything up.

"Mind if I give it a read?"

"Go for it," I said, and passed my laptop to him. Leaning back against the wall, I closed my eyes. Every now and then I'd peek at Edmund. I noticed his lips moving as he read, which I found charming. What I wouldn't give to lean over and kiss him.

When he finished my twenty-three pages he said, "This is really good, Evie. I don't know what you're struggling with." He reached over and awkwardly patted my knee, then rested his hand there. "All you need is a conclusion."

"You think?" I tried to sound normal, but his touch had me off kilter.

Our eyes met for a second before his gaze fell to my lips. "Yeah, it's great. Really . . . brilliant." His voice was soft and his breathing grew shallow. This sudden change in him sent tingles trilling through me.

Is this it?

Slowly, his head moved toward mine.

He closed his eyes, so I did the same.

My heart felt like it was going to explode straight out of my chest. Seconds passed and his lips didn't touch mine. My eyes flittered open as he cleared his throat and leaned back.

I inhaled sharply, mortification flooding my system. If I could disappear never to return, I so would.

Why didn't you kiss me? What do I have to do?

All I'd been thinking about since he sat next to me was how badly I wanted to curl myself into his arms and nestle my head in his nook. Unfortunately, we weren't on the same wavelength.

"What are you going to Caroline's Halloween party as?" he asked.

I was grateful he spoke first. Shaking my head, I said, "I haven't decided yet, you?"

"Well, I wanted to talk to you first." He glanced down at his hands.

"Why's that?"

Edmund smiled, his face flushing. "I wanted to ask you if you'd go with me?"

"As in a date?" My eyebrows shot up. *Okay, maybe we are on the same wavelength after all.*

"That's kind of what I had in mind." Not meeting my eyes, he ran his fingers along the edge of my laptop.

I paused, ignoring the reasons why I probably shouldn't. "I'd love to go with you."

He set my laptop aside and stood, a boyish grin on his now scarlet face. "Fantastic. That's bloody brilliant." Rubbing the back of his neck, he said, "Um, I should probably let you finish your paper. I'll meet you and the gang tomorrow at the costume shop." On his way to the door, his eyes never left mine. My desk chair nearly took him out when he walked into it.

I followed him over, neither of us sure if we should hug or not.

"See you tomorrow, Edmund." I feebly waved, my heart on rapid beat.

"Bye."

After closing the door, I leaned against it with a sigh. An actual date with Edmund. *Holy shit.* I jumped up and down, my fists pumping the air. If there was ever an occasion for the happy dance, this was it.

I was glad Mom brought me here. Right this very moment, I didn't care why. I just loved my life.

Chapter Nine

Best-Laid Plans

Caroline commandeered Suzy and me early Sunday morning. We trudged behind her in Marks and Spencer, shopping for party goods for her Halloween bash.

I glanced at Suzy. An awful queasiness settled in the pit of my stomach. I knew she was upset that Edmund had asked me out. I'd completely ignored her feelings. *I need to fix this.* "Is everything okay, Suze?" I whispered.

Caroline was on her phone, looking frustrated. She pointed toward the front of the store and mouthed, "Be back in a minute."

Suzy and I continued to wander, looking for munchies.

"I'm fine. Why?" She picked up a bag of chips and read the back label.

I sighed. "'Cause I'm a shitty friend."

"What?" Her head jerked up and she looked me in the eye.

"You like Edmund."

Her mouth opened and closed like a goldfish.

"I've suspected for a while, but I never did anything to stop him from flirting with me. I feel horrible. And now this date and the Halloween party . . ."

Suzy chewed her lower lip and tossed the crisps in the cart.

"I want to tell you everything's okay, but I can't." She spun the ring she wore on her right hand and looked away from me. "The way he looks at you—God, I'd kill for that, even just once. The moment he met you I could tell he fancied you. He's barely taken his eyes off you since then. I know it's mental, and I hate feeling this way, but I'm so damn jealous."

"Suze, I'm so sorry." I met her big blue eyes and felt worse. "I should've stayed away from him. I never expected he'd take an interest in me. When he did, I just . . ." I'd let my hormones overrun my senses. My stomach in knots, I felt like crying. I pulled my navy cardigan tightly around me, hoping its soft fabric would hold me together.

Suzy's hand came to rest on my arm. "I don't blame you. Well, not much anyway." She smiled and patted me. "Edmund's a great guy, a prince, and hot as hell. Any girl would be absolutely barmy to turn him down. If I were in your shoes, I'd have done the exact same thing. I'll get over it, but if I seem distant, it's how I'm coping, okay?"

I returned her smile. "Okay."

"Promise you won't chuck him because of me. I'd rather him be happy with you than miserable with that toxic Barbie doll, Jax."

I put my hand over Suzy's and gave a squeeze. "I promise."

"You girls haven't done anything. Come on, we've got to get moving." Caroline returned, tucking her cell phone in the butt pocket of her jeans. She grabbed the cart from me and rushed down the aisle, randomly tossing things into the basket.

"This party is going to cost a fortune." I chuckled.

"Caroline's family has money. This is pocket change." Suzy gestured for me to follow.

Never had I been this excited about a Halloween party. Nearly ready, I felt incredible.

Edmund suggested we go as a literary couple. Apparently, he'd noticed my Jane Austen collection. We ended up settling on Emma and Mr. Knightley. To say I was eager to see Edmund in his costume was an understatement.

My curls were piled atop my head and I kept my makeup light and fresh. *Gwyneth Paltrow, eat your heart out.* For the final touch I stood before the mirror and tucked a white ribbon through my curls. *Perfect.*

Satisfied, I slipped into my costume. It was a light green empire-waist dress with a sheer overlay embroidered with little white flowers. It reminded me of a dress Jennifer Ehle wore as Elizabeth Bennet in the BBC's *Pride and Prejudice*—by far the best version. The cut hugged the girls, making them look extra perky. *These dresses should make a comeback.* Comfortable and flattering, they were awesome in my book.

Shawl around my shoulders, I grasped the bonnet. Not wanting to mess up my hair, I opted to carry it.

Finished with myself, I went to check on Caroline. The sheer layer of my dress grazed the floor as I walked. For reasons I can't explain, this made me feel incredibly girly.

I knocked at Caroline's door and it flew open. There stood Suzy and Caroline, posed with hands on hips, looking bored. I burst into laughter. Standing before me were Paris Hilton and Nicole Richie, circa when they were still besties. It was perfect. The sequins on their skimpy dresses glinted in the dim light. Large sunglasses, lots of makeup, and a designer bag stuffed with a plush dog completed the look.

"Oh my God, you guys look fantastic."

"I know. We're hot." Suzy spoke in a nasally tone, trying to imitate Paris's American accent.

"You look gorgeous." Caroline broke character and came over, spinning me around as she pulled me into her room. "Edmund's not going to know what to do with himself."

"Thanks." I chuckled and smoothed imaginary wrinkles from the front of my skirt.

"You meeting him downstairs?" Suzy asked, closing the door behind me.

"No, Mr. Knightley is coming upstairs to pick me up." I tried to suppress my grin, but it was no use.

"You realize people are going to think you're Elizabeth and Darcy, right?" Suzy adjusted her pink minidress, attempting to pull it down further than it wanted to go. "You should slip your copy of *Emma* into your bonnet."

"That's a great idea." I spun and ran to the door.

When I stepped into the hall, I saw Edmund. He stood outside my room, black top hat in a leather-gloved hand, the other poised to knock.

Hello, Knightley.

He looked at me. His mouth popped open and then quickly transformed into a grin.

His navy tailcoat hugged his broad shoulders to perfection, and the tan breeches were snug in all the right places. It was the tall leather riding boots that did me in. I sucked in a deep breath after having momentarily stopped breathing.

"Wow, Evie, you look incredible."

A tingly sensation unfurled low in my belly and spread throughout my body.

"Thank you." I cleared the frog from my throat. "You make quite a debonair Mr. Knightley."

"Oooh, that's hot." Paris Hilton appeared in the doorway behind me. She pulled her big glasses down and gave us a cheeky wink. Edmund reached over, took my hand, and pulled me close to his side.

"Nice. Where's Nicole?" He laughed.

The rich sound warmed me to my core. A hand settled on my waist and I angled into him, wanting to be closer. It was wonderful, yet a little strange, to know that we were on a date. *An actual date.* My mind was already jumping to the end of the evening. *Will he kiss me?*

"Come on, Nicole. It's time to make our entrance," the Paris impostor called to her phony sidekick.

"Coming." Caroline appeared in the doorway. "Don't stay up here too long, you two." She sashayed past us in her white minidress.

"Are you ready to go down?" Edmund asked me.

"I just need to grab something. I'll be right back." I rushed into my room, snatched my worn copy of *Emma*, and placed it inside my bonnet. Back in the hall, I turned to him.

"Shall we?" He held his arm out to me.

Twining my arm with his, I met his eyes. "Let's go."

"I've been meaning to ask you, have you gotten your next task?"

"I have. It's just some research."

He held open the stairwell door. "On what?"

"My mom's side of the family, the Elliots."

"Have you started?" The look on his face was hard to decipher.

I lifted my hand and waved it back and forth. "A little. Not much."

"I'm happy to help. I'm good at research. Excellent at research, actually."

I smiled at his offer. He really was a great guy. "And so humble."

He laughed and placed his hand over mine. "Yes, yes, I am."

We hadn't opened the door into the commons yet, but I could hear, and feel, the bass thumping a steady beat. Edmund swung it open. The room was nearly dark, aside from orange and purple fairy lights strung from the ceiling in loops. Colorful and crazily dressed people filled the room, undulating in time to the rhythm.

I kept a firm hold on Edmund as he guided me around and through the chaos. If I lost him now, I might not find him again.

"Wow, I wonder if Caroline anticipated it being so crowded. This is insane," I shouted so Edmund could hear me.

He spoke near my ear. "Oh, she knew. You want to dance?"

I nodded. Edmund wove a way for us to the dance floor. As we arrived, the music transitioned to a slow dance.

Edmund and I looked at each other. He didn't appear nervous, but I sure was. His hands settled confidently on my hips.

Breathe.

Nervously I wound my arms around his neck and averted my gaze to his chest. When I glanced up, he was watching me, smiling.

I took a mental snapshot of the way the copper flecks in his eyes caught the light, how the soft waves of his hair brushed across his forehead, and how his lips . . . they were so invitingly close. I wanted to remember every detail.

If only I could spend forever like this. With him.

"Edmund!" The shrill call cut its way across the crowded dance floor.

We both turned toward the voice. It was none other than Miss BitchyBoobsInYourFace, Chloe Saunders. Dressed as a slutty devil, she held her pointed tail in her hand.

How appropriate.

"You'll never guess who I invited to Caroline's little party." Her voice was singsongy as she gestured to someone behind her. With a sneer on her thin lips, she aimed her smugly satisfied smile at me.

Edmund stiffened and his hand captured mine. I tried to see what he saw, but couldn't. A feeling of dread washed over me. If Chloe was this happy, it couldn't be good. I knew, without a doubt, this was her payback for our first meeting.

"Edmund, darling, you should have told me there was a party tonight." Jax appeared from behind Chloe and grabbed him. Wrapping herself, like a snake, around him, she planted a long, wet, slurpy-sounding kiss on his lips. Her fingers threaded themselves through his blond curls, knocking his hat off.

I felt like I'd been slapped. Edmund was forced to let go of me, or be knocked over by Jax's attentions. His eyes widened and his hands went to brace himself against her shoulders. I looked around the room, waiting for him to disengage. Jax's moans of satisfaction made me want to vomit.

Jesus, if this is who his parents want him to marry, why should I bother? I'm so not like her.

Blood pounded in my ears and my skin crawled. I wanted to run. I needed to be anywhere but here.

Air, I need air. The sea of people turned claustrophobic and overwhelming.

My eyes searched the room for anyone I knew, but with everyone decked out in costumes, I couldn't find my girlfriends. I didn't know what to do. I couldn't just stand there, watching some witch give my date a tongue bath. *Is she going to find a way to come between us every time?*

This was just too much. I liked Edmund far more than was safe for my heart. *I can't watch this.* Feeling shaky, I tried to find Caroline. As I pushed my way through the crush of people, anger pulsed through my veins.

"What the hell is going on with that?" Suzy surprised me and hauled me up next to her. She gestured toward Edmund, but I didn't turn around. I'd already seen it, from the front row.

"Edmund's wannabe princess sucking his face off, what does it look like?" I snipped at her, then cringed. "Sorry."

"That cow. Let's go find Caroline."

I followed Suzy, daring a glance back at Edmund. He was talking to Jax and Chloe, an angry scowl on his face. I watched him scan the room as he ran a hand through his hair and wondered if he was looking for me.

This was such a bad idea. *Lesson learned. Don't date guys whose parents have power over his love life.*

"Oh!" I plowed into the back of a frozen Suzy. "What's the matter?"

I leaned around her to see what caused the roadblock. Inside the kitchen Caroline sat on the counter, kissing a standing Marissa. Suzy pushed against me and backtracked out the door, stumbling over me in her haste.

"Did you know they were . . . ?"

"Didn't have a clue." Suzy chuckled. "It's actually kind of cool."

I nodded. "Let's leave them alone." I rubbed at my shoulder, tears burning. "You know, I think I'm gonna go. Maybe see a movie or something. I'll catch you later."

"Evie, you can't leave." She grabbed my hand. "Don't let Jax scare you off. Edmund will want to talk to you."

"You're probably right, but . . ." I shook my head and squeezed my eyes shut. "This date was such a bad idea. His parents already have his future mapped out with Jax and she knows it. So why am I even bothering? I'm just getting in the way. God, this is so humiliating. I need to be alone for a little while. Need to clear my head."

Suzy sighed. "Fine, but stay safe, okay? There's bound to be a bunch of loonies out. Find me when you get back if you want to talk."

"I will, and have fun."

I glanced back before I left. Edmund was nowhere to be seen. *Jax probably snuck him off somewhere private.* My rational side knew if she did, they'd only be talking, but my jealousy-riddled emotions won out over my rational thought process.

Why couldn't he have just pushed her away and told her off? Screw appearances and family obligations.

At the door to my freedom a crazy-looking mad scientist stopped me.

"Where do you think you're going?" Preston stood in my way, his blond hair in spikes. Weird little round goggles perched on his forehead. "Where's Edmund?"

I pasted a smile I didn't feel on my face. "Preston. Your costume turned out great. Are you entering the competition?"

He met my eyes, seeing right through me. "No, I'm not. You didn't answer my questions. What's going on?"

I shrugged. "This isn't really my scene. I'm going to take off."

"Not your scene, huh? So, why isn't Edmund with you? He's your date, right?" He looked like he was trying to sort out whether or not he should be mad at me for ditching his best friend.

"Edmund got sidetracked."

"By what?"

"Jax."

"Oh bollocks." He frowned and reached for my hands. "Are you okay?"

I looked into his concerned face. "I'm fine. I just want to get out of here."

"Right." Preston nodded. "Let's go." He grabbed my hand and tugged me out the door.

"I can't believe it's so late," I whispered to Preston as we returned to the dorms. A few stragglers were still out partying, but it was mostly quiet.

"I know. But I had so much fun tonight. Way better than the party would've been." Preston grabbed my hand and squeezed.

"Thanks for keeping me company." I pulled my shawl tighter around me. "Although after that ghost tour I doubt I'll be able to go anywhere alone on campus ever again." Our tour guide had taken us through the best-known Oxford University haunts. Super creepy.

Preston laughed as we walked up the stairs. "I'll happily escort you anywhere."

"You better. That was your brilliant idea and I'm a chicken." I pulled my hand from his and playfully pushed on his shoulder.

It felt weird, him holding my hand. Granted, throughout the spooky ghost tour it'd felt perfectly fine.

"Anytime."

"And thanks for dinner. You helped take my mind off . . . things. I'm really glad you came with me."

We stood on my floor's landing and he reached up, giving a gentle tug on a tendril of my hair that had slipped loose. "You deserve the best, Evie. If Edmund can't give that to you, there are others who'd gladly step up." He kissed me on the cheek. "I guess this is good night."

Was that an offer?

"Night." I gave him a shy wave and stepped through the door to my floor. I leaned against it and heaved a deep breath. *This isn't how I pictured the evening ending.*

This night had played out so differently in my mind. In my little fantasy world, Edmund and I would be about to have our first kiss. Instead, I was coming home alone, wondering if my date now had a brand new, parental-approved girlfriend.

I kicked off my shoes, anxious to crawl into bed. Frowning, I realized I never got a picture of myself as Emma. It would've been nice to have one to send to Dad and Abby.

Pushing away from the door, I padded down the hall, my shoes dangling from my fingertips. *Is someone sitting against my door?* I squinted my eyes.

Edmund.

I stopped in front of his sleeping form and stared, unsure what to make of this. Inside, my emotions pinged from annoyance to anger to happiness that he was here. *He's got me such a mess. Why is he even here? What does this mean?*

I crouched down and gazed at him. *Damn you, Chloe.* If she hadn't brought Jax tonight, where would we be instead?

"Edmund, wake up," I said softly near his ear.

"Hmm?" he mumbled, barely stirring.

"Wakey, wakey, eggs and bakey." I shook his shoulder. He cracked open a bleary eye. It took a moment to focus, but when he did, he snapped awake.

"Evie, you're all right. I looked everywhere for you." Relief spread across his face. He scrambled to his feet and grasped my upper arms, as if needing to touch me. "I was so worried. Why didn't you answer your mobile?" His hands dropped as if touching me had scorched him.

"I didn't have my phone. I forgot to grab it when I left." I shrugged. Waves of exhaustion crashed over me.

"I'm so sorry about tonight; it was awful. Can we talk?" His eyes pleaded with mine.

I nodded and unlocked my door with a sigh. Going in, I picked up some scattered laundry from the floor and stuffed it in my hamper.

Edmund sat on my bed, staring at his hands. I parked myself on my desk chair and turned to face him. I couldn't sit next to him, not right now.

"I don't know where to begin. Sorry isn't anywhere near adequate. Please believe I didn't know she was going to be there." He reached out and grasped my hand. "Can I ever make this up to you?"

"Edmund, I'm not mad." I shook my head and met his pleading eyes. "I know this wasn't your fault. I'm just really confused. Despite wanting to, I don't think I belong in your world. I'm just an average girl from Seattle."

I wanted him to tell me that I *could* fit into his world. That he wanted me to. Instead, he sat in silence, looking at his shoes.

She's still on track to be his future wife. My stomach turned. If I kept going down the path of more than friends with him, I was going to walk away with an utterly ravaged chest cavity.

"Evie, I . . ." He raised a hand, like he wanted to touch me, but stopped himself. "You're not average, furthest thing from it. I'm sorry for everything. You deserve so much better." He stood, startling me. "I'll see you in class tomorrow. Good night." He was out the door like The Flash.

Why is everyone so concerned with what I deserve tonight?

Chapter Ten

Shattered

"Paris? Christmas?" I squeaked. "I've always wanted to go there." I stopped walking across campus and leaned against a leaf-bare tree, buttoning the top of my pea coat.

"That's exactly why I thought we should go." The smile in Dad's voice warmed me through the misty fog. He lived to surprise me. It was one of my favorite things about him.

"This is going to be amazing. I can't wait."

"Me neither," he said, groaning like he was stretching. "I've got to get to bed, Peaches, early meeting in the morning. Give me a call tomorrow."

"I will. Love you, Dad."

"Love you, too."

I stayed against the tree, clutching my phone in my hands. Closing my eyes, I pictured a glittery Eiffel Tower with snow softly falling around it. Christmas lights. The Louvre. I opened my eyes and let out a squeal, clapping my hands together.

"Good news?" a voice asked, making me jump.

"Caroline, you scared me." I laughed and pressed a hand over my heart. "It was my dad. He's planned a trip for us this Christmas."

"Oh, where to?"

"Paris."

"Have you ever been?"

"No." I shook my head. "Although, I think my dad has."

"You'll love it. It's fabulous and it's not that far either." She smiled and changed the subject. "So, I've been thinking, we should do a girls' night and catch a movie this weekend."

"Oh, here comes Suzy." I smiled and waved to her to join us. Caroline smiled. "So, Suze, would you be up for a girls' night?"

"Absolutely."

I sighed. "I could definitely use some girl time. No men allowed."

"Brilliant. I'll see if Marissa wants to come, too, really do it up." Caroline pulled out her phone and started tapping away.

"So, how are things with Edmund?" Suzy pulled out her tube of lip balm and applied a fresh coat.

"Awkward, *extremely* awkward. We barely speak. Which makes our classes together painful. I miss how things used to be." I pinched the bridge of my nose. "If I could just stop having feelings for him I'd be better off."

Suzy chewed at her bottom lip, her eyes darting to the ground.

"What? You obviously want to say something; spit it out."

"I heard something at breakfast." She stared at me.

"Okay, and?" I'd been opting for early morning wake-ups to avoid running into Edmund and the weirdness of being near him.

"Well, while we were eating, Preston asked Edmund if it would be all right if he asked you out."

What? I stopped walking and turned, eyes wide. "What did Edmund say?" It was wrong how much I cared.

Caroline took over. "He didn't say anything. At first he looked shocked, then got cheesed off. He gave Preston a look, got up, and left. Preston said, 'I guess he doesn't like the idea.'"

"Okay, I don't know what I'm more disturbed by, Preston wanting to ask me out or Edmund being . . . whatever it is Edmund's being."

He doesn't like the idea of me being with another guy. I'd be a liar if I said this didn't thrill me. Yet, along with that bubbly excitement coursed irritation. "Guys are too confusing."

"Well, at least you've got two hot guys interested in you. I'm liable to be Single Suzy for the rest of my life."

"Suze, you're a great catch. Some guy will figure it out. You just need someone more mature."

"Hmm, maybe I need to start looking at graduate students." She winked at me with a silly giggle.

We cut across the grass to St. John's, the frosty leaves crunching under our feet. "Do you want to grab an early dinner? I'm getting hungry and I'd like to hit the dining hall before Edmund."

"So you *are* avoiding him. I thought so." Caroline smirked.

The sun had set and a chill descended in the air. I pulled my gloves from my pocket and slipped them on my hands. "I suppose I am. It's hard being around him when it feels like whatever chance we had is gone. Why would he let his parents have such a say in his love life? I get that they're the king and queen, but it's still his life."

"I think there's still a chance for the two of you. I mean, obviously he likes you and cares about you. Anyone with eyes can see that. How's he taking to you avoiding him?" Suzy sniffed, her nose red.

"I can't tell. We don't really talk above polite pleasantries. Even if he wanted to talk to me, which I don't think he does, there always seem to be too many cameras and no privacy."

Suzy put her arm around my shoulders and gave me a sympathetic squeeze. "Let's go get some early dinner."

It wasn't long before I was back in my room at my desk. The three of us had finished eating and left, just as Edmund arrived.

Pulling up Google, I typed in Mom's maiden name: Elliot.

It's well past time I started my fourth quest. Although nervous, at least I wasn't ditching Mom anymore.

Pages of results popped up. *Man, there's a lot of Elliots.*

I added *Lilliana* to the search bar, hoping to narrow down the results.

The first page of links pulled up and my stomach dropped.

No way.

They were all associated with the Duchess of Westminster. What were the odds she'd have a daughter named Lilliana?

I've got a bad feeling. It was like being at Welsington all over again; those same uneasy feelings assaulted me. My hand hovered over my touchpad as I skimmed the first three links. They all dealt with Lilliana Elliot's disappearance. I clicked on the top link. Eyes wide, I read.

The Duchess of Westminster has refused to answer any questions into the whereabouts of her daughter, Lady Lilliana Elliot. It's widely speculated that Lady Lilliana has gone against family wishes and eloped, making a most undesirable match. Sources close to the Duchess tell us Lady Lilliana's been disowned.

I studied a picture of the duchess. In the caption below, for the first time, her name was used: Clarice Elliot. *Her name's Clarice?* The only thing I knew about my mom's side of the family was that my grandmother's name was Clarice.

Dear God, is Mom leading me to Clarice?

Holding my breath, I continued scrolling until a photo made it all come out in a whoosh.

Mom?

I bounded down the stairs, the morning sun perking up my grumpy self. It'd been a long night of thinking and overthinking.

With my mind full of my mom, I stepped into the dining hall and immediately saw Edmund. He sat at our table, waiting. I sucked in a sharp breath. *Oh, shit.*

It'd been a week and a half since the great avoidance started. He didn't look pleased. My heart fluttered.

I leisurely gathered my breakfast, hoping one of our friends would show up and rescue me.

Taking a deep breath, I attempted to center myself. *It's okay. You'll be fine, no matter what happens.*

Carrying my tray, I joined him. "Morning, Edmund, you're up early."

"I am. Do you know why?" He looked at me, his copper-flecked eyes unwavering.

Swallowing, I said, "I could probably guess."

"Evie," his voice was soft, "why are you avoiding me?" He reached across the table, his fingertips nearly touching mine.

I stared at my breakfast, not about to confess how hurt and disappointed I felt.

"I miss you. Every day. There's so much I want to tell you. I need to be near you, to see your face. Please, don't cut me out." He ended on a whisper.

"I'm not. We sit next to each other in classes. I just . . ." I sighed with frustration and ran a hand through my hair. "Edmund, I don't know what you want from me."

The look in his eyes told me he wasn't sure what he wanted from me. Or maybe it was that he wasn't sure what he *could* offer me. He opened his mouth to speak, but something stopped him.

I pressed my palms against the cool tabletop. "I can't even begin to understand your world; I know that. But it's so opposite of everything I'm used to and it's confusing."

"I'll admit, my life is far from normal and I apologize for that." He swallowed. "And yes, my duty is to my family and I must uphold that. But I don't want it to get in the way of our friendship."

Friendship? Was I supposed to pretend that he'd never asked me out? Forget that we were on the verge of possibly something more?

Nodding, I looked away. "I guess I thought if I didn't spend a lot of time with you I wouldn't have to deal with this . . . this weirdness between us." *Or be reminded daily how I don't measure up.* I scratched a fingernail against a dent on the tabletop. "I miss how we used to be."

"I miss it, too." His hand reached across the table and covered mine. It was chilly. I stopped myself from placing my other hand over his to warm it up.

Our eyes met and in an instant I knew. Even though I wasn't sure if we had any sort of future together, and despite all the confusion running rampant inside me, I wanted him in my life. Smiling at him, I said, "Friends?"

His face lit up. "Friends. For now, anyway."

For now? The way his eyes twinkled made my heart do an erratic little prance in my chest.

"So, Preston told me he took you on a ghost walk."

"He did." I chuckled. "It was pretty cool." A line formed for breakfast; the morning rush had begun.

"Did you guys have fun?"

"Yeah, lots. Preston's always fun to be around."

"He is, isn't he?" Edmund looked away and stared out the tall windows.

I studied his face. The early morning light glowed through the leafless trees, leaving a stark pattern of light dancing across his chest. He was handsome, oh yes. But my attraction went so much deeper than his looks.

I loved how I could talk to him, *really* talk to him, and he understood me. And how just as easily we could sit in silence, not needing to say a word. Maybe it was his inner history geek speaking to mine. All I knew was I was drawn to him.

My brain flashed up reminders of how we'd nearly kissed on my bed. A tingle low in my tummy sparked at the memory.

That'd be my biggest regret. Not kissing him. I'd never know what his lips felt like or how he would've held me. I'd be stuck in the realm of imagination. A place I didn't want to be.

"You finally caught her." Preston's voice boomed through the dining hall, cutting through my thoughts. "Do you know how many mornings he's been down here trying to catch you?"

"Well, he caught me today. Morning, Preston."

"Aren't you looking lovely?" Preston sat beside me, smiling. "So are you up to anything fun tonight?"

"I was just about to ask her if she wanted to meet at the library and study, what with finals around the corner and all." Edmund took a sip of his tea.

I nodded. I could use all the extra studying I could get. My first finals at Oxford had me stressed.

"That sounds like loads of fun. Want to get supper together before?" Preston asked, dumping milk on his cereal.

I glanced at Edmund, who looked everywhere but at me. His hands were clenched so tight his knuckles went white.

Just friends. Time to move on. If Preston wants to grab dinner, why not?

"Sure, what time do you want to eat?"

"How about I meet you at your last class?"

"You know, Evie and I have that class together, so why don't all of us go to dinner? We can head to the library afterwards." Edmund met Preston's gaze, challenging him to suggest an alternative.

Preston grinned. "That'd be fun. I just assumed you'd be getting dinner with Jax. She's in town, right?"

She's here? Why had no one told me? Suzy and Caroline usually knew everything.

"Bollocks." Edmund closed his eyes and rubbed his forehead. "Why don't we all go to dinner? Then we can hit the library."

I chuckled. *So not gonna happen.* This chick had threatened me, humiliated me, and had her claws in the one guy I couldn't stop myself from falling for.

There was no way in hell. I was pissed he'd even suggest it.

"As delightful as that sounds, I'm gonna pass. I just remembered, I have some shivs in my dorm that I'd rather drive under my fingernails, sorry." I stood and took my tray to the trash. "I'm heading to class, I've got some reading to catch up on. Enjoy your breakfast." I tossed my bag over my shoulder and walked off, a little swagger to my step.

"I think I love her," Preston said, laughing.

A huge grin filled my face.

"Hey, Evie. Wait up," Preston called. "I'll walk you to class and we can discuss this shiv thing. It sounds way more enjoyable."

I glanced back and saw Edmund watching us with a scowl. I felt bad. For about a second. He was in this situation of his own doing. *Make up your damn mind.* Date Jax or date me. *Just pick one.*

"So, are we still on for dinner tonight?" Preston asked when we got outside. "Since I'm guessing the shivs were just a ploy to get out of dinner with the ice queen."

"Definitely, dinner sounds great." I wrapped my blue scarf around my neck and stuffed my hands in my pockets.

Preston fell into step beside me. I looked his way and smiled. Any girl would be lucky to catch his eye. He's smart, funny, and dorky in a charmingly good way. But could I ever see him as more than a friend? Could I lock my feelings for Edmund up tight enough and move on?

Preston would become collateral damage if I couldn't. *I don't want that.*

Stopped outside the looming gray stone building of my first class, I turned to him. "Thanks for walking me."

Preston's face lit up. "No problem; see you later."

"See you at lunch."

Preston bounced down the steps, his blond hair flopping, and waved at me.

I really hope I'm not starting more trouble.

Edmund slipped into the seat next to me just as lecture started. He didn't glance at me once.

When Professor Sawyer turned the lights back on, I stood and stretched. I didn't dare let myself touch Edmund. The frisson he ignited wasn't something I could handle. Standing, he hooked his thumb in his backpack strap. "Why don't I drop by your room tonight instead of meeting at the library?"

"What? Why?"

"Well, I don't know how long I'm going to be tonight. I'd hate to cancel last minute and I don't want you waiting for me or walking back alone in the dark."

His words sent a surge of irritation through me. I closed my eyes and inhaled through my nose. "Tell you what. Let's reschedule for a night when Jax isn't in town? I wouldn't want to cut into your time together." I gave him a tight smile. "This way Preston and I won't have to rush through dinner either."

I'm scum.

"You're still getting dinner with Preston?" His eyebrows drew together. He didn't look happy.

"I am." I was glad this bothered him. He may not like me enough to choose me, but he did care that I was spending time with another guy.

"Right. Well, I hope you and Preston have a nice time. I'm free to study tomorrow. Check your schedule and let me know if that works for you. See you in our next class." His voice was chilly.

Before I could reply, he left. Seeing him walk away hurt. He always walked with me.

What does he want me to do? Should I sit around and pine for someone who isn't, and probably never will be, mine?

"Edmund," I called after him. "Edmund, wait." I ran up the aisle and caught him near the doorway. This wasn't the best place for this conversation, but I didn't care. I needed answers.

Stepping outside together, I grabbed his arm to slow him down. "Are you serious? *You're* mad? It's dinner. With Preston. Come on."

He stopped and faced me with a sigh. Speaking quietly, he said, "I know I have no right to feel this way, but I absolutely hate the thought of you and Preston starting something." His fingers ran through his hair, messing it up.

"Why should it concern you? You're the one who can't seem to make a decision one way or the other. I'm not the one torturing you. Jax isn't either. You're doing this to yourself and you're dragging us along with you. You have to deal with your choice— or lack of one." I poked my finger in his chest with every point I made. "I'm not going to sit around, waiting and hoping one day you'll pay attention to me. I don't work like that, even if you are a prince."

He leaned his face close to mine and whispered, "You don't understand."

I moved in even closer, our faces a breath apart. "Then help me understand, because I'm lost and frustrated as hell with all these mixed messages."

"I can't do this here. I'm sorry." He turned and walked away, trying to appear unfazed, but failing miserably. I could just imagine the headlines tomorrow. *Prince Edmund in lover's quarrel and not with rumored romantic interest Lady Jacqueline.*

I quickly walked away, ignoring the photographers who turned their focus to me. Two students slipped in front of me, giving me a little shelter from the flashing cameras. Safely at my next class, my shields turned, curtly nodded at me, then disappeared into the milling students. *They're part of Edmund's security detail.* They had to be.

Outside the auditorium doors, I stopped. I couldn't bring myself to go in. A lump settled in my throat and my eyes stung. I looked at the ceiling, willing the tears to go away. When the first drop hit my cheek, I made a beeline for the bathroom, barricading myself in the first available stall.

No matter what I did, I couldn't stop them.

Trust me to fall for a guy who can't date who he wants.

My heart shattered. He felt so far away, so unreachable.

I had so much I needed to tell him. He was the only one who knew about Mom's letters. I wanted him to know what my research had uncovered. How I strongly suspected Mom was the daughter of the dragon duchess, making me her granddaughter. But I couldn't, not now, not with how weird things were.

Doubt it would make a damn bit of difference anyway.

I was late to class that day. And for the first time in my life, my punctual self didn't care.

Chapter Eleven

Unexpected Reunions

"Do you still fancy Edmund?" Preston tucked his hands in his pockets as we walked back to St. John's after dinner.

"What?" I asked, feeling a little tipsy from the half a beer I'd had. Normally I didn't drink. But he argued that I couldn't come to England, eat in a proper English pub, and not have a pint. Plus, I was of legal drinking age here.

"I know how he feels about you, but I'm curious if you still feel something for him?"

Shit. How do I answer that? The fact that he knew what Edmund felt for me was spinning in my lubricated brain. I held my jacket closed with a gloved hand, the night air misty and chilly against my skin.

Closing my eyes, I answered truthfully. "I'm confused. I want to stop liking him, to stop caring. But I can't. I *should* move on, right?" I didn't wait for an answer. "I just haven't figured out how."

"I was hoping you might be done. But I understand, it's not quite that simple, is it?" He smiled when I shook my head. "If you ever need anything, I'm here, whenever and whatever you decide." He reached over and grabbed my free hand.

His was warm and comforting, but that pulse of energy that surged through me whenever Edmund and I touched just wasn't there. "Thanks, Preston." I looked down the dark path at the dots of illumination. It'd be so much easier if I could think of him *that* way. Yet, all through dinner I'd been wondering what Jax and Edmund were doing.

"Just do me a favor?"

"What's that?" I looked up at him.

"When you're figuring things out, consider giving me a chance."

A sad smile touched my lips. "I will."

"We should probably get back. I'm sure you have as much homework as I do, if not more."

Inside the dorms, Preston walked me to my door and kissed my cheek. Although, if I hadn't turned my head, his original target just might've been my lips.

With a twinkle in his eye and a dashing wink, he said, "Night, Evie."

"Night."

As soon as I pulled my key out to unlock the door, Caroline was in the hall, questioning me.

"So it's Preston now?" She asked with a cheeky grin. "I guess I can see it, after his Halloween rescue of you and all?"

"Good evening, Caroline, how was your day? Mine was a little odd." I turned to face her so she wasn't breathing down my neck.

"Blah, blah, blah." She lifted a hand, making it talk, her black bob bouncing. "Enough with the chitchat. Spill the beans. You and Preston? He's a hell of a kisser, did you notice?"

A startled laugh escaped me. "Really? You and Preston?"

"It was once after a party." She waved it off.

"No, I haven't kissed him. He's interested in being more than friends, but I'm not ready."

"Edmund is going to hate this."

I scrunched my nose. "Well, that's his problem, isn't it?"

"I suppose so." She looked unsure.

"What? Do you know something else I don't?"

"Not really." Caroline shrugged. "You know his parents have always put a lot of pressure on him to be with Jax. One day he'll realize he doesn't have to sacrifice his own happiness for the status of his family. I just hope he's not too late when he figures it out."

I rubbed my eyes, feeling the tears well up again. "I know I'm not Jax and therefore not good enough for him. It was ridiculous to think I ever had a chance. I so need a break." I closed my door as a tear slipped down my cheek.

You survived and you didn't fail any classes. I took a deep breath and grinned as I sat on a metal bench, waiting in the baggage claim of Charles de Gaulle Airport. *Paris.* Dad's flight would be here soon and I couldn't wait to see him. This was the perfect thing to take my mind off Edmund and my quest letters.

Edmund. I wonder where he's at?

I'd been in a funk ever since my dinner with Preston. Edmund and I'd started our study sessions right after, which only made it worse.

Caroline had once told me that Edmund allowing himself to be alone with me was significant. That it made me different and special.

Well, things change. I'm no longer special.

I thought back to the first study session, how I'd been hoping to talk, just the two of us. When I arrived at the library, I spotted Edmund, and right next to him was Preston, waving.

"Hey there." Preston had grinned impishly.

"Hey, boys." I sat across from Edmund and pulled my makeshift flash cards from my bag, wondering how long Preston would be staying.

"You're probably curious why I'm here," Preston announced with a cheesy grin. "I begged Edmund to let me join you guys." He placed his hand over his heart. "My day just wouldn't have been complete without sitting here, listening to you guys talk about boring dead guys and their art." He gave me a teasing wink.

"Subtle, Preston, real subtle." Edmund sniffed and looked at his book. "I thought you might be more comfortable if someone was with us."

Nope, comfortable wasn't the emotion coursing through me. More like fury.

"I'd be more comfortable, or *you'd* be more comfortable?" I'd shivered when our eyes met. Angry or not, he still affected me. "I wasn't worried about being alone with you, Edmund. I can control myself."

"That's not what I meant. I thought we'd both be more comfortable." He didn't smile. A dull sheen had replaced the usual sparkle in his eyes. He looked wretched.

"Whatever, let's just study—it's what we're here for."

I snapped out of my memory as a large group of people scuttled into the baggage claim. The area swelled with conversations and people rushing to greet loved ones. I looked around, but Dad wasn't with them. Leaning back, I blew out a soft breath.

What's Edmund doing for Christmas? I shook my head, not wanting to think of him. I was still ticked. I thought we'd settled on being friends. *What kind of friends need chaperoning?* Did he really think I'd throw myself at him? Who did he think he was? *Wait, right. A prince.* Most girls probably couldn't control themselves around him.

While Edmund and I quizzed each other, Preston doodled in a notebook and hummed Justin Timberlake's "Sexy Back." I think he was trying to annoy Edmund. At first it was funny. After an hour, it was grating.

When Preston broke into the chorus of a Katy Perry song, I was over it.

"Preston!" Edmund said loudly.

"Ssssh," came from the surrounding tables.

Lowering his voice, Edmund continued, "Preston, I think we're good. You can go."

"Aw, and just when it was getting interesting." Preston packed up his backpack. "Took you long enough to get annoyed."

I smiled at Preston as I binder-clipped my note cards and tossed them in my bag. "I should go, too. I've got another study group to get to. Walk me back to the dorms?"

"Of course." Preston stood and waited for me. "You coming, Edmund?"

"No, I've got some things to finish up. I'll see you guys later."

"See you at dinner then." Slinging my bag on my shoulder, I waved.

Edmund watched us leave, looking troubled.

Through our tense study sessions, one thing remained the same. We were never alone.

I sat up straight and pulled my minty lip gloss from my pocket. As I put it on, I looked around again. A frazzled mom with three kids rushed past me. I smiled at her and scanned the crowd for Dad.

Reaching into my bag, I pulled out Mom's letters. Being here reminded me of her. She'd collected replicas of the Eiffel Tower. I'd brought my favorite one with Swarovski crystals to Oxford with me.

"Evie!"

My head snapped up. Dad rushed toward me through the crowd. I stuffed my letters in my bag and ran for him. Stopping, he dropped his carry-on and opened his arms, preparing for impact. We collided in a bear hug.

"Oh, my Evie girl," he said, breathless from running.

I hugged him tight. "I missed you so much."

"Let me get a look at you." He held me at arm's length. "How I've missed you." He wrapped me in another hug.

"How was your flight?" I squeezed him.

"Long, but worth it." He released me and draped an arm around my shoulder. "You look fantastic. I think England must agree with you." He chuckled. "There isn't another reason is there? Say a certain boy?"

"No, no guy, just enjoying England."

"Really? I would've thought you'd have caught the eye of someone special over here. At least that's what the tabloids are saying."

"Too busy with school, I suppose." Dwelling on my shitastic love life was not how I wanted to spend my holiday. "Wait a minute, tabloids?"

Dad nodded. "Your face has been on the cover of a few magazines, claiming a certain prince is falling in love with an American girl."

My mouth popped open. "Really? I know I've been on the covers over here, but that comes with being Edmund's friend. But back home?"

Dad nodded.

"That's crazy." I rolled my bag to the carousel, watching for Dad's.

"Well, I'm glad to hear you're so focused on your studies. If your mother were here, she'd tell you to enjoy this time, to have fun, and to leave some room for a love life."

Mom fell in love at university. Of course she'd want the same for me. It'd never happen if I couldn't get over this unhealthy crush of mine.

I sighed and smiled. "If only I could find a guy willing to fight for me, then I'd be set." That's what it ultimately boiled down to. I wasn't enough. Edmund would never challenge his family for me.

"Sounds like there's a story there," Dad said as he grabbed his suitcase. I knew my next birthday letter was tucked inside it somewhere. My fingers itched to hold it. The next quest letter, on the other hand, was an entirely different matter. I'd yet to pick it up from Anton.

"Probably, but it's one I'd rather not get into. You ready to go to the hotel?" I asked.

"You bet."

A short ride later, we stood before the Renaissance Paris Vendome Hotel.

The exterior was a striking black and white. Sleek black pots with well-tended boxwood bushes flanked the door and ran along the sidewalk under the windows. I smiled at its welcoming easiness. *I can't believe I'm here.*

After checking in, we went to dinner at a small cafe nearby. Miniature Christmas trees twined with glittering fairy lights decorated the window boxes. It was perfect.

I smiled at Dad as we nibbled on warm sandwiches made with fresh crusty bread and shared a small carafe of wine.

"I'm exhausted. I'm too old to go this long without sleep." Dad yawned and stretched.

"Did you sleep at all on the plane?"

He shook his head. He was like me, neither of us could sleep in-flight.

"Let's go back to the hotel and get you into bed." I patted his hand, so happy to have him here.

My thoughts were turbulent that night as I curled in bed. Edmund, my grades, the gang, Edmund, my birthday, Edmund, my next letter, Christmas, possibly being related to a duchess, and of course . . . Edmund.

I'd gone to Paris, yet I couldn't escape my stress.

Dad and I spent the next couple days museum hopping. The Louvre with its Nike of Samothrace was my highlight. Up close, the sculpture was breathtaking. All the slides and pictures I'd seen hadn't done her justice. She looked like the artist had captured in marble a real woman underneath a flimsy sheath of fabric. It was mind-bogglingly beautiful.

Sadly, not even Nike could distract me from Edmund. As I stood in front of her, I wished he were there, beside me.

The morning of my birthday, the sky was a bright blue. Dad took me for a chilly walk along the Seine. We passed bridge after bridge, talking and catching up.

"So, should we go to the Eiffel Tower to celebrate?" Dad asked.

I nodded as my phone rang. A glance at the caller ID made my heart race. "Oh, my God."

Edmund. My breathing quickened. *Why am I so nervous?*

I looked at Dad, and he smiled at me with a curious expression. "You okay?"

"Um, I need to take this. I'll be right back." I walked a little ways away as Dad leaned on the rock-and-cement wall. He didn't need to see what a lovesick idiot I was. "Hello?"

"Evie, hi! Happy birthday!"

The sound of his low voice sent a shiver through me. A familiar warmth enveloped me despite the chilly weather. "Thanks," I managed to say. "Um, how did you know it was my birthday?"

"Caroline told me. She said you mentioned it before you left. Told me you were excited to see your dad for your birthday."

"Ah, I see." I smiled.

"Did your dad make it to England safely?"

"Yeah, he's here, but we're not in England. I met him in Paris and we're celebrating my birthday and Christmas here."

"Wait, you're in Paris?" he asked with an incredulous laugh.

"Yeah?" I answered, no clue why this news was such a shock. "Why?"

"I'm here, too. My parents decided last minute, well last minute to me, to celebrate Christmas in Paris. Mum's sister lives here now."

"Well, wow!" My brain scrambled for something to say. "What a small world. Is your whole family here?" I kicked at the frost-covered grass. What were the odds we'd both end up in Paris for the holiday?

"They are. Well, Philip and Lauren are coming in today. Where are you staying?"

"Um, the Renaissance Paris Vendome." I pushed my sunglasses up my nose.

"Lovely, that's close to the Ritz, where I'm at. Since we're both here, we should get together."

"That'd be fun." I glanced at Dad. Still leaning against the wall, he watched me.

"What are you doing tonight? I'd love to give you your birthday present."

"You got me a present?" My voice rose an octave in shock. *Ah! What is he doing?*

"I did. I saw it and thought of you."

"I don't know what to say."

"Well, tell me I can take you to dinner tonight. That'd be a good start."

I hesitated. "Um, my dad's taking me to dinner."

"You could invite me to tag along, if that'd be okay."

Do I really want Dad and Edmund to meet? This holiday was supposed to be a break from him. Yet the simple sound of his voice made me crave to be near him. I wanted to see him. Closing my eyes, I shook my head at myself.

"Hang on." I hit mute and jogged back to Dad. "Would you be okay if I invited someone to join us for dinner?" I asked, slightly winded.

"Of course. Is this a *special* someone?"

I smiled coyly, not answering. Edmund definitely was special, in numerous ways. I gestured that I'd be one more minute as I took my phone off mute.

"Okay, you're invited. Where do you want to meet?"

"How about I pick you guys up at your hotel. Would seven o'clock work?"

"Sounds perfect. We'll see you at seven."

"Brilliant. See you soon, Evie." The way his voice softly caressed my name did unexplainable things inside me.

Once I hung up, I steadied myself against the rock wall and took a few deep breaths. My pulse slowly returned to normal. I grinned from ear to ear; I couldn't help it.

Dad sidled up next to me and put my arm through his, patting my hand. "So we're having dinner with a mystery person, are we? Is it a boy?"

"Yes, he's a friend from school."

"Anyone I've heard of?"

I looked at Dad, still unable to wipe the grin off my face. "It's Edmund."

"The prince?"

"That'd be the one."

"Well, my stars, how exciting." He laughed. "I'm guessing the Eiffel Tower can wait for another day."

I nodded. "Probably a good idea. I'd hate to rush through it."

Dad bobbed his head and walked on. "Your grandmother Elliot would be livid."

"Why?" I asked. Dad never willingly talked about Clarice. He always said he didn't know enough about her to say anything.

He blew out a breath and crossed his arms over his chest. "Your mom told me your grandmother has ideas about royalty mingling with commoners. Ridiculous, really."

I wondered if I should tell Dad about the letters and how I suspected Mom had quite the illustrious family background. I knew I'd need to sooner or later. "It's a good thing she doesn't care about me or I'd be quite the shock."

Dad frowned and looked across the street. A cigar shop had a massive cigar bolted on its front; the glowing tip let off a steady curl of smoke. "On some level she must care. Despite her disappointment in Lily's choices . . ." He pointed to himself. "She has to care; you're a part of Lily."

I shrugged, uneasy. Guilt uncoiled inside my stomach. I wanted to tell him about the letters and Clarice, everything. I just didn't know how to start.

Dad and I walked until we reached the Pont Neuf, the oldest and most famous bridge in Paris. I looked around at all the people out on such a cold day.

"You've gone awfully quiet. What's rattling around in that noggin of yours?" He reached over and tapped my forehead.

"Nothing in particular, just enjoying the scenery," I replied, looking out over the river. *And stressing over the things I haven't told you.* "It really is beautiful here."

"Don't for a second think I'm buying that. You're either thinking about this handsome prince we're dining with tonight or that old hag."

"Clarice." It was closest to the truth. All these years I'd never called her Grandma. She was always Clarice. She didn't deserve the title of grandmother.

"Don't waste your time. She's not worth it."

"You really never met her?" I looked up at him.

Dad sighed. "No, but I saw her from a distance once. I wanted to meet her, but your mother wouldn't let me. She said her mom would never approve of us. That meeting her would only make what we were about to do impossible. We had one choice if we wanted to be together."

"Did you never wonder why?"

"Oh, sure I did, but your mother hated to talk about her family. She told me she was from a very old and wealthy English line. Her mother had basically arranged a marriage for her and Lily couldn't stomach the thought of it. So, I rescued her and we eloped."

Just like Edmund and how his parents want him with Jax.

Mom left everything behind to marry Dad, the antithesis of wealth and an American to boot. Having seen Welsington in all its splendor, I knew what she sacrificed and what she'd been running from.

If only I could find a way rescue the prince.

Chapter Twelve

Flying

I stood looking out our hotel window at the Paris skyline. Nearby chimneystacks smoked and I could see the sparkling lights of the Eiffel Tower. Clasping my silver heart pendant around my neck, I jumped at the sound of the room phone bleeping. I momentarily closed my eyes and inhaled, willing my nerves to calm. My stockinged feet slid against the curlicue-patterned carpet to the phone. "Hello?"

"Good evening, Miss Gray, a gentleman guest is waiting for you in the lobby," the man at the front desk informed me.

"Thank you." I hung up, placing my hand on my somersaulting tummy. It's amazing how quickly my irritation with him vanished. *I can do this. We're friends.*

"Who was on the phone?" Dad asked, tying his tie.

"Front desk. Edmund's here." I tried to stop smiling, but I couldn't.

Dad slipped into his black suit coat. "So what's really going on between you two?"

I met his eyes. "Nothing. I mean, I like him, but his parents already have a girl all picked out for him."

"If he likes you as much as I suspect you like him, anything's possible. Love can work miracles. You just have to believe." He kissed my nose. "Come on, introduce me to this prince of yours."

My prince. I grinned and grabbed my coat as we went out the door.

In the elevator I straightened the front of my navy sheath dress, listening to the strains of Mozart being piped in. The closer we got to the ground floor, the louder my heart thudded, masking the music. Dad stood next to me and squeezed my hand.

"You look lovely. Don't be nervous," he whispered.

I frowned at him. "I'm not nervous." *Liar.*

I wonder if Edmund's nervous?

The elevator dinged and the doors opened to the modern lobby. A woman in an evening gown was with a man in a tux, waiting to get on. Smiling, I stepped out and looked around.

There he is.

Standing by the gas fireplace, hand against the wooden-slatted façade, he watched the flames. He turned and spotted me, and his face lit up. I froze. *Did he get even more attractive?* He closed the space between us and wrapped me in a tight, unexpected hug.

I melted against his chest; the scent of him, clean soap and sunshine, filled my nose. I wasn't used to this side of him, but I liked it. *A lot.*

"I missed you," he whispered in my ear, not letting me go. "Happy birthday."

Best. Birthday. Ever.

An older couple walked past us, heading for the elevator. The woman watched us, a soft smile on her lips.

Releasing me, Edmund took a small step back. Thankfully, my knees worked. I stood there, staring. His blond waves tousled to perfection, his eyes a brilliant blue. How I'd missed this face.

I shook my head to clear it. *I need help; this is pathetic.*

"Edmund, this is my father, Henry Gray. Dad, this is Edmund. We had a couple classes together last term." My pulse jumped. *Shit, I didn't introduce him as Prince Edmund. Should I add that now?*

Luckily, Dad came to my rescue. He bowed his head respectfully and said, "Your Royal Highness, it's a pleasure to meet you. Evie speaks very highly of you."

Edmund shook my father's hand. "Delighted to meet you, Mr. Gray. I must say, your daughter is quite remarkable." His eyes briefly alighted on me. "She's clever and she keeps me on my toes in class."

"Thank you, Your Highness, I'm glad to hear it."

"Please, call me Edmund."

Dad nodded and they both turned their attention to me.

Cheeks, flame on! I was tempted to burst into a Human Torch superhero pose.

Edmund stared at me, his eyes taking in every inch of me. "You look incredible."

"Thank you." I grinned and admired the fit of his black suit. His blue shirt made his eyes pop. "So do you."

We stood there, looking at each other. Dad cleared his throat, startling us back to reality. "I think we all look fantastic."

"Indeed, you're right." Edmund dropped his gaze guiltily and turned toward my father. "Shall we go? The car's out front."

Dad nodded and Edmund led the way through the lobby and out the front doors to a large black Town Car.

A driver in a smart black suit and little matching cap held the door for us as we climbed in.

"Did you guys have any particular plans?" Edmund glanced at Dad and me.

"No." I shook my head and looked at Dad to confirm.

Edmund's eyes glinted. "Then I'll take you to my favorite place." He leaned forward, opened the glass partition, and spoke to the driver. Turning back to us, he asked, "How are you liking Paris so far?"

I inhaled sharply. Where to start? "Everywhere I look there's something beautiful and historic. It's incredible. I could live here forever and I still don't think I'd be able to see everything."

"Paris has always been one of my favorite cities. I'm glad you're liking it."

"I don't like it." I shook my head. "I love it here."

Edmund smiled.

The car slowed and pulled up to a stone building. "Maxim's" was splashed in gold across its red awnings. Underneath, a line of shivering people waited to go in.

The driver opened the door and Edmund got out. Reaching back, he held my hand as I exited the car. When I was out, he released it, but stayed close to my side. Dad joined us on the sidewalk and stood a step behind me, waiting for us to lead the way.

Bypassing the line, we went straight in. There were some perks to having a royal with you.

"Good evening, Your Highness, your table is ready. Right this way."

"Thank you." Edmund nodded and followed the host.

The restaurant was an art nouveau masterpiece. There wasn't a straight line in sight. Everything was sensuously rounded and flowery. Looking up, I noticed the glass ceiling. *Holy cow that's gorgeous.*

The rooms we passed through were filled with fabulous glasswork and beautiful paintings. Petaled sconces glowed on the walls. I was in awe.

"Edmund, this place is incredible," I said as we sat down at a private table. "It's so beautiful."

"I thought you'd like it."

"It's perfect."

Our waiter was tall, with slicked back hair and a mustache. He reminded me of a mouse. Once our water goblets were filled and he had taken our drink order, he twirled away.

Edmund watched me and shook his head. "I can't believe you're here, in Paris. This is such a wonderful surprise."

"I agree." Dad nodded. "It's so nice for me to finally get to meet one of Evie's Oxford friends."

Conversation through dinner was easy and filled with laughter. I couldn't have asked for a better birthday present than these two men celebrating with me.

I nibbled at my pasta and watched them talk, thrilled they were getting along so well. I wanted so badly for them to like each other.

"Have you gotten your grades yet?" Edmund asked, interrupting my thoughts.

I shook my head. "Um, last time I checked nothing was posted."

"They went up this afternoon." He grinned.

"Really? Ugh, I'm dying to know how I did." Finished with dinner, I folded my hands in my lap under the white tablecloth.

Edmund smiled his crooked smile at me. "You'll do fine. You were running circles around me when we studied."

Dad sat back and watched. I knew he'd noticed the little glances between Edmund and me during dinner.

"So, how'd you do?" I reached up and brushed my hair back from my face.

"Top marks." He took a sip of his champagne. "I'm relieved."

I smacked his shoulder lightly and scoffed. "Like you had reason to worry."

A crackling noise caught my attention. I turned to see our waiter carrying a chocolate cake with sparklers blazing toward our table. In a beautiful voice, he sang what I assumed was the French equivalent of happy birthday.

When he finished his song he said, "Joyeux anniversaire à la belle jeune femme."

"Merci." I grinned up at him and nodded, only vaguely certain he'd wished me a happy birthday.

When he left, Dad and Edmund sang to me again, this time in English.

"Make a wish," Edmund whispered near my ear as I was about to blow out the candles.

I closed my eyes and held my breath. *Don't let this feeling ever end.* Opening my eyes, I exhaled.

Tendrils of smoke curled and danced off the extinguished sparklers. I looked to Edmund and smiled. Under the table, his hand grasped mine and gave it a squeeze.

Oh my God. It hit me in a dizzying rush. *I love him.* The colorful room tilted in my vision.

I'm in love with him.

There was no going back; I was in too far and felt too much. I wanted him. There was only one option: take the leap, enjoy the ride down, and pray the landing didn't kill me.

My heart's going to get so mangled.

We dropped Dad off at the hotel under the guise of lingering jet lag. The wink he gave me when Edmund wasn't looking told a different story. Now back in the car, Edmund sat beside me and turned to watch me.

"Close your eyes." He smiled.

My brow scrunched. "Why?"

One corner of his mouth hitched up. "I'm taking you somewhere and it's a surprise."

I eyed him before obligingly closing my eyes. He grasped my hand, making a grin fill my face. As we drove, the faint melody of holiday music filled the car. Tempted as I was, I didn't peek.

"We're here," Edmund's voice rumbled near my ear. "Ready for your surprise?" I nodded and he continued. "Open your eyes."

The Eiffel Tower lit up the night sky like a Christmas tree. *How beautiful.* The lights blinked on and off, creating a sparkly disco ball effect. A beam of light shot out the top.

Edmund's lips quirked up, then he whispered, "Come on."

"But it's closed."

The excitement in his eyes and the tenderness on his face gave me a warm, shivery sensation low in my tummy. We exited the car and I stood, looking up. "Incredible."

"I may have called in a tiny favor." He gestured to the tower glittering over us. "The tower, the observation deck, it's all yours for the night."

My mouth popped open, astounded he'd done this. "Are you kidding me?"

His lips curled in a sexy grin and his hand settled at the small of my back. I gasped as the electricity from his touch pinged through me.

Nothing in my life would ever be able to compare to this night, to this moment right now.

"Edmund." My voice came out in a breathy whisper. "I . . ." I shook my head. I couldn't wrap my head around this. Tears burned in my eyes.

"This way." He guided me to the coolest double-decker elevator I'd ever seen.

I watched the shimmering city slowly shrink as we made our ascent. The doors slid open and we stepped out.

I'm on the Eiffel Tower. With Edmund. Holy shit.

Below us, the city glimmered and gleamed in all its seasonal finery. Trees and buildings bedecked with lights and the neon glow of blinking signs lit up the sky as tiny snowflakes filled the air.

The view and the gift were overwhelming. A lump formed in my throat. *How can I possibly thank him for this?*

Facing him, I said, "No one has ever done anything this amazing for me. Thank you." Before I knew what I was doing,

I threw my arms around him. Eagerly, he returned the embrace. Pressed tightly against him, his heartbeat raced under my ear. I never wanted to let go.

Edmund leaned back, his eyes piercing mine. Softly, his fingers brushed against my cheek. I leaned into his hand.

"Has it been a good birthday?" he whispered, his nose reddening.

"The best." I inhaled, feeling lightheaded.

He was so close I could feel his breath on my lips. It was intoxicating. I closed my eyes. If he let me go now there was no way my knees would support me.

"Evie." My name crossed his lips on a soft breath. It was so quiet I nearly missed it.

Then it happened.

His lips grazed mine. I gasped and opened my eyes to look at him. His were shut and he slid a hand into my hair. My eyelids fluttered closed again as his mouth pressed firmly on mine.

My imaginings could never begin to compare with this. Arms threading around his neck, my fingers twined through his blond curls as sparks zapped through me.

A muffled groan escaped Edmund as he deepened the kiss. His fist clutched the back of my jacket, pulling me closer.

My senses went into overdrive, the smell of him, the taste of him, the feel of him. I was lost in everything Edmund.

The hand tangled in my hair held my lips against his. As if I'd dream of going anywhere.

A soft moan escaped my throat like a purr. *There's definitely no going back.*

A few kisses later, he pulled away and rested his forehead against mine, both of us breathing heavy. My hands slid down to rest on his muscular chest. Tingles coursed all over my body, making me feel weak. I've never had a kiss do that before.

"Wow." Edmund met my eyes with a huge grin.

His heartbeat slowly steadied under my fingertips. Reaching up, Edmund's hand found mine. He led me to the railing and put his arms around me. It felt like we were on top of the world.

Happiness surged through me. I closed my eyes, still tasting him on my lips. That had to be the best first kiss in the history of first kisses.

I opened my eyes and saw Edmund holding his hand palm up to the sky.

"I love snow." I stuck my tongue out, trying to catch one of the puffy white flakes. As the snow came down harder, I stepped away and did a little twirl.

"Does Seattle get much snow?"

"Not really. The mountains are close, though. We hit the slopes every season," I said as Edmund leaned back against the railing and reached for me.

"You ski then?" Catching me, he pulled me to him and wrapped his arms around me again.

"I can, but I prefer snowboarding." I reached up and brushed the icy flakes from his hair.

"Then you have to come skiing with us this year. My family always invites a group of friends to the château. The gang always comes."

"Sounds like fun." I cuddled up to him. *Is this really happening? Someone pinch me.*

"Then that settles it, you're coming with me." He gave me a squeeze and sighed. "As much as I hate to, I should probably get you back to your dad. I don't want him to worry. I want him to like me."

"I don't think you have to worry. You can usually tell right away what Dad thinks of you."

Edmund hesitated, his eyes darting away from mine. "So, what did he think of me?"

Smiling, I said, "I think he liked you."

"I'm glad to hear it."

"Were you worried he wouldn't?" I looked up at him. He hadn't seemed anxious in the least.

"A little," he admitted and rubbed my shoulders.

"You're so good with people, why would you worry?"

"When it really matters, I get nervous." He kissed my forehead and took a step back, releasing me. "Before we go, you need to open your birthday present." He handed me a small box wrapped in shiny pink wrapping paper and tied with a sheer ribbon.

"I thought this was my present."

He shook his head with a smile. "I set this up when I talked to you earlier today. I got your present a while ago, before I knew you had a birthday coming up."

I smiled and took the gift.

Biting the tip of my glove, I pulled it off my hand. Tearing the paper revealed a black velvet box. The lid flipped up with a snap. Inside, a small silver replica of the Eiffel Tower glinted at me. I pulled the necklace out and met his eyes.

"I noticed the one on your desk. It stuck with me, I guess. When I came across this, I thought of you. I wanted you to have it."

I rubbed my thumb over the pendant. "My mother had a collection of Eiffel Towers. Over the years, I've continued adding to it, for her. This is perfect. I love it." I smiled, trying not to cry. "Can you help me?"

Edmund took the necklace and waited for me to take off my heart pendant, then reached behind me, his face close to mine. I lifted my hair and he clasped his gift around my neck.

"It looks lovely."

"Thank you," I whispered.

Leaning down, he pressed his lips softly to mine once more. It was sweet and sexy and perfect.

Chapter Thirteen

Stalling or Moving On

With winter break over and classes resumed, things were difficult. Edmund and I hadn't talked about Paris or our kissing. There hadn't been any repeats either. Our time together in Paris seemed as if it were captured in a snow globe of perfection. If we talked about it or even looked at it too closely, the glass would shatter.

To make matters worse, he was still very much in contact with Jax. I was even more confused about where I stood with him now.

Which is why when another student in St. John's asked me to dinner, I said yes.

"You didn't seriously just agree to go out with Theron, did you?" Suzy's mouth gaped as she watched Theron walk away. She adjusted her lime green scarf and shook her head.

"You were standing right here, you saw me say yes." My irritation level was high and Suzy wasn't helping. Things were supposed to be different after Paris.

"It's just that, well, it's *Theron*." She sounded worried.

"So?"

"How well do you know him?"

I shrugged. "We had a class together last term and we're in a lit class together now. He's always been friendly. What's the big deal?"

Suzy wrinkled her nose. "He has a reputation of taking things too far, way too fast. Plus, he detests Edmund."

"I won't let things go too far." When she didn't respond I asked, "What's his deal with Edmund?"

"I don't know exactly, but the two of them can't stand each other. Plus, I thought you and Edmund *connected* when you were in Paris."

"Who told you that?" I was flabbergasted. I hadn't said anything to anyone, not even Abby.

"Edmund."

My head jerked back in shock. *Why would he talk to her and not me?* "Did he say anything about it being a gigantic mistake?"

"No, why would he?" Her delicate blond brows scrunched together.

"Because things are awkward again. I just assumed he regretted it. I mean, we haven't talked about what happened at all."

"Wait, what exactly *did* happen? I thought it was just a kiss." Her eyes opened wide and I could tell her mind was running wild.

"No, not *that,* geez. Kissing, only kissing, but still . . ." I shook my head, at a loss for words.

Suzy rolled her eyes and rubbed her forehead. "Oh my God, the two of you need to get your shit sorted out. It's exhausting keeping up with you. I've got homework to do. I'll see you at dinner."

Crap.

I watched her walk away, wanting to kick myself. I should've known better. *I'm such an idiot.* Then she stopped, turned around, and marched back to me.

"Evie, you know I love you, but someone has to say something. You're being a complete arse. If I knew Edmund liked me as much as he likes you, I wouldn't dream of dating another guy. So what if he hasn't talked to you, go and talk to him. Make the first move. Fight for him. He's worth it." With a stiff smile, she turned and left.

I stood frozen. *Did she really just call me an arse?*

Feeling like shit and beyond confused, I set off for my last class.

Once there, I slumped in my seat and tapped my pen against my lips. My memory replayed Edmund's kiss, how his mouth felt against mine, and how he held me like he never wanted to let me go. I smiled, wishing we were still in Paris.

"Is it true? You're going on a date with Theron Anderson?" Edmund slid into the seat next to mine, making me jump.

"He asked me to get dinner Friday. It's not a big deal. Who told *you*?" Suzy's words haunted me. I knew she was right.

He shook his head. "I heard Theron bragging to his mates on my floor about scoring a date with you, amongst other things." Looking away flustered, he said, "I don't . . . I wish . . . Look, Theron's not a nice guy. I know, it seems ridiculous of me to ask this, but please . . . don't go."

I pinched the bridge of my nose. "You're right, it is ridiculous and hypocritical. Look at you, one moment you're kissing me and the next you're hanging out with Jax. How is my getting dinner with Theron any different?" That last part came out too loud.

Professor Roth looked our way and cleared his throat. I sunk lower in my seat, feeling the other students' eyes on me. Edmund sat straighter, meeting their stares without apology.

Kill me now.

The lights dimmed and the white board up front glowed with the first piece of art. My brain wouldn't focus. Between the twinges of embarrassment, I was trying to decide if I was flattered or furious.

We're not together. I'm not his concern. He shouldn't care. Right?

My pen angrily scratched over my paper, scribbling out a word I'd misspelled. I hadn't been excited about this date to begin with, but now I was dreading it.

I'd only accepted Theron out of sheer petulance. Now, with Suzy and Edmund both warning me, my stomach tangled itself up in worrisome knots.

Maybe I should cancel? Then it'd look like I was doing exactly what Edmund wanted me to. I didn't want that.

This is so stupid. I closed my eyes and inhaled slowly. It's just dinner; everything will be fine.

Theron sat across from me at a dingy pub, *still* regaling me with stories of his cricket prowess. Bored out of my mind, I took another bite of my hamburger. *I wish this evening was over.* My pajamas and half an Aero bar were calling my name. Damn my stubbornness.

I watched Theron gesture with his hands as he spoke. Some people might call him attractive with his close-cropped dark hair, green eyes, and muscled chest. But he was also on the short side. It was impossible not to compare him to Edmund.

"So, then I scored another goal . . ."

The place was packed with students. They all looked like they were having way more fun than I was.

"After that, she couldn't keep her hands off me."

Every story he shared ended this way. He was one of those guys who thought every woman alive wanted him.

I lifted my arm off the table to grab my water, and my sweater stuck to the veneer. He was still on his highlight reel as I dipped a napkin in my water and tried to clean off the tabletop.

Noncommittal grunts and head nods were all the encouragement Theron needed. I'd barely spoken all night.

This might top Caroline's date from hell.

By dinner's end, I knew a lot about Mr. Anderson, and none of it remotely interesting.

In my purse, I fished around and pulled out my wallet, intending to split the tab.

"No, no, supper's on me," he said, waving me to put my money away.

I smiled. "Oh, okay, thanks."

"Do you want to catch a movie?" Theron asked, walking out the door I held open.

"I'm pretty beat and I have a lot of homework. We should call it a night and head back."

Theron nodded, his mouth a firm line.

Outside, fog had settled in, making it eerie and chilly. I blew out a long stream of misty breath as his hand grazed mine in a move to grab it. I stuffed it in my pocket, cutting off access.

"Brrr, sure is cold tonight." I said.

Theron launched into another cricket story. Blissfully, the dorm was only a few steps away. It was over.

Finally.

"Evie, I had a splendid time. I'd love to do it again." Theron blocked the front doors, not letting me in.

I was tempted to say, "Of course you had a good time, you talked about yourself all night." What I ended up saying was, "Dinner was yummy, thanks."

"This is good night, then." He leaned closer to me, smirking. I leaned back and tried to slip around him. "Don't play coy." Grabbing my upper arms, the threat in his voice was unmistakable.

"I'm not, I'm just ready to go inside," I said stiffly, alarm bells blaring in my head.

I should've listened.

"Come on, where's my goodnight kiss? I treated you to dinner, you can at least give me a little snog."

A nervous laugh slipped past my lips. "Really? You're not seriously pulling the I-paid-for-dinner-now-you-owe-me card?"

Theron's grip on my arms tightened painfully as he shoved me into a corner between the wall and a tall rectangular window. A loud thud sounded as my elbow collided with the glass.

Using his body to pin me, he forced his lips against mine in a rough kiss. The stubble on his chin scratched. I pushed at him and tried to pull my face away, but all that accomplished was a painful beard burn. His fingers dug into my arms, making me wince.

"I know you put out for that manky git, Edmund. I'm better at *everything*; I promise you'll enjoy yourself."

Panic rose in my throat and I tried to scream, but I couldn't escape his mouth. With shock, I realized just how much Theron enjoyed my struggling. I felt it pressed against my thigh.

My heart hammered in my chest. I had to get away. *Why the hell didn't I listen?*

"Let her go, now," a growl came from behind my date.

One minute Theron was there, the next he was ripped off me and tossed back. Slipping on the frosty pavement, he tumbled to the ground.

Edmund stood over him, shoulders squared, fist clenched, and eyes blazing. He looked ready to beat the shit out of Theron.

"Back off, *Your Highness*. She chose me over you. Get the bloody hell out of here." Theron rose from the pavement and got directly into Edmund's face.

"It didn't look to me like she was choosing anything," Edmund snarled.

Theron's face contorted with hatred. "She needed a little help to come to her senses. Someone had to show her what being with a real man was like."

Edmund snapped. He punched Theron in the face and knocked him flat on the ground.

I stared, shocked at Edmund as he towered over Theron.

The clicks and flashes of cameras got me moving again. I clasped Edmund's arm, his name tumbling from my lips. His eyes locked on mine as he slipped an arm around my waist and pulled me to him.

Preston rushed over and grabbed Edmund's free arm, pulling us inside. The palace security team pushed through the doors on our heels.

Two burly men stepped in to shield us and deal with Theron—who was still lying on the sidewalk, his nose bloody and dripping down his face onto his jacket.

"Are you all right?" Edmund turned me to face him as soon as we were inside. His hand caressed the side of my face, studying me, looking for injuries.

"I'm fine. Are you okay?" I reached for his hand. His knuckles were bright red.

"I was on the couch and I saw him touch you. You were struggling. I just lost it," he said in a rush.

"I'm so sorry." A tear trickled down my cheek and I buried my face in my hands, unable to look at him. *This is all my fault.* "I'm such a stubborn ass. I should've listened."

"You're okay, that's all that matters." He pulled my hands down and kissed my forehead as he wrapped me in a tight hug. It only made me cry harder. "It's okay. He's not going to touch you again. I promise."

I nodded against his chest, a shaky sob escaping.

Leaning back, his eyes met mine and he gave me a small smile. Slowly his lips lowered to cover mine in a gentle kiss. His hands rubbed my back. I felt safe in his arms.

I needed this kiss. I wanted to erase Theron's touch from my mind.

Edmund must have needed it just as much as I did. His kiss rapidly morphed into something fierce, passionate, and possessive.

"All right you two. We've got to go somewhere else. The paparazzi are outside the window enjoying the show, come on." Preston tugged at Edmund's arm.

Breaking the kiss, Edmund grabbed my hand and we raced up the stairs to his room. When he opened the door, I was surprised.

His furniture matched mine, but the walls were bare. It felt spartan and spotless. So not what I expected. Preston closed the door behind us and went to the couch.

Adrenaline thrummed through me. I ached to grab Edmund, but Preston's presence stopped me.

"Theron's been gagging for a punch in the face for a long time. That was bloody brilliant." He raised his fist in the air for Edmund to reciprocate the fist bump, which he did, but with less enthusiasm.

"If he thinks he can treat women in that manner, he deserves much worse than I gave him. That arsehole is going to milk this for all he can. It'll be all over the papers."

"I never dreamed he'd . . ." I trailed off as waves of guilt made my breathing difficult.

Edmund pulled me down beside him on his bed and brushed my hair over my shoulders. "It's okay. It's not your fault he's an arsehole who doesn't understand boundaries. I'd punch him again in a heartbeat if I needed to. You're worth it."

"I'll never forget how he looked, sprawled out on the sidewalk like that," Preston roared.

Edmund and I chuckled. Theron had gotten what he deserved. But at what price?

Wanting and needing to be alone with Edmund, I waited, hoping Preston would take off. After half an hour, exhaustion took over and I stood up. "I'm gonna say good night. Thank you both for everything."

"I'll walk you down." Edmund came over and placed his hand on my back, making my knees weak.

We walked downstairs in silence. At my room, Edmund stopped and leaned in. "Evie . . ."

He gently guided my hips with his hands and pressed me against the door. My pulse leapt in my throat as his lips touched mine.

From my purse, my cell phone trilled. Ignoring it, I twined my arms around his neck, my fingers playing in his hair. He deepened the kiss with a growl.

The second my cell phone stopped ringing, my room phone rang.

Edmund stepped back. "Do you want to get that?"

I shook my head and stood on my tiptoes, bringing my lips back to his. He lightly touched his tongue to my bottom lip. I gasped and Edmund seized the opportunity. His tongue found mine as his fingertips pressed into my back. A tremble coursed through me. It felt like he couldn't get me close enough.

Fingers tangled in my hair. I couldn't breathe; I was drowning in him.

Buried in the depths of my bag, my damn cell phone rang again. *Leave a freaking message already.*

"I think you should get that," he said, breathing heavily between little kisses. "Someone obviously needs to talk to you."

I pulled my phone out and saw Anton's name on my caller ID. With a resigned sigh, I answered. "Anton?" My hand slid down to rest on Edmund's chest.

"I know it's late, but I'm passing through Oxford right now. I was hoping to catch you and drop off your next letter. Well, assuming you've finished your fourth task."

"Um, yeah, sorry." I ran a hand through my hair, feeling guilty for essentially ditching my quest. "I finished it a while ago. I can meet you downstairs."

"Sounds good. I'll be there in twenty."

I hadn't called Anton because I wasn't ready to deal with anything to do with Clarice. I was still wrangling with my thoughts of my grandmother most likely being a duchess.

"Anton's coming by?" Edmund's arms were still clasped around my waist.

I nodded, wanting to get back to the kissing.

Slipping my phone into my pocket, I said, "So, where were we?"

Edmund brushed my hair over my shoulder and whispered, "Somewhere around here."

His lips grazed my neck, sending shivers down my spine. My breath caught in my throat as goose bumps covered my arms and rapidly spread. I wanted to grab him by the shirt and pull him into my room.

"Is he bringing your next letter?" Edmund's voice was muffled against the skin under my ear.

"Mmm hmm." I closed my eyes, enjoying the sensation.

He kissed his way down my jaw. "Did your research uncover anything?"

"I can't think when you do that." I pressed a palm to his chest and pulled away.

He chuckled. "My apologies."

Unlocking my door, I grabbed his hand and pulled him in. We sat on the bed, facing each other.

"So, when were you going to tell me?" His thumb trailed circles on the back of my hand.

I tried to focus, but he was making it difficult. "Tell you what?"

"About your research?"

I averted my eyes. "Oh, I, um, I may have found a relative. Nothing too exciting."

Confident in my conclusion, I still wanted Anton's confirmation before I said anything. Truthfully though, that wasn't the only reason I hadn't told Edmund about Clarice. My real motivation was entirely selfish. I wanted him to choose me for me. Not because I suddenly had an aristocratic relation paving the way.

Him not making a decision after Paris only strengthened my resolve. Jax lurked in the background because her family had a title. I needed him to want me how I was now—a simple American girl. In all likelihood, being the granddaughter of the Duchess of Westminster would change nothing.

"A connection to your mum? Evie, that's great. Are you going to visit them?" He flipped my hand over and lightly traced the lines on my palm.

My eyelids fluttered closed. I felt him kiss my palm. His touch drove me insane. "Haven't really decided."

"If you decide to pay them a visit I'd love to join you. Where do they live?"

He pressed his lips against my wrist, the crease of my elbow, my shoulder, and back to my neck. Eyes heavy-lidded, I said, "I'd really rather not talk right now."

The corner of his mouth hitched up. "As you wish."

Chapter Fourteen

Endings and Beginnings

Anton stood by the couch in the commons, my letter in hand. He walked toward me with a smile. He put his arm around my shoulder and gave me a little squeeze. "I trust you've been well."

I nervously nodded and sat. Please let it *not* be Clarice.

"So what did you discover with your research?" he asked, sitting beside me.

In a soft voice, I said, "I think I found my grandmother."

"I see. And is there anything particularly interesting about her?" His lips twitched.

My hair spilled around my face as I looked at my hands. I didn't want to say it out loud. Speaking the words made it real, made it true. I closed my eyes and spoke in a rush. "She's the Duchess of Westminster."

"Very good." He sounded impressed.

I looked at him and tossed my hair over my shoulder with a shake of my head. "So, it's true then?"

He nodded, tapping the corner of the envelope against his knee.

"I was afraid of that."

Anton's brow furrowed and he slid to the edge of the couch. "I apologize if this is out of line, but from everything I've seen and read, you and a certain prince seem to like each other quite a bit. So, why is this a bad thing? This could open doors for you."

"That's precisely what I don't want. I want him to like me for me."

"He does. Trust me." The look he shot me was reminiscent of Dad. A believe-me-I-know-what-I'm-talking-about kind of look.

"Yeah, well, maybe so . . ." I looked away. "But I don't want him to know yet."

Anton held up his hands. "I won't say a word."

"Thanks."

"I believe I have a letter for you." He handed it to me and grinned.

"They're leading me to her, aren't they?"

Anton cleared his throat. "I'll only say there's one letter left after this, and that this task might take a little courage to work up to."

I nodded, wanting to ask questions, but knowing I'd not get any details out of him. "Thanks, Anton."

"Night, Evie."

Letter in hand, I went upstairs. With no desire to open it, I pulled out my desk drawer and tossed it in with all the others. Then I stopped. The letter Dad had given me in Paris sat perched atop the pile. I needed Mom—I just didn't need her detailing my next quest.

I picked it up and looked at the "Happy Birthday" she'd written on the flap of the envelope. *Why did you even start this? What's the point?* I could've gone forever without knowing about Clarice.

My Evie,

Happy twentieth birthday, sweetheart! I hope your day was wonderful. What I wouldn't give to be there. To see you conquer university, fall in love, eventually start a family, and just grow into the amazing woman I know you're destined to be.

When I was your age, your father and I were secretly engaged and preparing to elope. I knew my mother would never allow me to choose Henry. She expected me to marry my social equal, meaning someone wealthy, British, with the right family connections, and impossibly boring.

When I called her from the States, a newlywed, she was beyond furious. She banned me from returning home and completely cut me from her life.

I always expected she'd forgive me. That eventually we'd repair the rift in our relationship. Apparently, falling in love with a man she deemed inappropriate was unforgivable. She couldn't embarrass the family, not even for her only daughter.

Your father and I agreed from the start, we'd never make the same mistake my mother did. No matter what you do, say, or whom you fall in love with, there is nothing in this world that could ever change our love for you.

May your twentieth year be full of amazing adventures, love, laughter, and joy. Be happy, my love, and follow your dreams. Anything is possible.

As always, I'll be watching over you. Love you forever, my darling girl.

Always,
Mom
xoxo

I folded the letter and put it away. The one Anton just delivered I pulled back out and sat it on my desk.

It's not like Clarice cares about me or wants to know me. Why should I want to know her?

I climbed into bed, so not thrilled with how Mom's quest was panning out. I'd had reservations at the start, but there was still the hope that she was guiding me toward something amazing. Clarice was far from amazing.

I picked up my phone and dialed Abby.

She answered just in time to keep me from going to voicemail. "Ugh, I have to head out in fifteen minutes, family thing."

I crinkled my nose. "Bummer, do you want me to call back?"

"No, it's been forever since we talked. I miss you, girl."

"I miss you too, Abs." These days, the further and further I delved into my quest letters, the more I ached for Seattle. Life was easier there.

"So, did you have a good day?" Her voice sounded like she was stretching.

"Meh, okay, I guess. You?" I refused to talk about that jerk, Theron. Reaching up, I turned off the desk lamp with a click. The room was now cloaked in darkness as I laid my head on the pillow.

"Can't complain much. So, how are things with that prince of yours?"

A flash of heat hit me as our kisses replayed in my mind. "They're pretty great."

I quickly caught up on how her holidays went and did a recap of Christmas and, quite possibly, the world's most perfect birthday.

"You finally kissed him?" She squealed. With a giggle she added, "And how was that?"

I sighed and pulled the blankets up around my chin, settling in. "I just don't have the words."

"Well, you better find some words, 'cause this is something I need to know." She laughed.

"I couldn't have dreamt a more perfect first kiss. He's an amazing kisser."

"I love you, but right now I hate you."

"Well, I'm glad you love me, because I need your advice on something."

"Yes, you should sleep with him."

I shook my head, smiling. "Abby, you're impossible."

"Seriously, there can't be many girls who could say they slept with a prince. Let alone that he was their first."

Chuckling, I said, "Not exactly what I was getting at, but I'll keep that in mind."

"Okay, okay, what's up?"

With a deep breath, I told her about Clarice. It felt good to get it out. "You can't tell my dad anything, not yet."

"Okay, my lips are sealed, but let me make sure I've got this straight. You're dating a prince and you've just discovered that your grandmother's a duchess, meaning you could be her heir." She scoffed. "Wow, it must be rough in your world."

I rolled into a fetal position. "It's not like that. She disowned my mom; there's like zero possibility I'll ever be a duchess." At least that's how I assumed it worked.

"So what's the problem?"

"I think Mom wants me to meet her. I really don't want to."

"What does Edmund think?"

I cringed. "I haven't told him yet."

Abby paused. "Is there a reason you aren't telling him?"

"I'm not ready to. I want him to send Jax packing before I tell him."

"I'm not following."

I switched my phone to the other ear and sat up. Clicking the lamp back on, I leaned against the wall. "I want to know that he likes me for who I am, Abs. Not because of who my grandmother is."

"You doubt he likes you? Really, Eves, come on. If he didn't like you, why the hell would he make arrangements to have the Eiffel Tower open just for you? Why would he be kissing you or making an effort to impress your dad or giving you jewelry?"

Sighing, I said, "Okay, I do think he likes me, but I need to know *I'm* enough. Just me. I don't want Clarice to be the reason he finally chooses me. Ugh, am I making any sense?"

"Not much, no. If you like him and he likes you, does it matter how you get together?"

I leaned my head back with a thump against the wall. "I'd always have doubts."

"He comes from a very different world than you do. If your grandmother being a duchess makes it possible for the two of you to be together, I'd be pretty damn grateful."

"Clarice is cold and vile. I don't want her having any part in my life."

"You should still tell him. This is something he should know. I mean, if you really like this guy, do you want to start things off with a huge secret? It's kinda like what your mom did to your dad."

"Stop being so logical, that's not why I called you."

Abby laughed. "Sorry, but if you didn't want the truth, you shouldn't have called me. You know I'm not going to lie to you."

"I know." I grinned. "What kind of best friend are you?" I chuckled. She was right, and I knew it.

My blue tray bumped its way down the metal rails. I was queued up near a griddle where the cook flipped long strips of bacon. I wrinkled my nose at the smell. *God, I hate bacon.*

"Are you okay?" Suzy appeared at my side, her face twisted with worry.

"I'm fine, why?" I asked, watching dust motes float through the sun-dappled air.

"After what happened with Theron last night, I thought you'd be upset."

"Did Preston tell you?" My brows scrunched together. I'd been trying to forget last night ever happened. Seeing the bruises on my upper arms in the mirror this morning had been a jolt of reality.

Suzy pressed her lips tight together and nodded. "But I also saw it here."

She held up a tabloid and there it was, splashed all over the front page, Edmund hitting Theron, El Creepo sprawled out on the sidewalk, and Edmund with his hands wound in my hair, kissing me.

Quite the pictorial synopsis. I grabbed the magazine and flipped through it. The article painted Edmund as my knight in shining armor. Theron came across like the scumbag he is.

I tucked the paper under my arm. "Theron is such an ass. Thank God they aren't buying his story."

"Oh please, who would choose Theron over Edmund? Even the press can figure that out." Suzy paid for her breakfast and waited beside the register.

"Good point."

"Look at you. Glad to see you're still in one piece." Caroline abandoned her tray and gave me a hug. Marissa did the same.

"Yeah, lesson learned—don't be so stubborn."

Caroline took the paper from me and looked at it. "I bet Jax and Lover Boy's parents have been relentless this morning."

I hadn't thought about his parents. My stomach clenched.

I led the way to our table by the windows. Preston and Edmund hadn't come down. I sighed, frustrated. Just when things were changing between Edmund and me. *Now we'll probably go back to being awkward.*

"I only wish I could've seen Jax's face when she saw the pictures." Caroline snorted a laugh and opened the spout of her milk carton to pour on her Frosted Shreddies.

I looked up, just in time to see the boys enter the dining hall. Edmund didn't look happy. Glancing in our direction, he met my gaze, a smile curling his lips.

A warm fuzzy feeling uncoiled low in my tummy. Maybe things wouldn't change between us after all.

"So, have you seen it?" Caroline asked and pulled the paper out, tossing it at Edmund as he sat on my other side.

Balling it up, he tossed it in the nearby trashcan. "Oh, I've seen it and heard all about it."

Suzy made a face, sucking air in through her teeth. "Was it bad?"

"Was what bad?" Edmund took a sip from his disposable coffee cup.

"Jax's reaction, your parents'." Suzy brushed her blond hair off her shoulder. "They must've been furious."

I sat frozen beside Edmund, barely daring to breathe, nervous to hear his reply. His shoulder rubbed against mine as he shrugged.

"I haven't talked to my parents, and when something's going down they're always the first to call." He took a bite of his blueberry scone. "As for Jax, I don't know what she thinks about the pictures and I don't care. She rang me late last night and I, hopefully, made it clear enough this time that there'll never be anything more than friendship between us. She was a tad bent out of shape about it."

My head snapped up. I stared at Edmund, who continued eating like he hadn't just said the most wonderful phrase in the universe. I looked at my breakfast, emotions swirling. *Does this mean he's choosing me?*

"Wow, do your parents know about this?" Preston asked from across the table, mouth gaping.

"By now I'm sure they do. She threatened to call them if I didn't change my mind." Edmund's hand found mine under the table. I went dizzy at his touch and the revelation.

Pulse racing, I blew out a shaky breath and glanced at him. *What does this make us now?*

"Well, congratulations, mate. This is the best bloody bit of news I've had all year." Preston slapped the shiny wood tabletop, his eyes glinting happily.

"Hear, hear," chimed Marissa and Caroline in unison.

Edmund cleared his throat. "So, my family's annual ski holiday is coming up over break and you're all invited."

"Awesome." Preston swirled the last of his tea around in his cup.

"Is it in Switzerland again?" Suzy asked.

How could they all change the topic so easily? Jax is out of the picture. *This. Is. Huge.*

Edmund nodded and looked at me. "Everyone in?"

A chorus of agreement went up. Edmund still had my hand captured in his. His thumb idly traced patterns on my palm, making me shiver. I closed my eyes a moment, enjoying the sensations. I so didn't want to go to class this morning.

Class.

"Oh crap, I'm going to be late if I don't move it." I stood and tossed my cereal and the lukewarm remnants of my tea into the trash. Spurred by my reminder, everyone else scattered to their classes.

Edmund, Marissa, and I headed in the same direction. They chatted about skiing and burying each other in the snow as my brain fantasized the possibilities of a Jax-free Edmund. We so didn't have the same priorities.

My boots clipped along the sidewalk and I tried not to slide on the slippery patches. I glanced up at the white sky and thought of the ski trip, excited to get out on the slopes. Then warm up by a cozy fireplace cuddled with Edmund after.

Lost in thought, I nearly stumbled when I realized that this ski trip meant something else entirely—something big.

Meeting his parents.

I had to make a good impression, especially after this tabloid debacle. And now with Edmund cutting out their first choice, it was crucial I got this meeting right.

My pace slowed as my stomach churned. They weren't just any parents, they were the freaking King and Queen of England. *Oh my God, I can't do this.*

Meeting the parents of the boy I want to do naughty things to won't be awkward at all.

Chapter Fifteen

Life with the Other Half

Tomorrow we leave for the château. Tomorrow, I meet the King and Queen of England. Tomorrow could make or break my future happiness. I'd been stressing for the past week and was now at the end of my tether. Ensconced at a table in the commons, I had papers sprawled around me.

Why did I take this stupid class?

Growling, I hurled my algebra book from the table and across the room. It nearly hit Edmund and Preston on their return from the dining hall.

Preston leaned down, picked it up, and looked at the cover. "Having trouble with algebra?" He sat beside me. "Show me what you're working on."

I flipped to the page and jabbed my finger at the offending section, then buried my hands in my loose curls.

"Breathe, I'll walk you through this. Just stop growling, I'm afraid you're going to bite me and I'm not current on all my shots."

Teasing, I gnashed my teeth at him.

He took a moment to scan the page. "Okay, this is easy."

"Not making me feel any better, Pres." I put my head down on my arms.

Chuckling, Edmund went and sat on the couch and pulled out his phone.

"No, what I'm saying is, you'll get it in no time." Preston grabbed my pencil and started scribbling in my notebook. "Watch this."

With a brief explanation and a few examples, he had me traveling down the right path. By the time we headed upstairs I had a good grasp of the concept and knew I could finish the last few problems on my own.

"Thanks, Preston. I don't think I'd have figured that out without you." I inhaled deeply and ran a hand through my hair. "I'm so relieved right now I could kiss you."

Stopping at the door to my floor, Preston faced me. "Anytime you want to kiss me, Evie, I'm completely willing. You don't even have to warn me, just grab me and do it." He waggled his eyebrows and moved closer to me.

Edmund grabbed Preston by the shoulders and turned him toward the stairs with a little nudge. "That's enough for tonight, Romeo, say good night, Preston."

"Good night, Preston," he said, mocking Edmund's low tone. "And I'll see you in the morning, Miss Evie." He flirtatiously winked at me.

"Night, Preston," I hollered before I heard the door above us open and shut.

"I'd be interested in that kiss you offered Preston, you know, if it's still on the table." Edmund moved toward me on the landing, slipping his hands into his pockets, looking charming and utterly sexy.

"Would you now?" I took a step closer to him and placed my hands on his sweater-clad chest. Standing on my tiptoes, I kissed his left cheek, then his right. "Good night," I chirped and turned for the door.

Edmund reached out and grabbed my hand. "Wait." He chuckled, his voice bouncing off the concrete walls. "That wasn't quite what I had in mind."

"No? Well, that's what I was offering Preston and you said that's what you wanted."

"Is that so? Well, then, what kind of kisses would you give me?"

"You? Hmm." I paused and looked up at the ceiling, pretending to think about it. "They'd probably be something a little more like this." I placed my hands on his chest again, and on tiptoes once more, I feathered small kisses along his jawline until I reached the corner of his lips. Planting a kiss there, I moved over his mouth and softly nipped at his bottom lip.

A sound of satisfaction escaped his lips. At their parting, I lightly touched my tongue to his. Edmund's hand slipped behind my head, pulling me closer. He transformed the kiss into something demanding and exhilarating. I was no longer the one in control. His free hand clutched the fabric of my shirt and he pulled me firmly to his chest.

I wound my arms around his neck and ran a hand through his hair, wanting him closer.

Footsteps above us skipped down the stairs. I leaned back, mentally cursing whoever was about to interrupt us.

"I much prefer the kisses you reserve for me," he panted.

"Good." I smiled. Still breathless, I backed through the door to my hall. Quietly, I added, "Good night, Edmund."

"Night." By the look on his face, "good night" was the last thing he wanted to say.

In my room I put my packed bags by the door and went to my desk. Finish up the algebra homework and I'd be all set.

Getting down to business, I opened my book and reached in my drawer for a pencil. My fingers brushed the letters. I sighed and looked down at them. The top letter, emblazoned with a dark number five, sat unopened. Picking it up, my fingertips ran along the edges, stopping at the corners. I spun it between my fingers.

It's time. You know it is.

My finger slid under the flap and popped it up. Closing my eyes, I pulled the single page out and opened it. It was silly, but I was nervous to open my eyes. Afraid I'd see the words: go visit your grandmother.

I cracked my right eye open a sliver and tried to focus on the script. When I couldn't decipher her handwriting I sighed and opened my other eye.

Darling Evie,

By now you've undoubtedly figured out my secret. My mother, your grandmother, is the Duchess of Westminster.

And I think it's time you met her. Try not to let my experience with her taint your feelings. I'm hopeful she's changed with all the time that's passed. Remember that everything you choose to do in your life is ultimately up to you. You're in control. Despite what your grandmother may try to tell you. I so wish I were there to do this with you. To guide you through this choice you'll have to make.

Always know anything is possible, my Evie. You can do and be anything your heart desires. I believe in you.

I love you,
Mom
xoxo

Caroline, Suzy, Marissa, and I stood outside our chauffeured car, the snow falling heavily on our heads. Before us stood an enormous château, beautiful and picturesque. I took it all in, mouth gaping. Tall evergreen trees surrounded us and a fresh layer of white glistened as far as I could see.

The château itself was made of gray flagstone and was several stories tall in some areas. No expense appeared to have been spared.

"Wait till you see the inside," Marissa leaned over and whispered in my ear. I noticed the snow sticking to her short haircut and smiled. She looked like a pixie.

I shook my head, needing to focus. This was a huge moment. His parents were somewhere inside. *Someone help me.*

I pulled my navy beanie down further on my head and nervously arranged my long curls.

Edmund and Preston pulled up behind us in a sporty silver car.

According to our driver, Edmund had business to take care of so he'd left early. I'd been nervous the whole drive. I didn't want to meet his parents without him.

Edmund walked toward us, opening his arms as if to hug us all. "Welcome to Château Eirwyn."

"I can't believe you left before us and we still beat you." Marissa chuckled.

A tall, handsome man, who looked like a slightly older version of Edmund, opened the door of the château and stepped out. At his side was a woman with long straight blond hair and a slim face. They looked like they'd just stepped from the pages of a Ralph Lauren catalog.

"Brother," the man called. Their footsteps crunched in the newly fallen snow as they made their way to us.

"Philip. Lauren." Edmund embraced each of them. "You remember my friends, Preston, Caroline, Suzy, and Marissa— they came on holiday with us last year."

"Yes, of course. So glad you all could make it back this year," Philip said. He and Lauren smiled warmly and shook everyone's hands.

"And this is Evie. She's a transfer student from America."

"Absolute pleasure to meet you, Evie. We've heard much about you." Philip raised one eyebrow at Edmund as he grasped my hand.

"Delighted to meet you, Your Highnesses." I shook his hand, then Lauren's thin one as she closely examined me. I wasn't sure what to make of her. Her closed-mouth smile revealed little. And I got the distinct impression I was being graded.

"Let's get you all inside and settled," Lauren said in a soft, silky voice. Sliding her hand into the crook of her husband's arm, they guided us to the massive wood doors.

Several staff members stood in a line, waiting to take us to our rooms.

A short woman approached me, head down. "Excuse me, ma'am, if you'll follow me I'll show you to your room." She glanced up only momentarily, as if afraid to look me in the eye. I was surprised to note she looked younger than me.

"Thank you." I nodded and glanced at Edmund, who was busy talking to his brother. I hoped he'd be able to find me.

Now separated from my friends, I followed the girl down a luxurious hallway, my footsteps deafened by the plush floral-print carpet. Famous paintings lined the walls. My eyes widened as we passed one after another. Some of these were pieces I'd studied at school. *How insane is this?*

Huge, fragrant floral arrangements in deep reds and burgundy were stationed every few feet between the doors. This place was incredible.

What's my room going to look like? I knew, without a doubt, it'd be the most extravagant place I'd ever stayed.

"Your room, Miss." The timid girl pushed open the large arched door.

I couldn't hold back the gasp.

"You'll be staying in the Champagne Room, Miss. It has quite a lovely view." After she spoke, she backed up against the wall, as if she wished the wallpaper would absorb her.

A man in dark blue livery, with red and gold detailing, brought my heavy suitcase in.

"Thank you." I wandered over to one of the large picture windows and took in the snowy landscape. From my vantage point on the third floor, I could see a large, fast-rushing river only a short walk from the house.

"Would you like me to help you unpack, Miss?"

"Um, no, I think I'm good, thanks."

With a bob of her head, the shy maid scurried out the door.

Sighing, I knew Edmund and I came from different worlds, but seeing this was astounding. Living in this kind of luxury and being surrounded by fascinating and glitteringly beautiful people—how had he ever found me interesting?

I wandered around, my fingers tentatively touching the rich surfaces. Cool glass vases, soft bed linens, and rough fireplace stones. Inside a hearth large enough for me to stand in, a fire blazed. The heat it put off gave the massive room a surprisingly cozy feel. I glanced at the large four-poster bed, smiling. It reminded me of a cloud. Its fluffy softness looked inviting. I couldn't wait to crawl in.

Soaking it all in, I did a slow spin. Everything was in beautiful shades of gold with a slight pinky hue. It was shimmery and lovely, perfectly feminine.

I sat on the cream chaise near the fire and pulled out my phone, sending Dad a quick text to let him know I'd made it safely.

Never in my wildest imaginings could I have pictured myself at the royal family's château in the mountains of Switzerland. Preparing to dine and socialize with the King and Queen of England. *Seriously, how did I get here?*

Dizziness hit me at the realization that I only had a couple hours until dinner. I said a quick prayer that I'd survive without looking like a stupid, arrogant American.

A quiet knock at my door pulled my mind back to the present. I tossed my phone next to a vase of pale pink and cream flowers on the coffee table. When I answered it, Suzy's smiling face greeted me and she flitted into my room.

"God, I love it here." She swiveled around and flopped on the chaise I'd just abandoned. "This place is incredible. Your room is fab. Please tell me we never have to go home. Let's just move in and live here forever." She giggled like she was tipsy.

"It really is amazing. I can't imagine owning a place like this."

She laughed and kicked her feet in the air before she got up and went to look out the window. "Wow, great view, much better than mine. I get to look out over the front entrance, which is very nice, but this is just, wow. It's like a painting."

"I know." I admired the scene with her. "This where you came last year too?"

"Yeah, I think this is where they always take their ski holiday."

"It won't be just us here, will it?"

"No, Philip and Lauren usually invite some friends, as do Edmund's parents. It'll be quite the full house this weekend."

I must've made a face because Suzy patted my hand comfortingly. "Don't be nervous; you'll do great. I know it."

My stomach dropped. *Oh boy, here we go.*

Chapter Sixteen

Ski Slopes and Firelight

I sat at the side of the hearth, full and contentedly surrounded by my friends. Dinner had just finished and I'd miraculously gotten a reprieve from officially meeting Edmund's parents. Which gave me the evening to try and relax. Or, in all reality, I'd just stress and stew about making a fool out of myself tomorrow.

Edmund and the gang were chatting about the snow and how the skiing would be. When I looked at him, he gave me a wink, making me blush.

"Your Highness?" A stiff butler approached. "Your parents will be ready to greet your guests within the hour. They extend their most sincere apologies that they were not available to welcome them upon your arrival."

Well, shit.

A cool chill settled over my body, despite the crackling flames behind me. Outwardly, I tried to stay calm. Inside, my heart thrashed around like a wild animal. Throwing up was suddenly a very real possibility.

Suzy subtly gave my hand a squeeze. I smiled, probably a little too brightly. She wasn't fooled for a second.

Needing a distraction, I stood. "So, is this strictly a skiing trip or does anyone snowboard?"

"I've always wanted to learn how, but we all just ski. I've seen a few people boarding, though. Not that I know them personally." Preston confirmed my suspicions.

"Gotcha. So, skiing it is." I smiled.

"If you want to snowboard, you can. It's not a big deal." Edmund stood beside me.

I shrugged as if I had no worries. "No, skiing's fine; I was just curious."

"Tell you what." Preston leaned over and bumped me. "One of the days we're here, you have to promise to teach me how to board. Deal?"

"Deal." I shook his hand.

The butler returned. "Their Royal Majesties are ready to receive you."

Following him, we stopped outside large double doors. Two guards swung them open, revealing Edmund's parents inside, waiting for us.

They stood stiffly, still in their finery from dinner. The king's dark suit made his queen's deep purple floor length dress pop. The small tiara she wore matched her teardrop earrings and necklace. When the light hit her just right, she sparkled.

Edmund let everyone enter before him and stayed at my side. He didn't hold my hand, but I wasn't expecting him to, despite how badly I wished he could.

I was positive my heartbeat echoed through the large room. Surely Edmund must hear it. At my side, my fingers fidgeted.

Oh my God, I can't breathe.

"How lovely to see you all again." Queen Beatrice came over and gave Preston a hug, then air kissed his cheeks. Everything about her looked serene and peaceful. Going down the line, she greeted each of us in turn. Everyone bowed or curtsied as expected.

King William stood close to his wife, watching her with a soft look in his eyes. I caught glimpses of Edmund in his expressions.

"Edmund, darling, I'm so glad you could come. Your brother worried you wouldn't make it this year," said the queen, giving her son a hug.

"Things fell into place."

"Well, thank goodness you're all here." She momentarily held his hand in hers, then turned toward me. "And you must be Evie." Her soft blue eyes considered me. "It's a pleasure to meet you."

"The pleasure is all mine, Your Majesties."

King William stepped forward, reached out, and took my hand to assist me up from my curtsy.

"Miss Gray, welcome. We always do so enjoy meeting one of Edmunds friends." His eyes had the same mischievous twinkle as his son's.

"Thank you." My nerves slowly calmed and I took a deep breath. They weren't nearly as scary as I'd imagined. Aside from their fancy clothes, expensive jewelry, and regal demeanor, they seemed normal, kind even.

After a short time, Edmund's parents excused themselves to their rooms for the night. Which left us to hang out by the fire. A tray of tea and cookies greeted us when we returned.

After all the stress and buildup of meeting his parents, my body ached. My shoulders were sore, my neck stiff. I needed a hot bath and a good night's sleep. "I think I'm just going to head to bed. I'm done for," I told my friends and yawned. "I'll see you guys in the morning."

I hoped Edmund would offer to walk me to my room. A little alone time with him would be perfect. When he didn't say anything, I waved to the gang and left, feeling self-conscious.

What if his parents gave him some secret signal of disapproval?

I stepped on the bottom stair and felt his hand settle just above my waist. My lips curled in a grin and I continued to walk up, comforted by his presence.

"I was hoping you'd join me."

"I thought it prudent. I didn't want you aimlessly wandering the halls."

"Is that the only reason? My intentions were nowhere near as innocent." I coyly looked up at him.

"Is that so?" Away from prying eyes, Edmund slipped his hand into mine. He whispered in my ear. "I freely confess that getting you alone was my primary goal."

"Well, thank goodness we're on the same page." We padded up the stairs, down the long hallway, and paused outside my door. "Want to come in for a minute?"

"I'd love to." The copper flecks in his blue eyes gleamed. Inside, he closed the door and turned to me. "You were wonderful today. My family thought you were lovely."

"Really? I was so nervous." I sat on the couch across from the dying fire as Edmund tossed on a couple logs. When he sat next to me, I curled into him, marveling at how well we fit together.

"I could tell you were." He played with the long strands of my hair.

"You could? How? Was I that obvious?" I raised my head from his chest and met his eyes, worried.

"You do this fidgety thing with your hands when you're anxious or stressed."

A breathy laugh escaped my throat. "You noticed?"

I'd taken sign language in high school and now, when nervous, I finger-spell random words that pop into my head.

"I could also see it in your eyes." Edmund took my hand in his and drew a heart just above the underside of my wrist.

Closing my eyes, I enjoyed the slight tickling sensation. His palm pressed flat against mine as he compared the lengths of our hands. I opened my eyes to see his fingers neatly curl over the tops of mine. I'd needed this, a quiet moment, just the two of us. Just being near him had an amazingly calming affect on me.

"You have beautiful hands, so delicate." He wove his fingers through mine, knotting us together. His chest puffed out as he took a deep breath, my head rising with it. "What are you doing to me, Evie?"

"What do you mean?" I asked, not daring to look at him as a jolt of panic shot through me.

"When I'm not with you, I think of nothing but you. I want to tell you things I've never told anyone else. I want to share everything with you." He shook his head and softly added, "You're sitting right next to me and I don't feel like I can get close enough to you. I've never felt anything like this."

I nuzzled into him, relieved. "This is new for me too. I just want to enjoy every minute we have together."

"I'm so glad you came to Oxford." He leaned down and kissed the top of my head before tilting my face toward his. Slowly he kissed my eyes, nose, and cheeks before finally settling on my lips.

Cuddled together, we watched the fire, stole kisses, and whispered. It was perfection. Well, okay, I would've preferred more kissing, but it was probably wise we kept things cool.

In the wee hours of the morning I woke up, lying on the large four-poster bed with a blanket draped over me, fully dressed.

I don't remember falling asleep.

Groggily, I peeled off my clothes, leaving them in a heap on the floor, and burrowed into the softest sheets I'd ever encountered. I drifted back to sleep and dreamt of Edmund lying next to me.

Preston and I stood at the top of the slope. Trees and snow covered the landscape as far as I could see. I watched other boarders cut slick paths down the mountain. Yesterday we'd been on skis; today he demanded I teach him how to snowboard. So, that's what we were doing. Much to my shock, Edmund's brother decided to give it a whirl, too.

"Are you sure you don't want to put skis back on? This doesn't feel right." Philip glanced down at the board attached to his feet. "You seemed to do just fine on a pair of skis yesterday."

"I never said I couldn't ski, Your Highness; I just prefer to snowboard. Give it a try, you might enjoy it." I laughed and gave him a friendly pat on the shoulder. After a few pointers, they shoved off.

"See you at the bottom, gentlemen," I called after they left.

I stayed behind them as we flew down the mountain. One of them let out a holler of excitement, making me laugh. The sensation of flying over the soft crystalline snow was thrilling. I'd missed this.

Edmund, Lauren, and most of our group were at the bottom, waiting to see if Preston and Philip would make it down without injury.

Philip's bodyguards trailed behind us on skis. The crown prince must stay secure at all times. And I thought Edmund had it tough. I pulled up on Philip's left and he glanced over with a loud "Woo hoo!" and two thumbs-up.

I returned the gesture, surprised Philip was such a cool guy.

At the bottom, Philip and Preston rushed me, gigantic smiles covering their faces.

"That was bloody brilliant." Preston gave me a high five.

"Fantastic. Let's do it again." Philip lifted his goggles and grinned.

After a few more hours and numerous passes down the mountain, the three of us were starved. When we arrived at the château for lunch, we found the skiing group huddled in the conservatory around one end of a large wooden table. The platters of food smelled delicious. I had my eye on the cucumber sandwiches.

"Ah, the intrepid snowboarders. How was it?" Queen Beatrice looked us over from head to toe, presumably assessing her son for damages.

"It was incredible. I think there's a chance Evie may have made a convert out of me. Don't worry, Mum, I'll still ski." Philip hurried to assure her as he pressed a kiss on her cheek.

Beatrice laughed. "What did you think, Preston?"

"I loved it. This girl here is fearless." He nudged my shoulder. "You should've seen some of the jumps she was taking, it was amazing."

Edmund smiled and stood to help me take off my jacket. Draping it on the seat next to his, he then pulled the chair out for me.

"Thanks." I met his eyes and a zing of warmth spread through my chilled body.

"Are you guys planning on going back out after lunch?" Edmund asked.

"Yes," both Preston and Philip answered.

"In that case, I think I'll join you and get my own lesson." Edmund winked at me and I, of course, went red from head to toe, although my already pinkened cheeks may have hidden it for me.

True to his word, Edmund joined us after lunch. He wasn't half bad either. He fell far fewer times than Philip had.

"I'm impressed," I said as the lift carried us to the top. "Is this your first time?"

"It is." He smiled at me, proud of himself.

I pulled up my goggles. "What do you think?"

"I think I'll always prefer a set of skis, but if you want to snowboard, I'll do my best to keep up." His eyes twinkled as he spoke.

Unable to resist, I leaned over and planted a kiss on his lips without thinking. When I sat back up I couldn't believe what I'd just done. In public. Eyes wide, I covered my lips with a hand, muffling my voice. "I'm sorry, I shouldn't have . . ."

"Yes, you totally should have." The corners of his mouth quirked upward.

I was glad Preston and Philip were on the seat in front of us. Our feet dangling in midair, Edmund threw his arm around me and grabbed me, elaborating on my little peck, not caring who saw us.

Yawning, I rubbed at my eyes, eager for sleep. A full day of snowboarding had done me in. Toasty and cocooned in the world's most amazing bed, I was about to turn out the lights when a knock sounded on my door. Grumbling, I threw the covers back and padded over the soft carpet in my bare feet.

"Who is it?" I whisper-yelled.

"It's Caroline; let me in."

I opened the door, curious what was so important it couldn't wait. Caroline grinned at me, a scary big, super happy grin.

Eyebrows raised, I said, "Is there something I can do for you, Caroline?"

"No, but there's something I can do for you." She came in and calmly sat on the corner of the bed.

I waited for her to continue but she stayed mute; clearly she wanted me to ask. "What can you do for me?"

"I have news." She rubbed her hands together in front of her. "I was sneaking into the kitchen for a snack and I overheard Edmund speaking to his family."

"So?"

"So? So, they were discussing *you*."

My nose crinkled. "Do I want to know?"

"They were all impressed with you. Philip thinks you're sensational and a blast to be around. Lauren said you seemed like a good match for Edmund. She thought you'd keep him on his toes."

"Caroline, you little snoop." Thrilled that his brother and sister-in-law liked me, I was even more curious about his parents.

The room was dim, aside from the bedside lamp and the glow coming off the fire. I sat beside her and wrapped my robe around my shoulders.

"That's not all I heard. His mum thinks you're charming. She said it was obvious you have feelings for Edmund and he for you. It sounded like she really likes you."

"Oh my God, Caroline! I love you!" I squealed and gave her a big bear hug.

Hugging me back, she added, "She did say it was a pity you weren't English."

"I'm half-English, does that count?"

"King William wasn't thrilled that you're an American either. But he thought you were very sweet and genuine. He said something about finding a way to make it work if Edmund was really serious about you."

"What did Edmund say?"

A sly smile brightened her face. "I couldn't see his expression, but he told them there was no chance he and Jax could ever be together. His mum admitted she'd never seen Edmund look at Jax the way he's been looking at you."

There was too much happiness inside me. I doubted my body's ability to contain it all.

"Then his dad shocked everyone and said he never really cared for Jax."

My lips parted in a grin. This was a great start. "That's awesome." I wished I could talk to Edmund.

"Sorry if I woke you, but I couldn't have kept that in all night. I'll let you get back to bed." She did the double-cheek kiss thing and flew out the door.

Before she closed it behind her, she leaned back in. "Edmund did say something odd, though."

"Oh yeah?" I sat on the bed in a daze. *His family likes me.*

"He said something about there possibly being more to your story than meets the eye. Or something along those lines; I don't remember exactly."

"Thanks, Caroline." *Wonder what he meant by that?*

With a wave, she closed the door.

Unable to support myself, I flopped back on the bed. My imagination slipped into overdrive. I saw Edmund in a tux, waiting for me down a long aisle lined with flowers. Next I pictured him carrying a little pink bundle in his arms.

Slow down, Evie. You haven't even made girlfriend status. I rubbed my hands over my face and took a deep breath, trying to descend from my happy little cloud. The view sure was fantastic from up here.

Our last day on the slopes, we skied. Just before lunch we took a break for Edmund's family to hold a pseudo press conference. It was basically a chance for photographers and reporters to ask a few questions and get some nice shots of the family.

I stood on the sidelines with the group, watching. Behind everyone, I kept quiet, attracting as little attention as I could.

A man in a blue parka held up a microphone across the tape barrier and asked, "Princess Lauren, when will you give us an heir?"

Shielding her eyes from the blinding sun and snow combination, she answered, "When it's meant to happen it will."

"Prince Edmund!" shouted a short woman. "Are the rumors true that you and Lady Jacqueline are seeing each other?"

"No. Lady Jacqueline and I have always been, and will continue to be, just friends."

"Prince Edmund! Prince Edmund!" Several people yelled his name.

He pointed to a tall, slender man with a bright red beanie.

"You've frequently been seen in the company of an American girl and most recently been caught kissing her. What's your relationship with her?"

The snow at my feet suddenly held a new fascination for me as I nervously awaited his answer. It felt like my future hung on his next words.

Edmund cleared his throat. "Currently I'm unattached and that individual is a friend from University."

Ouch. My little cloud was now on a collision course with earth. After what Caroline told me last night I wasn't sure what to expect. *So, still not his girlfriend.*

After a few more questions the press conference ended and we headed back to the château.

That evening, after dinner, I stood in my room and tossed my packed bags on the chaise. Too bad I couldn't squirrel the bed away in my bags and take it back to my dorm.

It was full dark outside, but still fairly early. I thought about crawling into bed. Instead, book in hand, I made my way to one of the great rooms. I knew I'd find a blazing fire in the hearth and could probably scrounge up a cup of tea. To me, the trio of book plus tea plus fireplace equaled heaven.

A large overstuffed chair next to the hearth welcomed me. Opening my book, I lost myself in the story. The next time I glanced up, the fire was dwindling. I felt a tap on my shoulder. Tilting my head back, I saw Edmund peering down at me.

"Trouble sleeping?"

"Just not tired yet. I thought I'd read for a bit." I folded the corner of the page back and placed the book in my lap.

Edmund motioned for me to scoot over. We ended up squished together, but I didn't mind.

"Are you ready to go back tomorrow?" he asked.

"Well, I'm packed, but I don't want to leave. It's amazing here. You're lucky, you can come here whenever you want."

"I'm a very lucky man, but this château isn't why." He reached over and brushed my hair off my forehead.

"Why do you consider yourself lucky, hmm?"

He thought a moment. "I'd have to say my family and friends." His face moved a smidgen closer. "There's also that I'm in a position to effect change. But the reason at the very top of my list would be that I get to do this." He slipped a hand behind my neck and guided my mouth to his.

I shivered; his lips were warm and soft. Three days of very little alone time with Edmund made this kiss that much sweeter.

My arms went about his neck as his free hand slid down my back to the waistband of my jeans. I nibbled on his lower lip, which elicited a low moan from him.

Pulling me so I leaned on top of him, his fingers twined through my hair, pinning my lips against his. The tip of his tongue played with mine, driving me crazy.

Heat welled low in my stomach; the more he touched me, the hotter I got. I wanted more. We couldn't get close enough. I wanted all of him. Now. His breaths were coming in ragged pants as he held me tightly against his chest.

"Well, well, well," a voice rang out behind us, startling us apart—not that we could get very far apart sharing an overstuffed chair.

We turned in unison to see Philip and Lauren watching us.

"We had the same idea, but it appears you got here first. Come on, Laur, let's leave these lovebirds alone." Philip patted Lauren's hand as they sauntered off, snickering quietly to themselves.

"Night, Philip, and thanks a bunch," Edmund called after his brother, shaking his head with a chuckle.

Philip gave Edmund a thumbs-up as he and Lauren retreated from the room. I closed my eyes, slightly mortified. *Of course we'd get caught.*

"That's certainly one way to ruin the mood." He didn't look angry, more amused. "Do you want me to walk you up?" His breathing still was not quite back to normal, but neither was mine.

"I probably *should* head up, but I'd much rather stay here with you. I'm not quite ready to say good night."

"Is that so? There's a chance you might be able to persuade me to stay." The low embers of firelight flickered in his eyes. I couldn't imagine a time when I wouldn't want him.

Quietly, I laid my hand on his chest and leaned against him. Laying my head in his nook, I breathed in the scent of him, sighing contentedly.

"Oh, you're very good at persuasion." He chuckled and smoothed my hair back, wrapping his arms around me. "We're probably lucky they came in when they did."

"Oh?"

"If we'd gone much further I'd never have been able to stop."

The spark that'd been ignited low in my belly earlier now burst into an inferno. I smiled, the mental images flashing through my head making me blush.

We sat there snuggled, watching the low flames of the fire fade.

"I wish we could stay like this forever," I whispered.

"Me too." He kissed my forehead and I closed my eyes, never wanting the night to end.

I really should tell him about Clarice. Later, I'll do it later.

Chapter Seventeen

Uncovered and Naked

We'd been back on campus almost a week, and still I daydreamed about the château. Remembering our kisses in front of the hearth put a smile on my face and a bounce in my step.

A crack sounded in the gray sky as I scampered across campus to class. Rain splattered down on my loose braid before I could grab my umbrella.

"You look far too happy."

I froze. *Shit.*

Rubber grip tight in my hand, I turned. Chloe Saunders, Jax's bestie, Miss BitchyBoobsInYourFace herself, stood smirking at me. This was going to be painful, she'd make sure of that.

"Afternoon, Chloe. How was your break?" I asked, monotone. We saw each other around campus numerous times a day. Up until now we'd ignored each other.

"Absolutely splendid." She twirled her bright yellow umbrella, spraying water around her and all over me. "I spent it off the coast of Spain with Jax and her family on their yacht. She wanted to pay me back for Halloween."

There they were. I knew it wouldn't take her long to whip out the talons.

"What exactly can I do for you, Chloe?" I stopped walking near a newsstand, hoping she'd walk on, but she didn't.

"I bet you like seeing your face on the cover of all these magazines, don't you?"

Does her bitch mode have an off switch?

"Such a little fame whore. You don't have any class and yet you think you belong with those that do. You're pathetic." She moved closer and got into my face. "Your fifteen minutes of fame are just . . . about . . . over."

I cocked my head to the side and matched her saccharine smile. "That's precious. You *actually* think you'd recognize class if you saw it? I bet it could run up to you decked out in a tiara and a fabulous pair of Manolo Blahniks and you'd still be completely clueless."

Her mouth opened and closed as she huffed, at a loss for words. It wouldn't last long. She'd stew over this and blast me with an insult the next time our paths crossed.

Blocking her face with my umbrella, I turned my attention to the newsstand. A cover caught my eye. There was a recent photo of me, side by side one of Clarice. Her silver hair was pulled back into a tight twist, just like in the paintings at Welsington. The headline above our photos read: The Duchess of Westminster's Heir Found.

What?

This is bad.

I haven't told Edmund.

Snatching the paper up, I paid and walked off.

When I looked back, Chloe glared at me, clutching a copy in her purple-polished fingernails.

Fabulous.

The headline swirled through my mind as I rushed across campus, splashing through puddles, heedless of the rain pelting down. *How had they figured it out? What did this mean?*

A few photographers approached me, clicking away. *I need Edmund.* If he were here, they'd have to keep their distance.

"How's the duchess?" a photographer asked, a camera held up to his face.

"When's the last time you spoke with the duchess?"

"When is Prince Edmund going to officially announce your relationship?"

"Does Edmund know you're related to the Duchess of Westminster?" They fired off more questions as their cameras clicked away.

I crammed the paper in my bag. Their growing numbers made me uneasy; I had to get out of here. Picking up the pace, I sprinted to class.

Professor Littleton began his lecture just as I settled into my seat. My brain was scrambled and unfocused. Has Edmund seen this? What does he think?

Dammit, I should have told him. Abby was right.

Class dragged on incessantly. My eyes kept darting to the clock. *Why isn't it moving?* My fingers itched to grab the newspaper in my bag.

What felt like eons later, Littleton wrapped things up. The second he was finished, zippers zipped and papers rustled as students filed out of the hall.

Okay, let's check the damage.

I whipped the newspaper from my bag and flipped it open. The article explained how Clarice had cut my mother off after she'd married an unknown American. The reporter couldn't locate any documents that formally disowned her, but it certainly appeared that way.

Felt that way, too.

Reading further in the abandoned hall, I learned the duchess was quite ill. Apparently, when she died, there was a good chance the title would pass to me. The end of the piece delved into my relationship with Edmund, not surprisingly.

Several pictures dotted the pages, including a picture of my mother and grandmother. It was from Mom's Oxford graduation day. I knew because it looked like Mom had been cut out of the picture of her and Dad on my desk and placed next to Clarice.

I felt violated. I closed the paper, not wanting to read more. *Me, a duchess?* It wouldn't come to that. *Would it?*

Bag on my shoulder, I peeked around the doorjamb, hoping my unwanted posse from earlier wouldn't be there. No such luck. Photographers flanked the entrance like vultures waiting for dinner.

I wrapped my jacket tight around my middle and kept my eyes focused straight ahead. When I got outside, I walked mutely toward the dining hall in St. John's, praying they'd back off once they'd gotten whatever they wanted.

They didn't.

"Evie," Preston called as he and a grumpy-looking Edmund walked down the tree-lined path toward me.

"Hey." I ran toward them.

"Are you okay?" Edmund asked, scowling behind me at my now retreating press crew. When I nodded he added, "Why didn't you just tell me?"

I flinched; the angry accusation in his eyes stung. There was no doubt in my mind what he was referring to.

"I . . . I meant to, I did." I glanced about, noticing all the people around us along with the paparazzi lurking nearby. "Can we go inside?"

"Evie, I've known about your grandmother for a long time. I've just been waiting for you to be ready to tell me. Instead, Chloe had the pleasure this morning."

"Wait, what do you mean you knew?" I popped a hand on my hip.

"What's going on?" Preston interrupted, his face scrunched in confusion.

I handed him the paper. "This. And yes, it's true. Not that it makes any difference."

Preston stared at the page. "Why didn't you tell any of us?"

"Because, it's . . . complicated, and I wasn't 100 percent sure until recently."

"Come on, let's get to the dining hall. We don't need to give them any more photo ops." Edmund spun and took off.

Preston hung back with me as we struggled to keep up with Edmund's power walk. I could tell by his speed that he was seriously pissed off. *How had he figured it out?*

Once we reached the dining hall, Edmund rounded on me. "Were you really planning on telling me?"

"How long have you known?"

Preston took a few steps back, like he was trying to stay out of the middle of whatever this was turning into.

Edmund folded his arms across his chest. "After Welsington I figured something was up, so I did a little research on the daughter of the Duchess of Westminster. It wasn't hard to connect the dots. Bloody hell, my parents know. They did a background check after they met you. It's not like it's classified material. Why did you keep it a secret? From me of all people."

Background check? Guess I should've expected that.

Closing my eyes, I sighed. I couldn't admit that I'd wanted him to choose me before I told him. Even to me, it sounded childish. Not to mention I'd had plenty of time to come clean. "Ultimately it doesn't matter. Clarice is nothing to me. She may be my grandmother, but I've never met her, never talked to her, and she wants nothing to do with me. She cut my mother out of her life, which cuts me out, too. Why would I care who or what she is? This—" I grabbed the paper from Preston and waved it around like a mad person "—isn't going to change anything. To her I don't exist and that's just how it is."

"But this *does* matter, Evie." Edmund ran a hand through his damp, tousled hair, making bits stick up at odd angles. "This changes things. You should have told me. Trusted me."

"What? How does my not telling you mean I don't trust you?"

"I thought . . ." He looked at Preston, then back at me, shaking his head. "I don't know what I thought. I should go."

"Edmund, wait. I trust you. I do." I grabbed his arm, my brows scrunched in confusion.

"Do you?" His blue eyes seared into mine. "Seems to me something this big would've come up in conversation a time or two, at least with someone you trusted." Shaking his head, he added, "I'll see you around."

My hand slipped from his arm and I watched him walk away, hating how angry he was. I felt stupid. This could've easily been avoided. I took a deep breath and tried to center myself. Unbuttoning my coat, I slid off my gloves, stuffing them in the pockets. *Don't cry. Give him space, some time to cool off. It'll be fine.*

The dreadful what-ifs danced around the periphery of my mind. I didn't want to let them in, but they pushed and shoved. *What if he hates me now? What if he never forgives me? What if I've just destroyed everything we had?*

"You okay?" Preston's face leaned toward mine.

I nodded, unsure what to say. Tears welled in my eyes and a lump formed in my throat.

"Don't worry, he'll calm down and come find you to talk. He usually does."

"Thanks." A weak smile crossed my lips as Preston put a sweatshirt-clad arm around my shoulder and gave me a reassuring hug.

"Duchess Evie, that's brilliant."

I laughed. "Right. Like that'll ever happen."

My craptastic day from hell was almost at an end. *I just have to survive dinner.* I looked across the table at the opposite end where Edmund sat, still ignoring me. A fact that the entire lecture hall of Professor Roth's class now knew. Miraculously, I'd managed not to die of humiliation.

Edmund scarfed his food and excused himself, eager to put distance between us. I picked at my meal and tried to eat, but nothing looked appealing.

"Guys, I'm not hungry. I'll see you tomorrow." I picked up my tray and dumped it. As I walked away I heard Preston giving them the Cliff's Notes version of my day.

Inside my room, the blue message light on my desktop phone flickered through the darkness. I tossed my keycard on my desk and clicked on the lamp. Receiver in hand, I dialed my access code.

"This is the secretary for Clarice Elliot, the Duchess of Winchester. The Duchess requests an audience with . . ." a brief pause while the man on the line rustled a paper ". . . a Miss Evangeline Gray. Please call to set up an appointment." He rattled off a series of numbers that I quickly jotted down before slamming the phone onto the cradle. I picked it up again just for the satisfaction of slamming it down again.

Now she wants to meet me. Twenty years and suddenly she has an interest. Isn't that just peachy? *What if I don't want to meet her, huh?* I stabbed the pen into the paper next to her number, leaving a divot in the pad.

Emotions swirled inside of me: anger, frustration, happiness, heartache, relief, sadness, bitterness. I couldn't reach out and grab just one; they were all too tightly woven together in an overwhelmingly large ball. I'd kept them at bay too long.

She can't order me around. I won't meet her. Screw my fifth quest. A tremble started in my stomach and spread through my body. *Why wasn't I good enough for her?*

All the years of rejection and the not knowing why bubbled over. Add my horrendous day, and great wracking sobs took over my body. Tears coursed down my cheeks. I curled up on the bed, grabbed my pillow, and released all the pent-up feelings of rage and inadequacy.

Startled by a loud knock, I tried to muffle my sobs. Intending to ignore whoever it was, I rolled to face the wall. Pushing my pillow away, I struggled to get control.

Deep breath in. And out. Deep breath in, blow it out.

"Evie, open up. Please?" It was Edmund. He rapped again.

I scrunched my eyes tight. Edmund was the last person I wanted to talk to. So, of course he'd pick now to try and work through this mess. *About par for the day.*

"Evie? I know you're in there. Can we please talk?" His weary voice filled my ears. "I'm not leaving until I talk to you."

No intention of getting up, I crossed my arms over my chest. Lying as still as I could, I tried to hold my breath. Which was impossible, since I'd just had a massive cry and was still gasping for air.

"Okay. Fine, I get it. You're mad, too. I'll wait. I'll sit here until you're ready." The door creaked in protest as he leaned against it and slid himself to the floor.

Ugh. Take a hint, dude, get lost.

I wiped the tears from my cheeks with the sleeves of my sweater. Black streaks of mascara stained the cuffs. *Whatever.* Knowing I was a mess, I got up and yanked the door open. Edmund nearly fell backwards.

"I don't want to talk right now. Please, just go away." The sight of him sent my tear ducts back into production.

Get a hold of yourself, Evie. A tear escaped and trickled down my cheek. I looked at the ceiling to stop crying. It sort of worked.

Edmund stood up quickly and cupped my face in his hands. His thumb traced the track of my tear, wiping it away and sending shivers through me. "Are you crying?"

I sighed. "Yes, I'm crying." My voice didn't sound right thanks to my plugged nose. "It's been a really rough day and I'd just like to be left alone. So, can you go?" I feebly pushed against his chest.

"Evie," he whispered, my name a plea. "Please, tell me I'm not the reason you're crying?"

The way he looked at me made me want to bawl even more. From his face, I could tell the idea that he'd made me cry was torturous.

I looked up at him, wanting him closer and hating myself for it. "Today was really crappy and yes, you're part of that." I pulled my face away from his hand. "But you're far from the only reason."

He pulled me into his arms and kissed my forehead. "I'm so sorry. I never wanted to make you cry. I was a complete arse."

"Yes, you were."

He leaned me back and smiled softly. "Well, at least we can agree."

I smiled and sniffed back the snot. "I should have told you. I know that. I just . . . I didn't know how and . . ." I shook my head and looked at the floor. "It's stupid."

"What do you mean? What's stupid?" His hand came up and brushed my hair over my shoulder.

Blowing out a deep breath I met his eyes, knowing I had to tell him my full rationale. "I didn't want you to pick me over Jax because of Clarice. I wanted to be certain you wanted me for me. Not because of some relative who'll probably never even know me."

"That's not stupid." He cupped my face again. The warmth of his breath caressed my lips. "I can understand that." He kissed the tip of my nose. "And for the record, Jax was never any competition. From the first moment I saw you, I knew . . ." His words trailed off in a whisper and slowly his mouth moved toward mine.

I could've turned away. His lips hovered in a silent last chance to deny him before they touched mine. The kiss was sweet and gentle. It felt like an apology.

He wants me. Only me.

My knees wobbled and I leaned into him. Releasing my face, his hands slid down my arms and came to a stop on my hips. A gentle tug and I was pressed against him. His lips met mine again.

Hands splayed against his back, I pulled him with me, into my room. He kicked the door closed behind him as I attempted to back us toward the couch.

"Oh!" I said, breaking our kiss, surprised to find the desk now under my bum.

My pencil holder clattered to the floor, spilling pens and pencils everywhere, and the pictures on my desk toppled over, along with Mom's glittery Eiffel Tower.

"I'll get the, um . . ." He grinned crookedly and gestured to the floor.

I stood and set my photos upright. My top was twisted and bunched up in the back. I straightened it and tried to compose myself before Edmund finished.

When he stood, he set the cup down and his eyes scanned the pad of paper with Clarice's name and number hastily scrawled across it.

"Did she call?"

Inhaling sharply, I nodded. "Well, someone who works for her called. They want me to call and set up an appointment with her. How weird is that?"

"What about your quests? Are you going to finish them? What was the next one?" He grabbed my hands in his and pulled me to the bed. He lay on his back; I curled next to him and rested my head on his chest.

"Ironically enough, to meet her."

"What do you want to do?"

My fingers played with the seaming of his blue shirt. "Part of me just wants to meet her and get it over with. But another part wants to run back to Seattle and never face her."

"But you have to."

"Why?" Under my ear I could hear his heart beating reassuringly steady.

"To get answers. Whether you like it or not, she's the one remaining person who connects you to your mum. Meet her, even if it's just to spit in her eye for how she treated your mother. Christ, Evie, this has the potential to change your life. You need to find out what this means for your future. And if none of these reasons are good enough, remember, your mum wanted you to meet her."

I propped my hands on his chest and used them to cushion my chin, meeting his eyes. "What about what I want? What if I really don't want to meet her? Why should I come running just because she calls?"

"Because this is huge. I'll go with you if you want me to." He slid his arm behind his head for support and looked down at me.

"You'd do that?"

"Of course I'd go with you. I've met the duchess before. She's a bit of an old hag, but she doesn't scare me . . . anymore." He grinned and ran his fingers through my hair, playing with it. "You need to do this."

Sighing, I said, "I know."

I laid my head back on his shoulder. His fingers continued combing through my hair, relaxing me. I closed my eyes, enjoying the sensation.

"How do you suppose the papers found out?"

My eyes snapped open. Edmund just asked the million-dollar question.

Chapter Eighteen

Be Our Guest

"Good morning," Edmund's sleepy voice rumbled underneath me.

I lifted my head off his chest and looked into Edmund's handsome face. "Morning?" I asked groggily and glanced at the window. Bright light glimmered through the curtains. "Oh my God, what time is it?" I craned my neck to see the clock on my desk: 7:00 A.M.

Holy shit. We just spent the night together. *In bed.*

Heat rushed from the top of my head to the tips of my toes. No guy had ever seen me in the morning. Well, aside from Dad. I knew I had cry-smeared makeup and my hair was probably a rat's nest. Top that off with morning breath and what a charming picture I must make.

"I can't believe we crashed like that." I tried to roll away, but he held me close.

His nose nuzzled my hair. "I didn't have the heart to wake you. Well, that, and I wasn't quite ready to let you go." He popped up on an elbow and studied my face. "You look absolutely fetching in the morning."

That did it; right then and there I melted. "You're trouble, you know that, right?" I couldn't help but smile. He looked incredible. The lids of his eyes, still a little heavy, and his disheveled blond hair gave him a carefree, easy sexiness.

"What do you mean, trouble?" His voice sounded deeper after sleeping. I loved that I now knew this.

"Just that you know exactly what to say and do to make me feel tingly all over."

He raised an eyebrow and gave me that irresistible crooked grin. "I make you tingly, do I?"

I chuckled. *You're doing it right now.* Clearing my throat, I said, "Um . . . I should go hop in the shower."

Awkwardly, I attempted to climb over him. Before I got very far his hand snaked up, stopping me. Perched atop him, my heart pounded against my ribs as he slowly rose and brushed a soft kiss across my lips.

"You should know, you're trouble, too." He grinned rakishly at me.

A girlish giggle, that I wish I could've stopped, escaped my lips.

Leaning down, I kissed him. Eagerly responding, his hand tangled through my messy bed head. A quivering sensation low in my stomach told me I needed to put a little space between us. The way he made me feel was unreal.

Pulling away, I looked down at him. One breathless word came out. "Shower."

"Okay, let's go." He grinned at me with a glint in his eyes.

I gasped, shocked yet thrilled at the same time. Hopping off him, I shook my head.

"So that's a no on the shower then?" He chuckled as he sat up. "I'll see you at breakfast."

I glanced back just in time to see him stretch. His muscular abs peeked out from beneath his now wrinkled undershirt. *Oh yum.* I sighed, then turned and spun the water dial to full blast.

Stepping into the noisy dining hall, I dodged students coming out the door and spied Edmund and Preston at our table. He'd changed into a long-sleeved gray T-shirt and, unfortunately, he'd brushed his hair. The sexy bed head of this morning was gone. *Bummer, I think that's my new favorite look.*

My stomach clenched, remembering the warmth of his arms wrapped around me. We'd slept together. *No, I slept next to him.* Nothing happened.

Inhaling sharply, I made my way to the breakfast line. The next time I peeked at him, Edmund saw me and smiled.

Good morning, belly butterflies. I smiled and waved. Preston returned it.

"I take it all's fine in Edmundlandia again?" Caroline asked as she, Marissa, and Suzy joined me with their trays.

"Very funny." I laughed. "But yes, we worked it out."

"Glad you're sorted." Caroline grabbed two apples and handed one of them to Marissa.

"Any news on your gram?" Suzy asked as she placed a mini-box of Corn Flakes and a carton of milk on her tray.

I grabbed some toast and a yogurt as we went farther down the line and paid. "Yeah, I had a message on my machine last night. Her secretary called to set up an appointment." I scrunched my nose. "I feel like I'm going to the doctor."

"Have you rung them back?" Suzy asked as we walked to the table.

"I did. I actually called this morning . . . after I showered." I shot Edmund a glance as I sat, blushing as he winked at me.

"And?" Marissa prompted.

"And now I have an appointment with the Duchess of Westminster." I used my loftiest voice, fake accent and all. "Saturday at two."

"You're finally getting to meet your gram, that's pretty exciting," Caroline said, tucking her black bob behind her ear.

"That's one way to look at it." I could tell from the look in Caroline's eyes she wanted to talk about Clarice.

"Do you still want me to go with you?" Edmund took a drink of his tea.

I nodded. "I'd rather not meet her alone."

"Then I'll be there." He nudged his shoulder into mine. I smiled, grateful he'd be there tomorrow.

The more I thought about meeting Clarice, the more nauseated I felt. She disowned her own daughter. What kind of person does that? I was terrified she'd be as cruel to me as she was to Mom. I didn't want to burst into tears in front of her and Edmund.

"You okay, Evie?" Preston asked from across the table.

I shook my head, snapping out of my thoughts. Everyone had finished eating and it was time to go. "I'm good. Just lost in thought."

My mostly uneaten breakfast got dumped in the trash. Slipping my coat on, I waved goodbye as we parted.

Edmund and I walked toward the side doors and Preston fell in step beside me. Normally he went with Suzy.

"You're really nervous, aren't you?" Preston's voice was softer than normal.

"It's that obvious?" I stopped and turned to face him.

"Don't let her get to you. She can only hurt you if you give her the power to. So don't give it to her." He pulled against his backpack straps as he spoke.

"Wow, Preston, that's really . . . deep." I got the impression he spoke from experience.

Preston scratched the back of his blond head. "Yeah, well, I'll see you guys later." With a wave, he jogged off in the direction of his class.

"Don't give her the power. I think I can do that." I turned to Edmund, smiling.

"You're going to be fine. I'll be there with you. Plus, she's awfully old and frail; you've got a definite advantage."

I laughed. "That's awful."

Dressed in an outfit Caroline had helped me put together, I went down to meet Edmund. From the stairs, I spotted him. Pausing, I admired how his build seemed perfectly made for suits.

He turned, smiling. In three steps he stood at the bottom of the stairs. I was tempted to jump into his arms and kiss him.

"You know, I can think of much better ways to spend our time. Are you sure you really want to go?" I slid my hands around his neck and played with the little curls of hair there. They were my favorite.

"Nice try. You're going." He pulled my hands down and held them in his warm ones. "Don't be nervous. You look quite smart. The duchess can't help but approve."

I slipped my hands from his and did a quick spin. "You really think so?" Caroline had selected a simple knee-length deep blue dress. I paired it with the Eiffel Tower necklace Edmund had given me. It rarely left my neck.

"I know so. You're beautiful." He clasped my hand. "Shall we? The car's waiting out front. Let's get this over with. What do you say, since we'll be in London, we hit the Victoria and Albert Museum before we head back?"

"That'd be fantastic." Having something positive to focus on after the meeting with Clarice helped.

Outside, photographers snapped pictures from a short distance as we climbed into the black Rolls Royce the duchess had sent. It was an older model, well preserved, but the windows lacked tinting. Flashes popped from either side of the car. I forced myself to keep my head up. *This is what it must be like to be a zoo animal.*

Once we pulled away, I blew out the breath I'd kept pent up. "So, what can you tell me about my grandmother? Aside from her being old, ill, and a bit of a hag?"

"She's quite well off financially. I know she has several homes and a pretty extensive art collection. From what my parents say, she's extremely opinionated. Although, you could argue that might fall under the hag category, I suppose." He softly chuckled.

I took a deep breath, feeling unsure and far from confident.

"You're going to be fine. Preston was right. Don't give her any power; she's not worth it."

I nodded and turned to look out the window. Trees and cars flew by as my stomach tied itself into queasy knots. I could picture it now, meeting Clarice and either crying or puking on her. Possibly both. If I puked, I'd definitely start crying.

Wordlessly, Edmund reached for my hand. A gentle squeeze and a sympathetic glance made me feel better. He didn't let go for the duration of the drive.

The closer we got to her, the harder my heart hammered.

"Breathe, Evie."

"Where are we?" I asked, taking a shaky breath. The area looked elegant and expensive, with fancy cars, large houses, and well-dressed people ambling along the frosty sidewalks.

"Kensington Square." Edmund leaned so he could see out my window.

"It's beautiful."

The chauffeur pulled to a stop in front of a four-story, white stone townhouse.

We can't be here already. I'm not ready. How would it look if I asked the driver to do a lap around the block?

I looked up the path to a black door, flanked by colorfully potted seasonal cabbage plants. A short, wrought-iron gate guarded the pathway.

My heartbeat sped up and my breathing sounded shallow. Edmund's hand squeezed mine. I felt his gaze on me.

"I can't do this. I don't want to do this." I frantically turned in my seat to face him. I knew I looked as terrified as I felt.

Edmund's hands cradled my face. "Evie, take a deep breath." He gave me a reassuring smile. "You're going to be fine. She's an old woman who has no power over you. Don't forget that. She should consider herself lucky you agreed to meet with her." He leaned in and kissed me.

What started off as a small graze escalated into something more ardent. My nerves disappeared and I focused only on Edmund and the sensations he created inside me. My fingers threaded through his hair until I heard someone clear his throat.

Edmund and I pulled apart and looked at the driver, who smiled at us in the rearview mirror.

"We've arrived at our destination." He then hopped out and came around to open our door.

I gave Edmund a sheepish look. He outright laughed as he clambered out. The driver in his crisp black suit offered me his hand as I exited. I couldn't meet his eyes. Looking at the ground, I turned as red as one of London's famous telephone boxes.

"I was hoping to take your mind off things for a moment. Did it help?" Edmund whispered when the driver walked away.

"Mmm, quite effective." I nodded and smoothed my skirt. I paused at the gate, staring at the beautiful house looming before me.

Mom lived here.

I stared at the four levels of white-latticed windows, wondering which one had been her bedroom. I imagined Mom walking through the gate and rushing off to some fabulous museum.

A longing for her struck me, so intense it nearly doubled me over. Clutching at my abdomen with both hands, I took a steadying breath.

"Are you sure you're okay?" Edmund rubbed my back and tilted my chin up with his other hand.

"Yeah, it's just that my mom was here, like *actually* here. She lived in this house. Maybe some of her stuff is still here." Looking up at his face, I felt the ache subside. Thank goodness he was here.

"Let's see if we can't find a bit of your mum in this old house." With a warm grin, he held the gate open for me. "You ready?" he asked, his hand hesitating at the doorbell.

At my nod, he pushed the button. Through the oversized door I heard the chimes. It wasn't long before a man in a sharply pressed jet-black jacket, wearing gray slacks and stark white gloves, opened the door.

Mentally, I named him Jeeves. He looked older than dirt.

"Yes?" He looked down his nose, squinting at Edmund at me.

I opened my mouth and a very undignified squeak slipped out. Clearing my throat, I managed, "Hello, I'm Evangeline Gray. I have a two o'clock appointment with the duchess."

"Yes, Miss Gray. Please come in. I shall notify Her Grace that you and a guest have arrived." He eyed Edmund from head to toe, clearly displeased to have an unannounced visitor, even if it was a royal one. "Please wait here." He pointed to the foyer as he walked through an arched doorway to the right.

"Why do I feel like I'm in trouble for bringing you?" I muttered, on the verge of nervously laughing.

"You're in so much trouble," Edmund whispered, as one corner of his lips twitched up.

The black-and-white marble floor was sleek and polished to a high sheen. Benches sat on either side, and a hall tree for coats, hats, gloves, and whatever else guests might bring perched just beyond.

A circular wooden table with a grand yellow floral centerpiece warmed the foyer. Above the table hung a glittering chandelier.

This is what Mom threw away.

The butler returned minutes later. "The duchess will be with you shortly. Please, have a seat." He indicated the benches then disappeared again.

"Okay." Edmund watched him, his brow furrowed. "This is different."

"How so?"

"Usually, you're taken to a parlor or sitting room. Leaving us out here is . . ." He shook his head. "Never mind."

Twenty minutes later, Jeeves shuffled back in. "The duchess is ready to see you."

Edmund stood stiffly. "About time," he softly huffed.

I suspected even the ancient butler heard him.

Jeeves glared at Edmund, his furry white brows lowering over his rheumy eyes. "If you'll follow me, Miss."

He guided us through the arched doorway on the right and down a hallway. Jeeves stopped at the last door and rapped lightly. "Your Grace, a Miss Evangeline Gray and guest to see you."

Guest?

"You may enter." A gravelly voice, deeper than I'd expected, called out.

Edmund and I exchanged a glance. Like me, he had to be wondering why he'd been labeled my guest and not properly introduced.

Jeeves had to recognize him, right?

Who wouldn't recognize the prince—well, aside from me?

The butler opened the large white doors and in we went.

Chapter Nineteen

You Can't Pick Your Family

Over the back of a tall brown leather chair, a little silver bun peeked out. The duchess sat unmoving, staring out the floor-to-ceiling windows.

Shelves of books, a massive dark oak desk, and two cushioned armchairs furnished the room. It reminded me of a man cave, not a feminine touch in sight.

I itched to reach and spin her chair around. *Please let this go well. Let her be nice.*

Edmund's hand settled on my back and rubbed. I wondered if he could feel my racing heartbeat.

The chair slowly turned.

I couldn't breathe.

This is it.

Clarice and I were in the same room. About to meet. This could be a new connection to my mother.

Now facing us, Clarice silently stared at me with a sour expression. She opened her mouth, but stopped when her eyes fully took in my *guest*. Her thin silver eyebrows shot up and a wrinkled hand went to her throat.

"Your Highness, what a pleasure. It's always such a delight to be in your presence. Please, forgive me for not getting up to properly receive you. I fear my health won't allow it these days."

"It's perfectly fine. There's nothing to forgive." He smiled warmly at her.

"Clearly, my staff needs to be educated. I did not realize my *granddaughter* would be bringing such an illustrious companion with her." The word "granddaughter" sounded acidic leaving her lips.

"Please, don't trouble yourself. I'm sure Evie is the one you're eager to finally meet." Edmund flashed Clarice his most charming smile and took a small step back, putting the focus on me.

"Indeed." She spared me a momentary glance. "How is your family, Your Highness?" She refocused her attention on Edmund, continuing to ignore me.

I shifted my stance self-consciously, feeling invisible. *I don't belong here.*

"All healthy and well." His voice sounded tight.

Clarice nodded and her smile faded to a grim, disapproving line. "Won't you both be seated and we can get down to business."

We sank into the cushioned armchairs opposite her. Clarice towered over us at her desk. Despite her frail stature, she looked menacing.

I clasped my hands together in my lap, trying to appear unaffected.

"I should warn you." She glowered at me. "I intend to say my piece. I'll not hold back simply because you've brought an audience with you."

"Fire away." I met her gaze with nonchalance, proud of myself for not showing the fear that coursed through every inch of me.

"I demand to know why you told the press of your association with me. I can only assume you did it to look more desirable to the prince and the royal family. Having some sort of titled connections would certainly help your feeble case for attention." Her face was full of disgust as she glared me down.

Beside me, Edmund stiffened. His hand tightly clutched the pommel at the end of his chair's arm.

Clarice's venomous words shocked me. They probably shouldn't have, but they did. So, that's how she wants to play this, embarrass and belittle me. Well, that isn't going to happen. She could try all she wanted, but I refused to let her make me feel small. *She doesn't have the power.*

Straightening my spine, I met her glare with one of my own. "Lovely to meet you too, *Grandma.*"

"Don't act like I'm the one being uncouth. You're the little chit who told the press." Her accusing eyes turned to slivers. In an icy voice she continued, "No doubt your father's subpar genes are surfacing."

She was old, sick, and frail, but I wanted to deck her.

"I forbade your mother to marry outside her class. She accused me of being elitist." She shook her head with a dry laugh. "No mother wants her daughter to marry common gutter trash. It's a blessing she never lived long enough to see you become the grasping, deceitful, little crown hunter you are. You can't possibly think I would ever claim you as my flesh and blood. You'll get nothing from me."

Fury flamed inside me. *How dare she.*

Edmund stood, nearly knocking over his chair, and leaned onto Clarice's desk. She sat back, startled. The muscles in his back were tense and taut under his jacket. Anger rolled off of him.

"Stop. Right. There. You are out of line. If you must blame someone for the press finding out, it's me. My *choosing* to be around Evie makes her a target and prompted the press to dig up anything they could find. Your Grace, Evie is amazing. Which is why I love . . . being around her. I pursued her, not the other way around."

Clarice's mouth popped open. Her eyes sparked with anger. She looked livid.

Edmund remained standing, as if challenging Clarice to say something cruel.

How did we end up here so quickly? My legs ached to run. I wanted to find a place I could curl up, hide, and cry. This had gone so much worse than I'd imagined. *Dammit, if Edmund hadn't insisted, I wouldn't even be here.*

Anger boiled inside me. I clenched my fists, unsure who to direct my rage at. I hated Clarice, but I was pissed at Edmund. Hell, I was even mad at myself.

Clarice's icy voice ended our standoff. "I think we're done here." She rang a small bell and called, "Denby."

Jeeves appeared at the door. "Your Grace?"

She gave the butler a stern look. "Please show Miss Gray and *Prince* Edmund out. That is all."

I rose from my chair, Edmund trailing behind me, and stopped at the doorway. This was the only time I'd ever set eyes on this woman. I needed to get this out, for me and for Mom.

"There's something you should know. Up until the very end, Mom never lost hope that one day you'd try to make amends. But, I get it now; you don't know how to love. You care nothing for me or her." A dry laugh left my lips. "She hoped her death would finally bring us together." I had to pause and take a deep breath. It was a struggle to speak past the lump of emotion in my throat.

How can this woman be related to my mother? I hovered in the doorway, my knees shaky.

"How could you not say goodbye to your only child? I was so young when she died, but I still knew you weren't there. That's when I started to hate you. My mother was a wonderful woman. How that happened with you for a mother, I'll never understand. But let me be perfectly clear when I say I'm ashamed of you."

I hate you. I wish I'd never met you. I sucked in a raspy breath. Why had I listened to Edmund?

"I have no desire for the world to know our connection. As far as I'm concerned, you're dead. You don't exist. Enjoy what's left of your lonely, hollow life." Spinning on my heel, I ran out of the room, not caring if Edmund followed or not.

I didn't wait for Jeeves. Instead I made a mad dash for the front door. Jerking it open, I slammed it behind me. My heels clacked against the paving stones in an angry cadence. I didn't care where I went, just as long as it was away and I was alone.

Why did you do this to me, Mom?

"Evie. Stop. Wait up," Edmund called, trying to catch up.

I winced. *Oh God, he witnessed all that.*

The blue skirt of my dress bounced as I stomped away. I'd blown out of Clarice's townhouse in a whirlwind, leaving everything behind. This had been a monumental disaster. Tears streamed down my cheeks.

His hand clasped my elbow. "Evie, slow down. Talk to me."

I turned to face him, my temper masking the embarrassment in my watery eyes. "I don't want to talk to you." I tried to pull away, but he held firm.

"Don't let her get to you. She's clearly not right in the head." He wrapped my coat around my bare shoulders.

His arms enveloped me in warmth, but I pushed hard against his chest. I didn't want to hear his voice or feel his hands on me. I wanted to be far away from him and the rest of the world.

"You're not mad at *me*, are you?" Dropping his hands, he took a step back. Worry lines etched on his forehead.

"I'm mad at her, I'm mad at myself, and yes, I'm even mad at you." I put another step between us.

"What did I do?" He held his hands up in surrender.

"You talked me into this whole mess."

Edmund's brows knitted together. "Rubbish, I was trying to help. I knew how nervous you were and that you wouldn't come if I hadn't prodded you to. I care about you, Evie, a lot." A strange wistful look crossed his face.

"I don't need your prodding and I don't need you pushing me into something that I don't want to do."

Edmund kicked a rock off the pavement, pinging it off one of the iron fences. "You're mad, I get that, but I stand by the importance of you meeting her. Now you know. You told her off and you don't have to wonder anymore. She's officially done in your life. I don't get why you're so bloody mad at me. Cross her off, move on."

"That's beside the point!" I stamped my foot. The realization that I might be being ever so slightly irrational hit me. Only problem, I was too upset and humiliated to back down.

Edmund turned away from me with an irritated sigh, then froze. I followed his gaze, dreading what I'd see.

"Ah, that's just bloody brilliant." He gestured toward the park, where men with cameras stood. "I'm calling for the car."

"I'll walk."

"All the way to Oxford?" With a laugh of frustration, he grabbed my hand. "Come on, be reasonable."

"Of course I'm not walking all the way to Oxford. I'll catch the train." I met his gaze with a challenging stare.

"Evie, I'm not just going to leave you in London. Where do you want to go? I'll go with you."

I closed my eyes, trying to rein in my anger before I said something I'd regret. When I looked at him again I said, "I really don't want to be around you right now, Edmund. I need some space."

"Let's get back to campus; you can be alone then. I promise I won't even talk to you in the car. It'll be like I'm not there." He was mad, but trying to smile it off for the cameras.

I looked to the trees lining the opposite side of the street. I wasn't ready to play nice. "Look, I already had a mother. I don't need you trying to take her place by smothering me. Just back off, would you?"

A flash of pain seared his face; he thrust my clutch in my hands, then tucked his hands in his pockets. "Fine, do whatever you want, Evie. I'll see you back on campus." Face like a mask, he turned away and walked off.

Way to go, Evie. You made him as mad as you are.

I watched as he left me behind without a backward glance. A small smidgen of relief swam in my mind, but it was quickly overwhelmed by the regret surging through me. I'd let my emotions overpower me. *Why didn't I stop?* Unsteady breaths burned my chest. I turned away, unable to watch his back any longer.

Arm outstretched, I hailed a taxi. One of London's famous black cabs pulled up to the curb and I hopped in.

"Where to, Miss?" The driver boasted a thick accent I couldn't place. He stared at me in the rearview mirror like he recognized me and was trying to sort out how.

"Victoria and Albert Museum, please." The cab jolted from the curb before I could buckle up. I grasped for the seatbelt, breathing a sigh of relief when I heard it click into place. The cab darted in and out of traffic. Just looking out the windows made me anxious.

We pulled up to the curb with a sudden lurch. "Your stop, Miss. That'll be a fiver."

"That was quick." I don't know if it was his driving, or the fact that I probably could've walked here, that made the trip feel like I'd been in warp speed.

He smiled as I handed him six pounds and jumped onto the curb. Behind me I heard him speed away.

Looking up at the large white stone entrance, I took a moment to just enjoy the beauty around me. I needed to get myself in a better mood.

Most of the building was red brick. Rows of windows glistened in the sunlight. With a contented sigh, I walked up the small flight of steps and through one of the large doors. Breathing in a deep breath, I thought, *this is exactly what I need.*

Inside, a massive rotunda greeted me. Suspended in the center was a chandelier. Not just a simple chandelier, oh no, it was an original Dale Chihuly. And it was breathtaking. Delicate blue-and-green tendrils of blown glass curled over, around, and through each other. It had to be at least thirty feet long.

A pang of homesickness hit me square in the chest. Chihuly was a Seattle artist. I loved his museum and gardens nestled under the Space Needle. I sighed, wishing I were home with Dad and Abby.

My hand slipped into my clutch, searching for Mom's letters as I set off to explore. This morning I'd grabbed them on my way out. I needed her with me. Now, here, I was doubly glad.

Wandering around the museum, I tried to push the hellish morning from my mind. I wanted to forget all about Clarice and my fight with Edmund.

Clarice, I easily chucked aside. Edmund, not so much. He stayed in the forefront of my thoughts.

Just being in a museum reminded me of him. The weekends we'd spent traipsing through other museums swam through my memories. Being here alone didn't feel right. It was too quiet. I was lonely without him.

I missed him.

I looked at the ceiling and I sent up a silent apology. *Edmund, I wish you were here.*

I explored and admired paintings by Botticelli, Rembrandt, Tintoretto, and numerous others, marveling at the artists' overwhelming talent.

But after only an hour I was ready to leave.

Edmund probably would've had some interesting facts to share. He always did. I imagined him standing beside me. I could almost feel his hand in mine. We'd stare at the Botticelli and he'd lean a little closer and whisper some obscure fact in my ear.

How could I have been so awful to him? My breath hitched in my throat. He'd only been trying to help, looking out for my best interests. He was right, meeting Clarice was closure. *Oh, God, the way I behaved.* I cringed. Bet he wasn't having any trouble seeing the family resemblance.

I walked a little farther and stood in front of a Tintoretto, my vision blurring. I put my face in my hands and pressed my palms against my eyes, attempting to turn off the tears without smearing the crap out of my mascara. Someone grazed my shoulder and stood beside me. I froze, wishing whoever it was would go away and leave me to cry in private.

"Did you know his father was a dyer? Which they would have called a *tintore* back then. That's how he got the nickname of Tintoretto; it means 'little dyer.' His real name was Jacopo Comin."

I dropped my hands and turned. A smile burst from my lips at the sight of him standing so close to me, hands clasped behind his back. Wiping at my eyes, I couldn't manage anything above a whisper. "What are you doing here?"

"I thought I might find you here. There was no way I could just drive off and leave you in London. Especially not as upset as you were." His eyes softened as he looked at me. "I had to make sure you were all right. You still mad?" He tucked his hands in his pockets, looking contrite.

I shook my head. "I've had time to calm down. I'm pretty sure I'm sane again. I can't believe I blew up at you like that." My hands twisted together in front of me. I wanted to touch him, but I couldn't bring myself to reach for him. "I'm really sorry."

"It's okay." His hand caressed my cheek. I leaned into it with a small sigh. "This morning was a little intense. And maybe I shouldn't have pressured you. I just didn't want you to regret not meeting her while you had the chance." He broke into a grin. "But honestly, the way you took her on was cracking."

I chuckled, then scrunched my face, reaching for his hand. "She's awful, isn't she?"

"She is." Edmund nodded and pulled me into a hug.

"I'm sorry you had to see that." I curled into his chest.

"No worries. We all have at least one family member we'd rather not claim. I've got an uncle whose goal is to party it up and sleep with the entire female population of Britain. You don't want to know the problems he's caused." He laughed, leaned back, and stared into my eyes. "So you've got a mean, old harpy for a grandmother. It could be worse."

"Oh really?" I held onto his hands as we stood alone in the hallway. "How could it be worse?"

"Well . . ." He paused to think. "I suppose she could take up body painting herself and then go jogging in Kensington Gardens every Sunday." He waggled his brows playfully at me.

"Touché." I laughed.

"Come on." He grabbed my hand, his eyes full of mischief. "Let's get lost together."

Chapter Twenty

Coming Clean

When I hung up from talking with an apologetic Anton, I bundled into my blanket and went to the couch in my dorm room. Knowing I'd reached the destination of the quest letters made me miss Mom more. At least there was one final letter waiting for me, according to Anton. Staring out the window into the dark night, my mind wandered back to Clarice.

I've got to call Dad and tell him about her. And I needed to do it before he read it in some sleazy tabloid. It'd be much better coming from me, but I really didn't want to do it.

With a deep sigh, I looked up at the stars. "I wish you were here, Mom."

Scrolling through my phone to Dad's number, I held my finger over the call button. His day was just starting. *Maybe I should save this for after work?* The thought of shattering his image of Mom didn't sit well with me. Dread settled into my bones, making me feel heavy.

I tossed my phone on the black cushion next to me.

There was one positive in all this. I now knew for certain nothing would change. Having a duchess for a grandmother wouldn't make any difference to me. My life would eventually go back to normal, which was reassuring.

The sun was just starting to set as I walked back from the student bookstore. It was staying light longer now. A sure sign spring was on its way, which made me giddy.

"I have some interesting information." Preston fell into step next to me, the dimple in his cheek coming out with his playful grin.

"Oh? And what would that be?" I zipped the front of my black, fitted fleece jacket.

"I overheard Chloe talking to one of her friends about you."

"About me? Really?" I impatiently gestured for him to continue. "And?"

"Well, she was bragging about Jax. She's the one who told the tabloids about you and your grandmother." His jacket flapped behind him in the wind.

What the hell? "Jax? How did she know?" My face scrunched and I tucked closer to Preston as a large truck lumbered down the street, too close to the curb.

"Apparently she hired a private investigator to dig into your past."

I stopped. "Ew, creeptastic much?"

Preston chuckled. "Apparently, she's trying to find something to make Edmund lose interest in you. That's what Chloe told her friend anyway. It sounded like she and Jax aren't getting on anymore, though."

"I guess that solves the mystery." I looked up at the blue sky as a V of birds soared overhead. It was naive of me to think Jax would quietly fade into the background. I started walking again. "Why would she want the world to know I had connections to a duchess? How does that help her?"

Shrugging, he answered, "Maybe she knows Clarice is a horrible old witch who'd make your life miserable."

Maybe she hoped Clarice would denounce me to the world. I shook my head, my pace picking up an angry momentum.

"Are you okay?" Preston struggled to keep up.

"Who does she think she is?"

"Oh, she knows she's *Lady* Jacqueline. In her world, she can do no wrong. She'll stop at nothing to get what she wants. Her whole family is ruthless."

"What's your history with her?"

Preston shook his head and tucked a thumb in the strap of his backpack. "It's nothing huge. Basically, her mum and mine used to run in the same circles, they were friends. That is, until Jax's mum decided to cut my mum out. All her friends turned against my mum. It changed her." His brow wrinkled. "She was lonely and fell into a deep depression. Thanks to the whims of Jax's family, our family's had to live on the outskirts of society ever since."

"Even with Edmund as your best friend?"

He nodded. "We're not titled."

"Is your mom okay now?"

"She's okay; she's still ostracized and a little lonely, but she makes do. Therapy and medication have done wonders for her. She has a much quieter life now."

I grabbed his hand and gave it a squeeze. "I'm sorry she hurt your mom and your family."

"Yeah well, watch your back. She wants Edmund and you know she's not going to give him up without a fight."

Sighing, I released his hand. A breeze made the naked tree branches sway and dance. "Lovely. I'll add it to the pile of things I don't want to deal with right now."

Preston threw his arm around my shoulder. "Edmund's smart; he won't get caught in her trap. He knows better."

"Do you think he suspects she's responsible?"

"Doubt it." Preston held the door to our dorm open for me.

I blew a raspberry. "My head hurts. I'm gonna go lie down. Thanks for the scoop." I gave him a hug.

"See you later," he called as I hiked up the stairs.

Unlocking my door, I tossed my bag on the couch. The light on my desk phone was blinking again.

What now? A small part of me was afraid to push the button.

My head pounding, I grabbed my bottle of ibuprofen. Glass of water in hand, I chugged back two capsules and hit play.

"Hello, this message is for Miss Evangeline Gray. The Duchess of Westminster would like to schedule an appointment with you for tomorrow, Saturday, afternoon at one o'clock." The nasally man's voice filled my room again. "She requests a *private* audience with you. Please call back to confirm." He rattled off the same string of numbers he had left the other day.

What the hell is this about? I threw myself on my bed. *I can't do this again.* Draping my arm over my eyes, I took a deep breath. What could she possibly want from me? There's no way she wants to see me again any more than I want to see her.

So why am I even considering it?

I stood and slipped out of my clothes, tossing them into the hamper. I didn't feel like going down to dinner tonight. It was a good thing I'd grabbed some snacks earlier.

Tank top and boxers on, I groped in my bag for my phone. I needed to call Dad. The proper thing probably would've been to call Clarice back. But I didn't feel like it. The old dragon could wait.

Comfortable on my bed, I tapped the little green phone icon. Pressed tightly to my ear, it rang. I looked at the clock. It was the middle of the night back in Seattle.

A groggy Dad answered. "Evie? Everything all right? What's wrong?"

I rubbed a hand on my forehead. "Everything's fine, I just really needed to talk to you. Do you want me to call back later?" My throat tightened. I knew I sounded on the verge of tears. *Please say no.*

Through the phone I heard the rustle of his sheets. "What's going on? What happened? You sound upset."

"I met Clarice," I blurted. The phone line went silent. "Dad? You still there?"

He cleared his throat. "I'm still here. But did I hear you right? You met Clarice? Clarice your grandmother?"

I nodded. "Yeah, and there's something you really ought to know."

"Oh boy, what's that?" His half-asleep voice was tinged with worry.

How do you tell your father that the love of his life had lived a huge lie? That she'd kept things, big things, from him? It's better to just get it over with, right? *Like ripping off a Band-Aid.*

"She's—she's a duchess. A very wealthy one at that."

I could hear his smile when he spoke. "Okay, wait, are you trying to tell me your grandmother's a duchess? Very funny, Peaches."

"Dad, I'm not joking. She's Clarice Elliot, Duchess of Westminster. I saw a painting at her country estate of Mom as a little girl. When I met with her she knew about Mom. She still hates you. And she's not too fond of me either."

He was silent a moment before asking, "Why didn't your mother tell me?"

"I don't know." I closed my eyes and rubbed a hand over my face. "I've also been getting more letters from Mom. Not the birthday ones, but new ones, with tasks to accomplish. She led me straight to Clarice. Apparently there's a choice I have to make."

"How are you getting these letters?"

"Anton."

"You've met Anton?" Dad's voice cracked with surprise.

"Shortly after I got here."

"Why have you been keeping this from me?" The pain and confusion in his voice pulled tight in my chest.

I sighed. "I don't remember why I thought it was a good idea in the beginning. I think I wanted to see what Mom was guiding me to first. And . . . it's weird, me telling you something about Mom."

She should've told you. Not me.

"I'm not sure what to say." He blew out a long breath. "This explains why she never let me meet her family and insisted on eloping. I suppose in a weird way it makes sense."

My finger traced along the satin binding of my blanket as my pulse raced. "You okay?"

I didn't want this to change his memories of Mom. If he was mad at me for keeping her secret, I couldn't really blame him.

"Yeah, just surprised. So what's your grandmother *really* like?" He voice sounded distracted and far away.

"Awful. She was cruel, hateful, cold—nothing like Mom. I can see why Mom didn't want you to meet her. She was probably terrified that if you saw the kind of life she came from, you'd never have dared take her away from it."

"That impressive, huh?"

"Oh yeah." I sniffed and rolled my eyes.

Clearing his throat, he asked, "So what does this mean for you?"

"Absolutely nothing. Clarice wants nothing to do with me. She made that crystal clear. But at least I met her, right?"

"I suppose so. Have you told Edmund about this?"

"He was with me. He saw me blow up at her and thought it was pretty badass."

"I knew he was a good guy."

I chuckled. "Thanks, Dad, I really needed to hear your voice tonight. Sorry to call so late."

"Eves, you can call me anytime. You know that. And as for Clarice, she's gone from your life. Don't give her any more space in your mind."

"I kinda have to. She wants to see me again." I pulled the strap of my tank top up and leaned against the wall, gasping as my bare skin met the cool paint.

"After her behavior, why would you go back?"

My face screwed up. An uneasy guilty feeling ran rampant through my brain. *I shouldn't go back.* "Because I'm curious. Why does she want to see me again after what we said to each other?"

"I wouldn't call her back."

Reaching for my backpack, I pulled it onto my lap. "Maybe you're right. I'm still intrigued, though."

Dad sighed. "Well, let me know what you end up doing. But be warned, if she hurts you, I'm going to come over there and she'll have to deal with me. After what I suspect she did to your mom, I'm tempted to anyway."

"Thanks, Dad." My heart felt lightened, unburdened by the sharing of my secrets.

Chapter Twenty-One

Choices

Outside the gate to Clarice's townhouse, I looked up at the overcast sky and took a deep breath. Even the heavens matched my mood today.

What the hell am I doing here?

When I told Edmund this morning about going to see Clarice, he offered to join me. He was less than thrilled when I insisted on going alone. He'd called me mental. *He's probably right.*

Refusing to be at her mercy, I took the train in. On the ride there I prepped myself to walk out if she laid into me again like I suspected she would.

Straightening my spine, I walked up the steps to her front door and rang the bell. Jeeves promptly answered.

"Miss Gray." He nodded. "Please come in. I'll let the duchess know you're here."

I sat on the bench, pumping myself up for another long wait then an ensuing battle. To my surprise Jeeves returned right away.

"The duchess will see you now. Please, follow me."

Instead of guiding me toward her office again, we climbed the flight of stairs just beyond the foyer. After a brief knock on an oversized door, he opened it.

"Your Grace, Miss Gray to see you."

"Send her in," Clarice called. "Thank you, Denby."

Denby smiled and allowed me to pass through the arched doorway. I surveyed the room. My eyes widened when I realized we were in a bedroom. It was clean and feminine, decorated in creams and violet.

This wasn't where I'd imagined our epic battle taking place. *Where are we?*

"This was your mother's bedroom. Everything is just as she left it," Clarice answered, as though she'd read my mind.

My mom's room?

I walked around, glancing nervously at Clarice, who reclined on a pale lavender chaise lounge. She'd caught me completely off guard. I hated how vulnerable that made me feel.

Without a word, I went to the window. Beside it sat a vanity, covered with half-used perfume bottles and silver-framed photos. I bent and looked closer. Most of the pictures were of Dad. There was a fantastic one of both of them standing in front of the Victoria and Albert Museum, smiling, arms around each other.

She's been there. I smiled as tears welled up in my eyes. She was so beautiful and they looked so happy. *This is incredible.*

I spotted a handwritten letter and picture lying on the desktop. I recognized Mom's handwriting instantly. The photo was of her and Dad on their wedding day. Mom wore a short, white, lacy summer dress, and Dad, khakis with a navy blue blazer. He had a pink peony in his lapel, matching Mom's small bouquet of peonies. His arm was around her, and he kissed her cheek. *Young and in love, just how it should be.*

I cleared my throat, not wanting to get swept up in emotions. Backing away from the photos, I brushed the wetness from my eyes, and rounded on Clarice. "Why did you ask me here?"

Clarice sighed and stiffly said, "I wanted to apologize for my behavior at our last meeting. I fear you did not catch me at me best."

When her eyes flashed to mine I saw the same anger and irritation that'd been there the first time we met. I didn't believe for a second she wanted me to come just so she could apologize. That was too big a change of heart. Especially when I'd yet to see any evidence of her actually having a heart.

"Is that so?" I met her eyes challengingly.

"Indeed," she spoke, her lips tight.

"Right." I chuckled. "Why am I really here? We both know you aren't sorry."

Clarice raised her chin and sized me up. She looked paler than she had at our last meeting.

Here it comes. She's going to unleash the beast. I nearly giggled at the thought of some foul creature bursting from this frail old woman's body. This was ridiculous. At least I wasn't as terrified as I was last time.

"Fine, I'll get straight to the point. I want to strike a deal with you." She raised a withered hand to her hair, smoothing and patting the silver bun.

Okay, wasn't expecting that. "What exactly do you have in mind?"

Clarice took a deep breath and gazed out the large window the chaise was positioned in front of. "I went to my doctor earlier this week. I've been battling breast cancer for the past year and a half." She paused and met my surprised gaze.

Just like Mom.

"Apparently, I haven't been as responsive to treatments as the doctors would have liked. They're suggesting I get my affairs in order, quickly." She looked away from me. The words seemed to have left a bitter taste in her mouth.

I scoffed. *I know what this is about.* "You don't have to worry, Clarice. You made yourself perfectly clear. I don't expect or want anything from you. I know you disowned my mother and I have absolutely no expectations of you or your estate." I waved my hand around the grand room. Turning on my heel, I went to the door.

"You are so like your mother, far too headstrong and stubborn. You don't know what I was about to say. Sit down and listen to me, you impertinent girl," she chastised me curtly.

I slowly turned, meeting her icy blue eyes. "What then? What do you want from me?"

"I want to add you to my will."

"What?"

Clarice impatiently huffed, "I have every intention of adding you to my will."

"Why? You disowned my mother. You *hate* my father, and you've proven you don't like me either. Why would you want to claim me?" What the hell is she trying to pull?

"You're right, I don't like your father. He took my only daughter away from me. But, I *never* disowned Lilliana." She looked me straight in the eye, her jaw tightening. "I have little choice in the matter of whether I live or die. So, despite being part of your father, I have accepted that you are also my heir."

"Why didn't you come to her funeral?" The words burst from my lips. This one question had bothered me my entire life.

She sniffed and looked away. "I doubt your father would've allowed me entrance."

My temper prickled as I spoke softly to keep myself from yelling. "He would have welcomed you. My father is an amazing man, kind and loving. He's not the monster you've built in your imagination. How can you judge him when you've never met?"

She adjusted the blanket on her lap.

"You could've called—"

Clarice's fiery eyes snapped to mine. "I told your mother, should she marry Henry, I would never see her again or speak to her. I was true to my word."

"And you're proud of that?" I made no attempt to hide my disgust.

She glared. "Perhaps we might return to the subject at hand. My will, I'd like to add you to it."

"What exactly would that entail? I don't want anything you have. So, what's the point?"

"The point is, I'd like you to inherit everything. Including my title."

I paused, feeling dumbstruck and struggling to keep my face blank. "Are you telling me you want me to be the next Duchess of Westminster?"

"Yes. It is my family's title and should have passed to Lilliana. Which makes you next in line. I feel, under my tutelage, you should be able to pull off the role, at least marginally."

Gee, thanks, you're too kind. "And what if I don't want to do this? Surely there must be someone else you could saddle with this responsibility."

This is the choice Mom was talking about. I closed my eyes, letting that sink in. She knew.

"Aside from you?" She paused. "No, the other alternative is simply unacceptable." She turned back toward the window.

"But there *is* an alternative, right?" I pushed.

"No."

"Who's the 'simply unacceptable' alternative then?" I unsuccessfully mimicked her voice, which earned me an unamused glower.

"There is a distant family member lined up to inherit should no direct heir be available. But here *you* are, an heir."

"Who is this distant relative?" I walked to the bench at the bottom of the bed and debated sitting down.

"His name is Julian Musgrove. He's a distant cousin, very distant. He's one of the last remaining members of our family line. Beside you and me, that is. Should you reject the title, he'd become the Duke of Westminster."

"So, there's not a single soul in all that distance between the two of you who could step up?"

"Trust me, everyone else in our line has passed away."

"This Julian fellow, what's wrong with him?"

"Wrong?" She snapped and met my eyes. "Julian is a drunkard who's squandered away his entire family fortune. He's been foaming at the mouth to get at my money for years. Should he succeed, I have no doubt it would be obliterated within the year. On top of that he's a cheat, a womanizer, and completely dissolute."

"What a catch." I watched her chest heave with each breath.

"I'd much rather see my title pass to my worst enemy than that man." She scowled, making her look like a gargoyle.

"I'm the lesser of two evils then, am I?" Did she know how to make a girl feel special or what?

Clarice sighed and glanced heavenward. "If you want to look at it that way, then yes. You are the lesser of two evils."

I backed my way to the door. "Flattered as I am, I don't see any reason why I should do this for you."

"No? Then do it for Edmund."

My eyebrows shot up. "Excuse me?"

"He's clearly in love with you. As a commoner you'll never fully be accepted. You might manage to marry him, but you'll be lonely. Our society would be polite to you around Edmund, but you'd never be fully accepted. You'd be the subject of gossip. It would take its toll on your relationship. Do it so Edmund doesn't have to deal with the scandal that being with you would create."

What a hateful woman. Is that how she treated outsiders who dared enter her social sphere?

Yes, I could see her point. I knew Edmund's world was vastly different from mine. Still her words had the opposite effect she was hoping for. Sick to my stomach, I was determined to turn her down and leave.

"Your Grace, I appreciate the offer, but no thank you. Quite frankly, I don't want, nor do I need, the acceptance of people whose primary concern is whether my blood is blue enough or if I'm titled. If Edmund loves me, as you say he does," I began thinking, *because he sure hasn't said anything to me,* "he'll love me regardless of what his friends say. Otherwise, he's not worthy of my time." My hand was on the doorknob when she chuckled.

"Despite her not raising you for long, you are your mother's daughter. You're *just like* Lilliana. She couldn't be forced or coerced into anything and you appear to be the same." Clarice's face softened and she actually smiled.

Without a thought, I went to the bed and sat. *I'm really like my mother?* Warm fuzzies sprang up all over my body.

Clarice looked up into my face and spoke softly. "Please, as the dying wish of someone you owe absolutely nothing to, I ask you to do this. It'll give us the chance to get better acquainted during the time I have left."

She was playing the sympathy card. I tucked my hands under my thighs, not wanting to fidget in front of her.

What would Mom want me to do? She'd always hoped Clarice would come to her senses. It was Mom who guided me here after all. The answer was obvious.

"I'll agree to this on one condition." I waited for her to nod before I proceeded. "If you're mean, or say anything negative or hateful about my parents, I'm done. I walk away. My choice is made. Do you understand?"

She took a moment before answering. "Understood and agreed."

We sat in brief silence before Clarice picked up a little silver bell and jangled it.

Denby appeared in the doorway and bowed unsteadily. "Your Grace?"

"Denby, please assist me to my rooms. I wish to lie down. Miss Gray is going to see if there's anything she wants from her mother's belongings."

My eyes bulged. *Pick anything of my mother's? How would I ever carry it all?*

"Yes, ma'am." The doddering butler stepped behind the chaise and produced a wheelchair. Locking the wheels, he turned and assisted her into it.

Clarice covered her cream pantsuit with a white chenille blanket and turned to me. "Denby will return to check on you in a little while. Let him know if you need anything."

"I will, thank you." I watched Denby slowly roll her out the door.

There was a very high probability this would end in a disaster of epic proportions. But maybe, just maybe, it'd be a good thing.

As I looked around I tried to envision Mom here. I could picture her painting her toenails on the chaise, doing homework at the little desk in the windowed alcove, or draped across the bed reading with her long red hair spilling behind her.

I smiled and went over to her bookshelf. My eyes tumbled over the titles on the spines, stopping when I came to a set of the Bronte sisters' books. *You guys are coming with me.* I gingerly pulled them from the shelf and set them on the bench at the end of the bed.

By the time Denby returned to check on me I'd rounded up a few pictures of my mother and several with my father, a well-worn Oxford sweatshirt, a wire replica of the Eiffel Tower, and a delicate golden chain with a matching disk monogrammed with an L.

"Do you need anything, Miss?"

"Yes, do you have something I can carry these in?"

"Certainly." He disappeared for only a moment and returned with a cloth grocery tote. "Will this do?"

"That's perfect. Thank you, Denby." I loaded up my treasures, and Jeeves and I walked to the front door.

"The duchess will be in touch with you. She said you should expect to meet with her several times a week for the foreseeable future."

My mouth popped open. Several times a week? *What does she have planned?* "Okay."

I bid Jeeves farewell, turning down his offer of a car, and made my way to the Underground. After a short ride I hopped onto the train at Paddington Station, where I tried to relax. I laughed out loud at the idea of having duchess lessons. It was absurd. *Me? A duchess?*

The woman sitting across from me eyed me warily, then abandoned her blue seat and moved to the back of the train. *At least she doesn't recognize me.* I giggled.

By the time I'd made it back to campus it was past dinnertime. I pulled my phone from my pocket, realizing I'd forgotten to un-silence it. I went through the texts I'd missed. Most were from Edmund.

Edmund: You okay?

Edmund: Did she eat you alive?

Edmund: Evie, text me.

Edmund: I'm praying you didn't kill her.

Edmund: Don't panic, I have connections, we can make it look like an accident ;)

I chuckled and quickly texted him back.

Me: Sorry, we both made it out alive. Just got back on campus. Meet me at my room?

Edmund: See you in five.

I hurried and grabbed some fresh fruit, a microwave pasta, and a pint of Ben and Jerry's Chubby Hubby. Bags in hand, I went to my dorm room. When I saw Edmund leaning against my door, waiting, I smiled.

He immediately straightened and walked toward me, reaching for my bags. "How did it go?"

I fished my key out of my pocket. "Totally not what I'd expected."

"Tell me it wasn't worse than last time."

"No, definitely not worse." I slid the key in the lock.

"What a relief. I was nervous with no word from you all day."

"Sorry about that." I cringed.

Inside my room Edmund set the bags down. "Do you want to talk about it?"

"Well, I get to have duchess lessons." I watched the confusion cross his face.

"What?"

"Duchess lessons."

"I thought that's what you said. How did you get from our disastrous meeting with her to having duchess lessons?"

"How long do you have?"

"For you? All night." He grinned and wrapped his arms around me, pulling me tight.

Chapter Twenty-Two

Limbo

I sat in Clarice's office, waiting for her to put down her pen and acknowledge me. Studying my nails, I smiled thinking back to my last phone call with Abby. As excited as she was for me and my potential future as a duchess, she was mainly interested in hearing about Edmund.

"Have you told him yet?" Abby had asked.

"About Clarice? Of course."

She laughed. "No, that you're in love with him."

"What makes you think I'm in love with him?" I mean, I knew I was, but I hadn't told anyone.

"Oh please, your voice alone whenever you talk about him just oozes love—and lust," she added with a giggle. "If you weren't in love with him, you would've told your grandmother to blow it out her old wazoo."

I sighed. "No, I haven't told him. I don't think he's ready to hear it. I don't want to rush this."

"I think he'd be thrilled. You should tell him." She yawned.

Yeah, easier said than done.

"Evangeline?" Clarice cleared her throat. "Were you listening?"

My eyes snapped to hers, feeling guilty that I'd been caught daydreaming. "I'm sorry, what were you saying?"

Clarice sat up at her desk and looked down at me disapprovingly. "Your holiday starts next week, correct?"

"Yes, ma'am." I straightened myself in the chair across from her, feeling small.

At the start of duchess lessons, I hadn't a clue what an upper-class woman ought to know. But, one thing I did know, Clarice hated the term *duchess lessons*—so I used it as often as I could.

"Plan on spending your holiday here. You aren't learning these skills as quickly as I'd hoped you would."

"Are you saying you want me here for my entire break?" I asked as my eyebrows shot up to my hairline.

"Was I unclear?"

Whatever, Hagatha.

I didn't answer her. There was no way I could handle a week and a half of nothing but Clarice. Weekends were tough enough. Staying in Mom's room was the only thing that made it bearable. Being surrounded by her things was next to heaven.

"I believe it's vital that you spend a significant amount of your holiday here. Your etiquette and household maintenance skills are shabby, at best."

I rolled my eyes. The past week she'd hounded me on proper etiquette and how to best remove stains, along with other household remedies. It was like Emily Post on crack meets Martha Stewart on acid. I couldn't sit through more of that. Besides, I seriously doubted Clarice had ever removed a red wine stain herself.

"Plus, there are several areas we haven't even begun to touch upon," she continued, tapping a silver pen against the palm of her hand.

"Really? Like what?"

"Music appreciation, horseback riding, flower and tree identification." She ticked off the items on her fingers with her pen as she ran down her mental list. "The art of bouquet making, wine differentiation, architecture admiration, table etiquette, and how to properly address your aristocratic peers. Oh, and I'm afraid your conversational skills leave much to be desired."

"Flower and tree appreciation? Seriously? Is this really necessary? Seems silly if you ask me." I pretended to scratch my cheek to cover my amusement.

"I *wasn't* asking you. You may keep your opinions on the subject to yourself. My only concern is when you'll be here to proceed with your lessons. Which brings us back to your holiday." As she shifted in her chair, I heard the worn leather creak underneath her.

I hated when she spoke to me like a ten-year-old. "I'll try to be here for duchess lessons, but I have plans I'll need to work around." Okay, that was a total lie. Between Clarice's lessons, classes, and studying, I hadn't seen enough of the gang to know if there were any plans.

"These lessons should be your top priority. Do sit up straight, child. Don't slouch. How many times must I remind you?" She slapped a hand against her desk and sighed in frustration.

Ah, yes. Posture, carriage, and personal dress. That'd been a fun lesson. I sat up straight and blew out a deep breath. My shoulders achy and stiff, I was ready to slip into my grubbies and veg.

"I should head back to campus. I have early classes tomorrow." I stood and twisted from side to side, hoping she wouldn't notice.

"Until Wednesday then." Clarice ripped into an envelope sitting in front of her.

I knew my cue. Gathering my bag, I left.

Denby met me in the foyer. He had a car waiting outside.

"Thanks, Jeeves," I said with a wink.

"Of course, Miss." He smiled warmly and opened the door.

I may not have cracked Clarice's icy exterior, but Denby was warming to me. Hurrying down the darkened steps to the idling Town Car, I couldn't wait to leave. It was a long drive back to school; lucky for me, I slept most of the way.

At breakfast I didn't bother trying to catch up on homework. This morning was reserved for my friends. I sat at our table, my head resting on my palm, staring at my toast and jam. I popped a grape in my mouth and thought of Edmund.

God, I miss him.

Yes, technically I'd been around, but with duchess lessons taking over it felt like I was only lurking on the edges. Any time with Edmund was while I studied, wrote a paper, or basically did anything that sucked my full attention away from him.

I thought back to last Thursday night and smiled. I'd been apologizing . . . again. Edmund had grabbed my hands and said, "Evie, I don't mind, really. I know you're crazy busy with your studies, the duchess lessons, and dealing with Clarice. I'd much rather just sit by your side while you study than be out with anyone else."

I steamed up, remembering what happened next. Lord, did that boy know how to kiss. He stirred feelings inside me that I didn't even have a name for.

"Morning, Evie." Preston sat down across from me. "How's it going?"

"All right. I'm so ready for break."

"I bet you are," Suzy chimed as she walked up and placed her tray beside mine. "You've been running yourself ragged. When will you be done getting duchessified?"

"Your guess is as good as mine. Feels like it'll never end though. Apparently, I'm not a quick enough learner for her."

Suzy scrunched her face, her blond ponytail swishing as she shook her head. "So, do you get any free time over break or is Clarice going to monopolize it all?"

"I told her I was still sorting out my plans. What are you all doing?"

"My family's headed to Spain," Suzy answered and bit into her apple.

I looked over and spotted Caroline and Marissa grab their breakfasts, then head our way. "What about you, Preston?"

"My parents are taking a short trip to Scotland. Mum has a sister up there and Dad's got some business in the area. So I get to tag along," he replied.

"Sounds like fun." Caroline patted his shoulder as she sat, her sapphire shirt highlighting her flawless skin.

Preston smiled. "We go there nearly every break and it's the same boring people every time. I tried to get out of it, but Mum thinks it'd be rude if I skipped it. It means a week and a half of dealing with my cousin, the daft git."

"Too bad we can't go with Edmund," Suzy cheekily said.

"No kidding, I'd love to be on a yacht in the middle of the Mediterranean." Preston poured cream into his tea.

Mediterranean? What? "When's he leaving?" I tried to act like I knew he was going and this wasn't a surprise.

"Friday, right after classes." Preston lifted his mug to taste test.

"Lucky guy." *Why hadn't he mentioned this before?* Then again, between studying and making out, we hadn't had much time for an in-depth conversation.

"Speaking of the lucky guy, here he is." Caroline waved. "Hey, Prince Charming. We're just talking about you jetting off to the Mediterranean for spring break. We're all insanely jealous."

Edmund slid onto the bench next to me, his arm resting against mine.

"Meh, I'm not looking forward to it. I wish you were all coming. Unfortunately, it's with a group of my parents' friends. So I have no say in who comes."

"Poor you." Preston laughed. "I'll trade places."

"If I could get out of it, I seriously would." Edmund's eyes met mine. I could tell he was speaking truthfully.

I rested my hand on his shoulder, a playful grin on my face. "A week on a yacht in the middle of the Mediterranean is going to be tough. My thoughts are with you."

Edmund stole a quick peck, then turned and took a bite of cereal. "So, are you caught up with your homework?"

"Not quite. I still have a couple papers to write and, of course, exams. I'm so not ready."

"Tell Clarice you need a break. Surely she can't want your education to suffer." Edmund pushed up the sleeves of his Oxford sweatshirt.

"I don't know about that. My *actual* education doesn't seem to matter to her. Training me to be a duchess feels like the only thing she cares about. Plus, she didn't look too good last weekend."

"Not many options then, huh?" Preston said.

I sighed and shook my head. "Doesn't seem to be."

"I've got to get moving," Marissa announced. "I'm meeting with a professor before class. I'll see you guys tonight."

"Bye, babe." Caroline turned her face up for a quick kiss before Marissa darted out the door. Ever since Halloween they'd been inseparable. I loved that they were together.

"So do you two have plans?" I asked Caroline.

"We do. Her family has a little cottage on the coast we're going to use. I can't wait."

"Wow, a holiday away together. That's pretty serious." Suzy's eyebrows shot up.

"Yeah, it is." Caroline grinned as she bit her lower lip. She looked over the moon.

I envied them. It was clear what they were to each other. We all knew.

If only it was that simple for Edmund and me. He'd never once called me his girlfriend, yet I knew I was way more than just a friend.

So what did that make us? Friends with minimal benefits?

Dwelling on this and knowing I'd be alone over break curdled my mood. This meant I'd be stuck with Haggy Hagatha Clarice.

I couldn't sit there any longer. Standing to dump my tray, I said, "I'm gonna run. I'll catch you guys later."

"You want me to walk you?" Edmund asked.

"No, stay and finish your breakfast. I'll see you at lunch."

Once outside, I took a deep breath, hoping it would help clear my head. It didn't. My life felt like it was spinning faster and faster out of my control.

Which, for a control freak, is utterly terrifying.

Chapter Twenty-Three

A Glimpse

The first day of spring break I caught the train and headed into London. Clarice had been pleased when I told her I'd spend my break with her.

Standing on the sidewalk outside her townhouse, I sighed. I so didn't want to do this. Slowly, I climbed the steps and rang the bell.

I'd rather be on a yacht with Edmund.

Denby opened the door.

"Hey, Jeeves." I plastered on a smile I wasn't feeling.

"Miss Gray." He opened the door and ushered me in. "Her Grace is in the music room."

"Thanks, I know the way." I started down the hallway.

Last time, she'd made me walk around the music room with heavy books on my head. I'd spent most of the time laughing, which made the books fall off, which in turn annoyed Clarice. I'd felt like I was in a bad remake of *The Princess Diaries*. The Duchess Diaries.

"That is highly against protocol, Miss. Her Grace would be very disappointed in me if I didn't set you straight."

I shook my head. "Then by all means, Jeeves, lead the way."

Denby knocked on the door and announced me.

"Come in." Her low voice echoed through the large room.

I noticed the light-colored furniture had been shoved away from the epicenter of the room. Off to the side sat a grand piano. I glanced through the sheer curtains to the street below, nervous. *What does this wily old woman have up her sleeve now?*

I glanced to where Clarice sat in a wingback chair, beside a large stereo. She looked thinner. "So, I'm not balancing books on my head again today?"

"Well, that was highly unproductive, so I thought it best to move on." She looked down her thin nose at me. "Some creatures apparently can't learn new tricks."

"Evidently not." *Whatever, you stuffy, old, ungrateful cow.*

I thought about leaving, but I knew the dorms would be deserted, which freaked me out. I vividly remembered the ghost tour Preston took me on.

"Today I thought we'd work on music appreciation."

"Fabulous." I took a seat near her.

Clarice pressed a button and classical music filled the air. "Surely you know this composer."

I did. "It's Vivaldi, the Spring movement from his *Four Seasons*."

"Correct." She looked impressed.

We spent the day talking about nineteenth-century composers Liszt, Wagner, Berlioz, and Chopin, just to name a few.

It was actually kind of fun. I found something I didn't suck at.

All those years of piano lessons helped. Well, that and art history. My lectures presented the whole picture of any given time period. Composers and their music were always an element.

"All right, we'll work on other eras later. What a relief, we seem to have finally found a strength of yours." She picked up her little silver bell and gave it a jingle.

"Your Grace?" Denby entered the room.

"Denby, do you waltz?"

"Waltz?" He looked confused.

"Yes, you know, the dance. Waltzing."

Jeeves straightened his black tailcoat. "I do, ma'am."

I could see where this was going and I didn't like it.

"Good. Come, take Evangeline in your arms. You're going to teach her the waltz." Her brittle fingers selected a song.

"Maybe I already know how." I didn't like her assuming.

"Do you?" She turned, giving me a look that suggested she didn't think I could.

Pausing, I didn't want to answer. I had a general understanding, but no actual training. "No."

"Precisely what I thought. Denby?"

I sighed and Denby cleared his throat as he walked toward me. I didn't know about him, but I was as uncomfortable as hell. His right hand slipped around my waist and with his left he held onto my hand.

"All right, Miss, it's a simple box step. Lead with your right foot." He tapped my foot with his shiny black toe. "One, two, three. One, two, three." He swept me around the room in an effortless dance.

Well, I'm sure for some people it was easy. I looked more like a wounded gazelle trying to escape a hungry lion. It wasn't pretty. I crunched Denby's toes so many times it was obscene.

"I'm so sorry," I said, watching him wince.

"It's fine, Miss."

"Evangeline, straighten your back. Lift your head. Stop clomping around." She continued to call out criticisms.

If I wasn't so busy looking like an idiot, I'd be over there telling her to pipe down. My brain wandered from the dance to Edmund. What's he doing right now? Probably working on his tan and relaxing on the deck of their yacht.

God, I miss him. I missed them all.

"Stop peering at your toes. They're not doing it right, anyway." Clarice angrily sighed from the sidelines.

I glanced at Denby. He was biting his lip, his eyes shining with mirth. I smiled at him.

"You're doing just fine, Miss," he softly told me.

"Thanks, Jeeves," I whispered back.

We practiced through a few more songs, and by the end, Clarice was yelling less. That might be because she was giving up, but I hoped it was because I was getting better.

Clarice abruptly shut off the music with a shaky hand. "That's enough for today. Thank you, Denby, you may resume your duties."

Denby bowed and left us.

"Am I done here?" I asked tiredly.

"Until tomorrow." As if an afterthought, she added, "You may eat in the dining room tonight if you like, but it isn't necessary. I'll be taking dinner in my room. You're excused."

Lying on the four-poster bed in Mom's old bedroom, I stared at the high ceiling. As cool as it was to be surrounded by her things, this place had a cold loneliness that bothered me. It didn't feel like a home. I missed my friends.

I picked up my phone and noticed I had new texts. Sliding my thumb across the screen, I pulled up the first one.

Suzy: Wish you were here. Spain is incredible!

Me: Wish I was there too.

I went to the next.

Dad: How are you doing with Clarice? Do I need to get on a plane?

Me: We're working together the best we can. Although, I'd like to tell her where to shove her title more often than not. Love you.

I smiled when I saw who the last one was from.

Edmund: I miss you.

Me: I miss you too.

There was a knock on my door. Denby poked his gray head around the corner. "I brought you a dinner tray, Miss."

I made room on the lavender bedspread. "Thank you, Denby."

"Good night, Miss."

"Night. Oh, and Jeeves?"

"Yes, Miss?"

"Thanks for the dance lesson earlier."

"It was my pleasure, Miss." He nodded with a smile as the door clicked shut behind him.

Mom's journals and books were spread around me. A Moleskine full of doodles, sketches, and cool drawings was opened in front of me. She was an incredible artist. Considering her job as an art conservationist, I guess it made sense.

Tucked inside, I discovered a gorgeous pencil drawing of Dad. She'd caught him perfectly, from the sparkle in his eye to the dimple in his left cheek. *This is coming back to campus with me.*

Flipping through the pages, I stopped and traced a petal of a flower she'd drawn. As I followed the line of ink, I wondered who else had seen these. Was this something she only shared with me? *I hope so.* The idea made me feel special.

Her loopy script filled the pages in between the doodles. My heart fluttered as I read the passages, searching for anything that would tell me more about her. A page scattered with red hearts caught my attention. "I met someone amazing today. He has the most adorable dimple in his cheek. His name's Henry."

Dad. I leaned forward, absorbed in her words.

"He's so friendly and his accent is charming. After class he walked me back to St. John's and asked if I wanted to study together. I'm looking forward to getting to know him."

I laughed. "You're gonna do more than get to know him." I couldn't wipe the grin from my face. These journals were a window to her life, her voice. I wanted to read them all right now, tonight. But I stopped myself.

Once they're gone, that's it, there's nothing more.

Like the letters, they had to end sometime, but at least with these, I could slowly work my way through them. Get to know her, see her life from her point of view. *Did she ever imagine her daughter would read these?*

Closing the journal, I set it with the stack of others next to me. A sigh of contentment left my lungs. Here, in her room, it felt like she was sitting beside me.

Shifting on the bed, I pulled the tray Denby had left closer. I lifted the silver lid with a soft chink of metal against metal. A delicious aroma of carrots, chicken, and roasted potatoes wafted to my nose.

As I took a bite, another message from Edmund pinged through. Grinning, I read it.

Edmund: I'm lying here in my room, thinking about you and how badly I need to kiss you.

I pressed a hand to my hot cheek. Only five more days and we'd both be back on campus. That is if I survived Clarice.

He's thinking about kissing me. A jolt of pleasure ripped through me. *I want to do so much more than kiss.*

Dear God, what happened in here?

I stepped into what had been Clarice's kitchen. Big white buckets of flowers lined the counters and floors. The large granite island in the center supported partially arranged vases.

"Morning, Miss Evie." The cook smiled as she walked through with a cup of tea. She sat on the opposite side of the island from the two housemaids, who were busy tucking greenery and flowers into vases.

"Good morning, Letty." I took a seat beside the elderly woman and yawned. Clarice's personal maid woke me at the butt crack of dawn, informing me that Her Ladyship wanted to see me in the kitchen in twenty minutes. It was a rush, but I made it. In fact, I even beat her. "Mmm, could I get a cup of that tea?"

"There's a pot of it behind the ranunculus," Letty said between sips as she pointed to the counter. "Help yourself, sweetie."

I got up and went to the counter she indicated. *Hmm, ranunculus?* "Letty, which ones are ranunculus?"

"The little colorful ones that look like tiny cabbages."

I went to a bucket filled with light pink, pale yellow, white, and peach flowers. They did look like lovely little cabbages. They were small and round, with tightly compact petals that curled on top of each other.

Sliding the bucket aside, I grasped the pot and poured a mug full of the steaming liquid. It smelled like English Breakfast.

"All right," Clarice said as Denby wheeled her into the kitchen. She eyed the young maids working on the arrangements. "Lucy, Anna, stop right there. Evangeline will be doing the house's flowers this week."

"I'm what now?" I asked, leaning against the counter, mug midway to my lips.

"Studying flower identification and floral arranging. Two birds with one stone, I think. Not only will you be able to identify these flowers and foliage, you'll be capable of preparing a lovely bouquet as well."

I took a swig and closed my eyes, steeling myself. I could think of a million things I'd rather be doing. "Okay, let's get started."

Reaching in my pocket, I pulled out a hair-tie, twirled my long curls into a ponytail and left the end tucked under, creating a bun.

Clarice smiled kindly. "Can you identify any of the flowers?"

"Um, roses." With a smile, I glanced conspiratorially at Letty. "And ranunculus."

Letty grinned back at me.

"Well, at least it's a start. Let's begin with the greenery."

The maids obliged by holding out whichever plant Clarice called out. I was only allowed to move onto the flowers once I'd passed the leaf quiz.

"Now, you know, of course, there are many more types of greenery. These are just a few." Clarice motioned for Lucy and Anna to put the greens away.

I nodded. Why on earth do I need to know this to be a duchess? What does a duchess even do? *That's what I need to learn.*

Clarice ran through the flowers. They were easier to remember. "And this . . ." She rolled her chair closer to a bucket on the floor I hadn't realized was there. Pulling a long stem out, she smelled it. "This is a peony." She trailed a finger over the light pink petals. "It was your mother's favorite. We always have them in the house."

Clarice's face took on a faraway look. *She misses her.* I looked away. The threat of tears burned my eyes.

Shaking her head and clearing her throat, Clarice gestured for me to begin. "Let's see what you can do."

I chuckled internally then rubbed my hands together. *This is gonna be lovely.*

"So, did my mom know how to do all this stuff?"

"Of course; she started learning as a young child. She was excellent. She'd have made an amazing duchess."

I grabbed a stem of a flower that looked like a giant snowball. Clarice had called it viburnum. I plunked it into a silver vase and grabbed a few more. No clue what I was doing, I picked flowers and greenery willy-nilly and shoved them in.

Huh, who knew you could make flowers ugly?

"Did she want the title?"

Clarice quietly watched me create my monstrosity. I slid in one last peony and stood back. Bear grass hung haphazardly around the bottom and one side was decidedly heavier with viburnum. It was a mess.

"Wow, I'm horrible at this." I giggled.

"Glad you said it and not me." Letty chuckled and took her mug to the sink. When she turned around she added, "Oh my, its even prettier from this angle." She snickered as she wiped her plump hands on her apron.

"Thanks, Letty."

"Pull it apart; let's start this over." Clarice motioned for Denby to wheel her closer to the table. "This time, greenery first, then the larger flowers on the bottom, save the smaller flowers for the top, and finish off with the filler flowers." She grabbed a fern rod and handed it to me. "Lily did want the title. She was set to marry the son of a marquis. Together they would have been very powerful."

"And she wanted that?" That didn't sound like Mom. I slowly remade the arrangement, following my new instructions.

"She tried to convince me to let her have the title and marry whom she wanted. I was stubborn and stood my ground. I had such a promising future planned for her."

Holding a peony in my hand, I looked up at Clarice. "What about love?"

Rolling her eyes, she answered, "Our set doesn't marry for love. Love is for the young and idealistic. You spend enough time with someone and love eventually comes."

I shook my head and tucked in the peony. "You're wrong. Love is something special. Something that if you're lucky enough to find, you don't throw away."

Clarice sighed and fingered a thread on her soft blue knit throw. "I'll not apologize for what I did." She paused, pulling the thread taut until it snapped off in her fingers. "But I will concede I may have been too stubborn. I doubt I would have approved of your father, but I could have met him, at least given her choice a chance."

For something that wasn't an apology, it sure sounded like one. The corners of my lips turned upward. *If only you were here, Mom.*

By the time I finished my second arrangement I'd made a pretty remarkable recovery. I took a step back and admired my handiwork. It wasn't perfect, but it was at least prettier.

"Very nice," Clarice said, nodding in approval. "Lucy, please take this to my room."

I smiled. Praise from her was rare. In my pocket, my phone vibrated against my thigh. Pulling it out, I saw a new text from Edmund.

"Please put your mobile away." Clarice eyed me, then with a swift clap of her hands, she motioned for Denby to see to her chair. "Now, a car is waiting outside to take you to the stables. Grab your jacket."

"Stables?"

"Yes, a proper young lady must know how to ride." She took an unsteady breath.

Horses and I weren't friends. I'd tried to ride once as a child and been terrified ever since. *There's no way I'm getting on a horse.* "Can we do this later? I'm not feeling well."

"No. Your lesson is in an hour. Go." She waved me away as Denby wheeled her from the room.

I sighed and got my coat. Taking a moment, I pulled out my phone and read my texts.

Edmund: How's your break going? Clarice playing nice?

In the car I shrugged out of my raincoat and settled in to return Edmund's message.

Me: No, she's torturing me. Right now I'm on my way to learn how to ride a horse.

Edmund: Fun, I love riding.

Me: No, not fun. I don't like horses.

Edmund: How can you not like horses?

Me: I was traumatized as a small child. A birthday party gone horribly wrong.

Edmund: lol, well maybe you'll have a better experience today. I'd love to take you out riding sometime.

Okay, *that* I'd get on a horse for.

Chapter Twenty-Four

Friends

When I got back to campus, I spied Caroline outside sunbathing. Yes, technically spring had arrived and the sun was shining, but it was still chilly.

After running my bags to my room, I hurried to join her.

Blanket spread out in the middle of the quad, Caroline sprawled on her stomach and read a magazine. Suzy had joined her since I last walked by.

"Hey girls," I called as I approached the short-shorts and T-shirt clad Caroline.

"Evie." Suzy stood, sensibly dressed in jeans and a sweater, to give me a hug. "How was break?"

"Probably about as fun as you imagine it was." I laughed and leaned to give Caroline a hug too. "Caroline, you're going to make yourself sick. It's too cold to be dressed like that."

"Evie, this is England. When we see the sun we take advantage of it. If we didn't, we'd never get tanned or any vitamin D." Caroline shot me a smug smile.

"Seattle weather is pretty much the same, and guess what? We take a vitamin and we have these awesome places called tanning salons, or even better, spray tans. You can avoid skin cancer later in life."

"You're cute, Evie." Caroline patted my knee.

I rolled my eyes and laughed. "Yeah, I know I am. You'll be even cuter when your nose looks like Rudolph's from the cold you're going to catch."

Suzy chuckled in agreement with me.

Caroline made a face and stuck her tongue out at us, casually flipping the pages of her magazine. "So, Suze, who's the hot guy I saw you snogging last night?"

Suzy's head snapped up. Once she closed her mouth and stopped looking like Edvard Munch's *The Scream*, she started sputtering excuses. "I-I don't know what you mean. I was in my room all night."

"Not when I saw you. You were at the corner of the library, plastered up against some—from what I could see—totally hot guy. Spill it." Caroline set her magazine down, her gaze challenging Suzy to deny it.

"It was most likely just someone who looked like me." Suzy brushed it off.

"I thought that at first, but then I saw your lime green scarf and knew without a doubt it was you. What's the big deal? You were making out with a hot guy; it's not like you were doing anything wrong—wait, were you? Who was he?" Caroline sat up and leaned close, her eyes glinting with intrigue.

Suzy glanced at me, her eyes pleading for help. I shrugged my shoulders apologetically.

"Suze?" Caroline pressed.

"If she doesn't want to tell, she doesn't have to. Sometimes sneaking around can be sexy and exciting. She'll tell us when she's ready," I said. In my opinion, sneaking around loses its appeal rather quickly.

"Bollocks!" Caroline dismissed my words.

I put my hands up in the air and conceded defeat.

Caroline was on a mission and about to pull out the heavy artillery when Suzy finally caved.

"He's a professor." She buried her face in her hands.

"One of yours?" I ventured. She didn't say anything, only nodded her head. "Oh, boy."

"Are you serious?" Caroline softened her voice.

"I don't know how it happened. I went to talk to him about a problem I was having. The next thing I knew, we were kissing." She lowered her hands, her cheeks flaming. "I guess you were right, Evie."

"About what? I never said go date a teacher."

"No." She laughed. "When you said I probably just needed an older man to date."

"Ew, how old is he?" In my mind I was picturing one of the sixty-plus crowd that filled a good portion of the faculty positions.

"He's twenty-eight and an adjunct professor," she answered on the defensive.

"Well, that's better than what I was thinking. I was picturing wrinkles, white hair, and tweed coats with elbow patches."

"Ew, no." Suzy wrinkled her nose and laughed. "Well, he does look pretty hot in a tweed coat actually."

"What's his name?" Caroline picked her magazine back up.

"Leo. Leo McMurty," she mumbled.

The breeze had picked up and I could see goose bumps on Caroline's skin. "You guys better be careful. What happens if you get caught?"

"I'm not sure. But I think he'd lose his job." She frowned.

"He must like you an awful lot if he's willing to take that big a risk." A twinge of jealousy streaked through me.

Caroline gasped and closed her magazine abruptly, tucking it under her arm. She stood and began to pull the blanket out from under us. "Okay guys, I'm ready to go in. You're right, I'm freezing."

"Are you okay?" I asked. Caroline never admitted someone else was right.

"I'm fine, why?" She looked up innocently as she wrapped the blanket around herself.

"What's going on?" Suzy eyed her warily.

"Nothing. Come on, let's go. Brrr."

Suzy and I exchanged a glance, then followed Caroline back to the dorms.

In the common room I spied Preston and Marissa. *Is Edmund back?* Stopping, I waved, then realized the girls hadn't stopped. In a rush, I caught up with them on the stairs.

When we reached Caroline's room she opened her door and immediately threw the magazine in the trash.

"Did something in there upset you?" I grabbed it from the bin and scanned the pages.

"Evie, you don't want to read that," Caroline cautioned.

"Why ever not?" I flipped through the pages and discovered why. I stood there and stared. Not wanting to believe what was so plainly before my eyes.

"That's why." Caroline's voice sounded flat and disappointed.

Suzy came to my side to see what all the sudden drama was about.

"Is that Edmund?" Suzy grabbed the magazine, pulling it in her direction.

The photo was of Edmund on a yacht with a group of friends I'd never met. He was smiling, an arm draped around a very scantily clad Jax. Her bikini left little to the imagination, and I do mean *very little*.

The back of my throat burned and my eyes stung. *Why didn't he tell me she was there?*

"Looks like he's having fun." Suzy's brow creased with worry. "Those are the kids of his parents' friends. They're awfully wild. Edmund got into a spot of trouble with them when he was younger."

Caroline sat at her desk. "I wouldn't go to the next page if I were you."

I glanced at her and nervously turned it. I knew it'd be painful, but clearly the masochistic part of me just had to do it.

Under big black letters saying, "Apparently The Grass Isn't Greener in the States" was a picture of Edmund and Jax. Kissing. Edmund's hands were gripping her shoulders and her arms were just starting to wind around his neck. I sucked in a sharp breath as my stomach churned.

What the hell?

"Have you guys seen Edmund?" I asked, fighting to stay calm and not cry.

"He hasn't gotten back yet," Suzy answered as she took the magazine from me.

I was glad she'd taken it. I didn't want to see Edmund with Jax draped all over him. *Are they together now?*

"It's probably nothing." Suzy rubbed my shoulder. "I know it's hard, but try not to jump to conclusions. The press can make anything look horrible."

She was right. I knew without a doubt there was probably more to the story, that tabloids can't be trusted. But a big part of me was hurt and angry. I looked at Suzy and blew out a deep breath, nodding. "You're right, I know you are."

"I'd be narked," Caroline chimed in. "He's kissing her."

It'd be so easy to lose my cool over this. But truth be told, I found it hard to believe. *He wouldn't intentionally hurt me.* At least that's what I kept reminding myself.

"It could be the angle that made nothing look like something." Suzy looked pointedly at Caroline. "Are you okay, Eves?"

"Right now, I'm fine." I grabbed the magazine and rolled it in my hands. "Ask me again after I talk to Edmund for my final answer." I slapped the roll against my thigh. "Why don't we go get some dinner and see a movie? I need to get my mind off this." Sitting alone stewing in my room was the last thing I wanted to do.

"Evie? You there?" It was late when Edmund knocked. "I just got back and wanted to see you."

I went to the door and paused. Standing in my pajamas, hand poised at the knob, my nerves took over. They'd been *kissing*. What if he says his parents convinced him to give Jax a chance?

I shook my head. *Stop being a chicken and answer the damn door.* I took a deep breath and steeled myself. Opening the door a crack, I poked my head out.

He stood there smiling, looking amazing.

"Evie."

Seeing his face sent a shiver of happiness through me. It scared me how much I'd missed him.

I pulled the door open the rest of the way and he walked toward me, opening his arms. Palm on his chest, I stopped him. "We need to talk."

"Okay, about what?" He looked confused by my less than eager reception.

I spoke calmly, despite my erratically thumping heart. "About why you didn't tell me Jax would be on the yacht with you."

"I didn't know she was coming." He shook his head, his eyes searching mine.

My eyebrows drew together. "I'm guessing you knew she was there when you were texting me."

He shrugged his shoulders. "It wasn't a big deal. At least I didn't think it was."

I reached into my trashcan and pulled out the magazine. I thrust it at him, cover up. The magazine had blurred out the head of the girl with the headline: Who's Prince Edmund's New Love?

He flipped through it, scowling. He stopped at the picture of them kissing. Sighing, he said, "It's not what it looks like. I mean, yes, she tried to kiss me, but I was pushing her away. You've seen her firsthand do this. This is all bollocks." He chucked it back in the trash.

I sniffed. "I get that. But if I'd known she was there, I'd have been better prepared. Honestly, I'd expect her to try something like this. But not telling me . . . it feels like you're trying to hide this from me. That's what bothers me." I crossed my arms over my chest, protecting my heart.

"I didn't want her to be there and I most certainly didn't want her to kiss me. You have to believe me."

"I want to, I really do. But . . ." *But what?* I rubbed my hands over my face, feeling tears burn my eyes. *I'm acting like a jealous girlfriend, and I'm not even his girlfriend. What the hell am I doing?* Tired and frazzled by a life that felt like it was no longer mine to control, my mouth went on autopilot. "Do I even have any right to be irritated by this? I'm not your girlfriend." I closed my eyes and sighed, rubbing my forehead. This was too difficult and I needed sleep. "You know, maybe we should go back to when we were strictly friends. Simplify things for a while."

"Wait, what are you saying?" He took a step in my direction, his face screwed up in confusion. He extended a hand toward me, pausing before he touched me, and let it drop.

"I don't know." I slipped a hand through my hair. "I'm struggling to balance everything and I'm hardly ever here. You, you're making out with the girl your parents would love for you to be with. This . . . it's just not . . . good. I can't do this."

"Evie." My name left his lips in a hoarse whisper. "Please."

"I'll see you at breakfast." I turned wearily away from him.

He clutched my arm before I could close the door on him. "Being just your friend will never be enough for me. You are so much more than that. Maybe we never put a label on us, but that doesn't mean we aren't something more." His hand reached up and cupped my cheek. "I'll back off, if that's what you need, but we're far from over."

I sucked in a breath, my eyes watering. An overwhelming wave of emotion crashed over me. I couldn't handle anymore. Missing Dad, stressing over school, never seeing friends, craving Edmund, trying to please Clarice, learning to be a duchess, and now Jax resurfacing—it was too much.

Tears trickled down my face. Silently Edmund enveloped me in his arms. We stood in my doorway, him holding me. When I stopped crying he looked at me very seriously.

"I won't lose you."

I looked up at him, not sure what to say.

"How about this. Get some sleep. We'll talk about this later." He dropped his hands from my shoulders.

My desk phone rang. Turning, I lifted a finger to Edmund. "Wait a second." It was nearly midnight; this couldn't be good. "Hello?"

"Miss Gray?"

"Denby?" I didn't try to disguise my surprise.

"Yes, Miss." He sounded exhausted. "I'm afraid I have some bad news."

I felt a lump settle in my throat. Clarice must be sick, maybe she'd been taken to the hospital. "What is it?"

The normally unflappable butler sounded on the verge of tears. "It's your grandmother, Miss. I'm afraid s-she's no . . ." he cleared his throat. "She's no longer with us."

"What? When?" My knees went weak and I sank into my desk chair.

"Late this afternoon, Miss." Denby sniffed.

I shook my head. "Why wasn't I told earlier? I should've been there."

Edmund sat on my couch and watched me, his brow furrowing.

"There wasn't time. After you left, she went to lie down and was unresponsive when I went to rouse her. When the ambulance arrived, her pulse was very weak. They got her to hospital, but she passed before they could do much of anything. I'm so very sorry, Miss Evie."

My vision blurred. Taking a deep breath, I asked, "Can I come to the house?"

"But of course, Miss. The house is yours now."

"Okay. Um, I'm going to try to get down there soon. When's the funeral?" I didn't look at Edmund, but I didn't need to. His hand found mine and he clutched it tightly.

"It hasn't been sorted out yet, Miss."

"Will you need my help with that?" I wondered how I'd plan a service for a woman I'd barely gotten to know.

"No, Miss, your grandmother sorted everything out a long time ago."

I cleared my throat. "All right, please keep me updated. I'll see you soon."

"If you need anything, Miss Evie, don't hesitate to ring me."

"Thank you, Denby." I sniffled, trying to stop the snot from running onto my upper lip.

"Jeeves, at your service, Miss." He softly chuckled.

I smiled through my tears and barely managed to answer, "Thanks."

Clarice and I weren't close, but I was still glad I'd gotten to know her a little. The tears I shed were for what might have been, what *should* have been. I closed my eyes and took a slow deep breath.

Edmund leaned closer, waiting for my reaction. I blew out a breath as I met his steady gaze.

"Clarice?" He reached over and rested a hand on my leg.

I nodded. "She died this afternoon."

"I'm so sorry. Is there anything I can do?"

I met his watery blue gaze. *What did I want from him?* I wanted him to hold me and stay the night with me, but that blurred the lines of my "let's just be friends" notion.

"I think it's best if you go."

A pained look crossed his face. "Are you sure?"

I nodded, unable to speak.

"If that's what you really want." Unsure, he stood and went to the door. "You need to know something. The only reason I haven't yelled it from the rooftops that we're together is for you. To protect you. You think the press are insane now?" A dry laugh left his throat. "I saw what they did to Lauren and my brother. I don't want that for you. Not until you're ready." Looking back once, he left.

As the door clicked softly behind him, I curled on my bed and sobbed, regretting this whole conversation.

What have I done?

Chapter Twenty-Five

Finality

I hate funerals.

From the back of a black Town Car, I stared out the tinted windows. The church was a short drive ahead, but we were in a long queue of similar vehicles. Clarice might've been an old harpy, but there were hundreds of people here for the service.

Closing my eyes, I thought back to the last time I did this. I was only six, but I remember my mom's funeral. I wore a little white dress with pink rosebuds on it. Dad told me she'd picked it out specifically. He said she wanted me to look happy, not sad. There was a picture of it. Dad was holding me against his side, talking to Abby's parents, his eyes rimmed with red, my head leaning on him, looking lost and sad.

Sorrow descended over me and a tired heaviness settled in my chest.

Will Edmund come?

The morning after Denby phoned, I'd left for London. Edmund had called and messaged me, but I'd been inundated with lawyers, household employees, and numerous people—strangers really—coming to pay their last respects. When I could answer the phone, we were interrupted. My texts were quick one-word replies.

I really hope he comes.

The driver stopped in front of the church and came to open my door, his eyes not meeting mine. Photographers flanked the entry. *Who'd want to photograph a funeral?*

I climbed the steps to the church. A few people who'd visited the townhouse saw me and nodded with tentative smiles. Some even came over and hugged me, like they knew me.

Since coming to England, this was the loneliest I'd felt. Dad offered to come over, but I told him not to bother. Clarice would've sat up in her coffin and shooed him out.

I walked down the hardwood aisle and sat in the front. The first few pews were ribboned off, reserved for family and close friends. I was relieved her lawyer, Thomas Collingsworth, and Anton were sitting there already. I'd spent so much time with them recently they felt like family. It also meant I wouldn't have to sit alone.

"Hello, Thomas, Anton." I nodded.

Anton stood and hugged me. "Evie."

"Your Grace." Thomas smiled warmly.

Him calling me that still startled me. Heck, when anyone did, it threw me for a loop. I shook Thomas's hand and sat next to Anton.

Organ music reverberated through the large stone church as people took their seats. I glanced back at the doors, hoping to find a familiar face from school. I wasn't counting on it, though; finals were too close.

The benches filled quickly. I spun around and saw the bishop come through the side door near the pulpit. *Here we go.*

I blew out a deep breath. Today had just begun, yet I was drained.

"Have you given any thought to the advice I gave you, Your Grace?" Thomas leaned around Anton and spoke softly.

"I have, and I agree. I intend to keep her staff on at all the houses." Houses, plural. Clarice was like a female Daddy Warbucks. My bank account now held a staggering amount of money and I was officially the Duchess of Westminster. My life was unrecognizable from the one I'd known when I'd first arrived in England.

What seriously blew my mind was that from my title alone I made an income—a very large one. It apparently had to do with the land I now owned. And I owned lots of it. Well, I would once I got my dual citizenship sorted out. In addition to all this land, I now had the townhouse in London, Welsington Manor in Brighton, a villa in Italy, an apartment in Paris, and a cottage in Ireland.

What the hell am I gonna do with all that?

"I think that's a wise move." Thomas's eyes crinkled as he smiled at me.

"Agreed." Anton gave my knee a comforting pat. I was glad he was here.

I felt someone sit beside me on the end of the pew. I turned to say hello. My pulse jumped. *He came.* Edmund wore a black suit, but it may as well have been silver and metal, because at this very moment, he was my knight in shining armor. My shoulders relaxed and I gave an appreciative nod.

"Is this okay?" he whispered, as the church dramatically quieted.

I didn't trust my voice at the moment, not with my eyes stinging. With a small smile, I nodded. He knew I was about to cry. Taking my hand in his, he squeezed it tight and gave me his endearing grin.

"We are gathered here today to remember a remarkable woman. The Duchess of Westminster, Clarice Augustine Eustace Goddard Elliot."

The bishop continued to speak, but the only thing I could concentrate on was Edmund. I didn't have to face this by myself. He came for me.

Afterwards, he didn't leave my side as I accepted the condolences of Clarice's friends and acquaintances.

"Do you mind if I ride with you to the gravesite?" Edmund whispered in my ear at a break in the mourners.

Clarice had arranged to be buried next to her husband, Maxwell. They would spend eternity together in a small churchyard in Brighton, near their country estate.

"Please do," I said, glad I wouldn't be alone with my thoughts.

Anton approached us and gave Edmund a nod. "Your Highness."

"Anton." Edmund shook his hand.

Turning to me with a smile, Anton reached in his jacket pocket. "Evie, I must apologize. I've been carrying this around with me, meaning to get it to you, but it kept slipping my mind." Out came a letter. *My final quest letter.*

I took the envelope from his hand and stared at the scrawled number six on the back. "I forgot about it, too. Thank you, Anton."

"Of course. I'll see you at the gravesite."

I nodded. As Anton left, I saw the bishop on a path toward us.

"Your Highness." The bishop addressed Edmund, then turned to me. "Your Grace, we'll be ready to proceed to the burial site shortly, once people are finished paying their last respects." He inclined his head toward the coffin where people were standing, waiting to have a moment of silence, prayer, or whatever with Clarice.

"Thank you." I nodded.

"Have you had a chance to say your goodbyes?" Edmund asked as the bishop walked away.

"I have. Last night, I went to the funeral home with Mr. Collingsworth and Anton to make sure everything was to Clarice's exacting specifications." I smiled at the memory of the long list of dos and don'ts regarding her funeral.

"I'm glad." He lifted my hand and pressed his lips tenderly to the back of it before releasing it. Once the majority of mourners left, Edmund asked, "Are you ready to go?"

I nodded. "Yeah."

Edmund guided me down the church steps then helped me into the car. He grabbed my hand again and we sat in silence as the car wove through the crazy London streets, taking us toward the motorway and *my* country estate. I still couldn't believe all this.

In the end, it hadn't been as much of a choice as Mom thought it'd be.

Edmund's deep voice startled me. "My timing is crap, I know, but we have a bit of a drive ahead of us and this is making me mental. Can I ask you something?"

I nodded, curious where this was going.

"This only friends thing, are you sure it's what you want? Because I don't."

I stared at my hand in Edmund's and shrugged. "I'm tired and burnt out. I haven't had a chance to think of anything but Clarice and her estate."

Edmund turned to face me; his eyes never left mine as he spoke. "There is nothing between Jax and me. If you look at the picture, my hands are on her shoulders because I'm pushing her away. She and I agreed to be friends and *only* friends. I told her how I felt about you."

How about telling me how you feel? In all the months I'd been here, neither of us had really said anything about our feelings. Yet here he is confiding in *her*, which bothered me.

When I didn't say anything, he continued. "You have nothing to worry about."

I stared into his eyes, unsure what to say. A warm itchiness overtook my body. I pulled at the collar of my dress with my free hand. The car seemed to shrink and close in on us. "Give me time to process everything. Right now, I just . . . I can't."

He gave my hand a reassuring squeeze.

I stared out the rain-spattered window. My stomach churned. I needed to get out of the car, get some fresh air into my lungs.

My hands were starting to sweat, as was my upper lip. I ripped my hand from Edmund and leaned toward the driver.

"Can you pull over, please?"

"Now, Your Grace?" The driver's eyes met mine in the rearview mirror. The "Your Grace" was the final straw. I wasn't sure I wanted this life. I hadn't been able to properly breathe since I'd met Clarice. I needed space.

"Yes, now," I said louder than I intended. Softening my voice, I added, "Please."

"Are you okay?" Edmund looked worried.

"I just can't be in here right now."

The car pulled off the road. As soon as it was going slow enough that I wouldn't kill myself, I opened the door and jumped out.

I walked down the embankment into someone's pasture, surrounded by green grass and tall trees, not caring where I went. My heels sank into the soft, damp earth. Inhaling deeply, I continued to put distance between the car and myself. Rain softly pattered on my head and misted my skin.

"Evie, where are you going?" Edmund caught up to me, slightly out of breath.

I stopped and turned to face him. "I just can't do this. All the drama with Jax, Clarice's death. I'm a freaking duchess now. What the hell am I supposed to do with that? I miss my dad, school is slowly killing me, and everyone's calling me 'Your Grace.' I just . . . I just don't know if I want any of this." I walked over to a low stone wall and sat down, mindless of the wetness, burying my face in my shaking hands.

Edmund sat next to me quietly, letting me catch my breath.

"I'm sorry." I don't know why I was apologizing. Edmund put his arms around me. Dropping my hands, I laid my head on his shoulder and wept.

"*You* have nothing to be sorry for. I'm the one who's a bloody sorry git." He stroked my hair, trying to calm me down. "Evie, you'll be a great duchess. You'll figure it out. You're intelligent and kind. You can't go wrong with that combination. You're an excellent student, we can study together, and you'll ace the exams like you always do."

I looked into his face, my eyes welling with tears.

"Your dad would fly over here in a heartbeat if you needed him. You'll get through this. It feels like a lot right now, but you're going to be incredible. You always are. And you'll get used to the 'Your Grace' thing. It just takes time." He leaned down and gently kissed my forehead. "Take all the time you need. I'll wait for you. I promise."

I closed my eyes, took a deep, cleansing breath, and slowly blew it out.

"I'll always be here for you. *Always*."

I curled back into his arms. One day at a time, that's how I had to do this. Right now, I just wanted him to hold me.

Chapter Twenty-Six

A Royal Pain in the . . .

I switched my phone to the other ear, took off my diamond stud earring, and placed it on the desk with its mate. Edmund and I'd just got back from Brighton. The clock glowed a red four-thirty in the morning.

Down my back, I slid the zipper of my black dress. Today had done me in.

Dad answered on the first ring. A clear indicator of how concerned he'd been. We didn't talk much about the funeral. After I assured him I was fine and didn't need him to fly over, the conversation took an unexpected turn.

"I saw the pictures of Edmund and some girl. They seemed pretty friendly. What's that about?"

Kicking my dress in the direction of my hamper, I said with a tired sigh, "I guess she tried to kiss him or something." I slid into my pajama pants and pulled the phone away from my ear while I changed into a worn, baggy, black T-shirt. "At the moment, we've decided to be just friends."

"Just friends?" He sounded surprised.

I slumped onto my bed. "Yeah, I need time to get my life sorted out."

Dad huffed. "If he hurts you, I'm going to hurt him."

"I'll warn him." I chuckled.

"He better treat you right, friend or boyfriend."

Silence blanketed us. I didn't know what to say.

"I want you to take it easy." His office chair creaked. He must've leaned back.

"That's not really an option." I groaned as I sat on the side of my bed. "How've you been?"

"Aside from worrying about you? I'm good." He cleared his throat. "Um, I actually wanted to talk to you about something. Do you remember Mrs. Therazauld?"

I laughed. "Of course I do. She only lives across the hall and babysat me every day after school while you worked."

"Right, well, I ran into her recently and we decided to grab some dinner. She's quite an interesting woman. I never realized. It's been nice to have her company. I guess you could say we're seeing each other. You don't mind, do you?"

Sliding between my sheets, I turned my desk lamp off. "No, it's time you started dating again. I was worried you were becoming a recluse."

He sniffed. "You know me too well. It'll be good to have you home. Well, until the fall at least."

About that. "Dad?"

"Yeah?"

I hesitated. "Do I have to come back to Oxford next fall?"

"What?" His voice rose in surprise. "Why wouldn't you want to go back?"

I sighed. "It's just my life here is so out of control and chaotic. Plus, I miss you, and home, and Abby, and . . . just everything."

"Sweetie, the choice is up to you, it always has been. I'm not going to tell you where to go to university. If you want to come home, fabulous. I'd love to have you closer. But I think you'd find there's a lot at Oxford you'd miss just as much. Don't make any decisions because of what you're feeling right now. Think it over."

What if I'd already made up my mind?

"Please tell me you're not spending the weekend in London." Caroline came and sat next to me at our lunch table, her short yellow dress reminding me of a ray of sunshine.

"Why? Do you have plans?" I asked groggily. It'd been a week since Clarice's funeral and I hadn't been sleeping well. My brain wouldn't shut off. I couldn't stop pondering leaving Oxford for good, being just friends with Edmund, and kicking Jax's interfering ass.

"Darling, I always have plans." Caroline grinned wickedly.

"She's still dealing with Clarice's estate, aren't you?" Suzy sat, opened her bottle of water, and took a sip.

"According to the lawyers, things are mostly finished. So, I'll be sticking around here and trying to catch up."

"Are you planning to run it like your grandmother did?" asked Preston, who'd been sitting silently at my side.

I shook my head. "She didn't run it, not really. My grandfather had it all set up, with a business manager, estate managers, the works. Right now, I'm going to let them keep doing what they do. Then I'll slowly figure out what to do with it all."

"Deal with things as they present themselves. Sounds like a good plan." Preston smiled and patted my hand.

"Where's Edmund?" Suzy asked Preston as she looked around.

"Um, he sort of had plans." He shifted uncomfortably.

"God, Preston, you suck at trying to hide things." Caroline rolled her eyes. "Spill it."

Preston sighed and looked at us. "Jax is in town and they're getting lunch together. Please, don't shoot the messenger. I'm no happier about it than you guys. Besides, I don't think he intended for me to find out. I ran into them on my way here."

"Jax is here? Why?" I asked.

"I haven't the foggiest, but Edmund looked pissed. He wasn't pleased to be with her, if that's any consolation."

It wasn't. Why couldn't she just disappear? "Whatever." I shook my head and smiled, hoping my disappointment wasn't obvious. "What's everyone's summer plans?"

As they talked I only partially listened. *Just friends were they? I don't have to worry . . . right. Why the hell isn't Edmund telling her to buzz off?*

"What about you, Evie?" Preston pulled me back into the conversation.

Summer. "Um, I'm bound for Seattle."

"Wouldn't it be easier to stay here over the summer?" Caroline asked.

Not if I'm not coming back. "Probably, but I need to be home."

"At least you'll be back in the fall. Hey, us girls should get a flat together; that'd be fun." Suzy bounced happily in her seat.

Only if I'm here.

I walked into my last class and looked for Edmund, curious how his lunch with Jax went. He sat in his usual seat, but he wasn't alone.

You've got to be kidding me.

Jax sat next to him, in my chair, clinging to his arm. I stared at the backs of their heads, anger spreading from the pit of my stomach.

I ducked back in the foyer, trying to decide what I should do.

Do I sit next to him anyway? Pick a new seat? Skip class altogether?

As much as I wanted to call it a day and go back to the dorms, I couldn't. Finals were coming and I needed the lecture material.

Plus, why should I let her win? She may be trying to push me out, but I certainly didn't have to let her. I flipped around and marched back into the auditorium.

"We missed you at lunch." I slid in front of Jax and went to sit on the other side of Edmund.

He opened his mouth to answer, but Jax was quicker. "I couldn't resist coming and kidnapping him for lunch. You know, just friendly like." She smiled, her gaze icy, and did an awkward shoulder shimmy.

Edmund turned to gauge my reaction. His brows furrowed and his lips frowned. "She surprised me this afternoon."

"What else brings you to Oxford, Jax, aside from kidnapping Edmund?" I smiled sweetly and flipped my desk top down with a bang.

"Well, the old gang of ours is up here this weekend for a party. Oh, those were the days weren't they, Eddie?"

Eddie? Blech. My upper lip curled at the endearment.

She rested her hand on his bicep possessively. I wanted to smack her like a bug and squish her to a skid mark.

"We used to get into such trouble with them. Do you remember the time Mimi got so plastered she could barely walk?" Her head tilted back as she cackled. "We had to carry her out of the nightclub and Tyler just tossed her into a cab and sent her on her way. So hilarious. I don't remember where she said she woke up."

Edmund shifted uncomfortably in his seat.

"Oh, and what about that time on bonfire night? I think we had a little too much fun, didn't we? Well, the nude photos suggest we did." She snorted a giggle and leaned over to nudge his shoulder. "If I remember right, your parents were livid and had quite the struggle to keep that one under wraps."

Edmund wasn't smiling, reliving the good ol' days with her. His mouth was set in a grim line. He looked pissed. "It was also when I stopped hanging out with them."

"You should come out with us this weekend, for old time's sake. That is, if you're finally done slumming it." She pointedly looked at me.

"What did you just say?" Irritation laced his voice.

Feigning innocence, she opened her eyes wide. "What do you mean?"

"You know what? Enough. I've tried to make it clear and tried to be nice, but I can't take it anymore." Angling himself toward her he said, "I don't want to do this with you. I never have. You and I both know we're not really friends and we never will be. I'm done being nice solely for our parents. And I don't care how awkward things are when we're around each other. Don't call, don't text, and *definitely* don't just show up."

Jax looked up at Edmund her eyes squinting. "But—"

"No, Jax, no buts. I'm so bloody done with you. I know you tipped the press off about Evie's grandmother. I'm not stupid."

My mouth involuntarily popped open.

He knew?

"You take pleasure from hurting the people I care about most. That's not okay. You aren't anyone I want to be friends with. And it's well past time you left." Edmund turned in his seat and gave a nod to his security team. They came down the aisle and escorted a shocked Jax away from Edmund.

"Don't touch me!" She slapped at their hands. "My parents will be very disappointed, Edmund!" Jax hollered, her voice echoing in the auditorium.

"I don't give a monkey's arse what your parents think. They can bugger off with you for all I care." Edmund turned and noticed our professor standing, waiting at the front. "My apologies, Professor."

Reaching over, Edmund grabbed my hand and gave it a squeeze.

Okay, that was hot.

Chapter Twenty-Seven

A First

Only a day and a half left in England. The sunset hit my window, casting shadows on my walls. I sat on my bed studying for my only remaining final. It was a miracle I'd ever managed to catch up with all my coursework. Edmund was due any minute so we could quiz each other. These would be my last moments with him.

Possibly forever.

Since my brilliant "let's just be friends" plan, he hadn't tried to kiss me. Not even once.

It royally sucked.

I missed him.

So, my plan for my last hours at Oxford was to cram every last minute as full of him as I could. Preferably, kissing would be involved. I just hadn't figured out how to achieve that goal.

"You ready to study?" Edmund's head popped in my open doorway.

Smiling, I scooted closer to the wall. "Yup, come on in."

He shut the door, then came over and sat beside me on the bed. Pressed against each other, I shivered at the warmth from his body. *Goodness, I want him to kiss me.*

"I can't believe the year is over or that you're heading home tomorrow." He was so close I could smell his minty breath.

I sighed and shook my head. "It's all been a bit of a blur."

He angled his body toward me; his steady eyes met mine. "I feel like I've wasted a lot of time."

My eyebrows scrunched together as I turned toward him. "How so?"

Edmund tossed his notebook and text next to mine on the bed.

"It's just that I . . . I didn't do this right." The look on my face must have prompted him to continue. "Us. I feel like I made a right cock up of it."

I looked at my lap, not sure how to reply. "Are we in that bad of a spot?"

"Evie, friends isn't enough." He tilted my face up and whispered, "I want you. All of you. I always have."

He cupped my face, running a thumb softly over my bottom lip. My pulse quickened as he hovered momentarily before slowly coming down to kiss me.

When his lips met mine, fireworks shot off inside me, and a breathy moan left my lips.

How I missed this.

It may have started soft and sweet, but quickly morphed into the whole world seeming to dissolve around us. A rumbly sound in the back of his throat sent a tingle, like a shockwave, down my body.

Edmund trailed soft kisses down my neck onto my collarbone, his hands slid under my shirt, caressing the bare skin of my back. My breath caught and I closed my eyes, savoring his touch, memorizing it.

I twined my fingers through his hair. His lips returned to mine. I shivered as he lifted my top little by little. Where our skin touched, flames ignited. His lips left mine only long enough for him to slip my shirt over my head. Where it ended up I had no clue, nor did I care.

I was completely lost in him, his touch, how he tasted of spearmint and smelled like summer sunshine. He felt warm and wonderful under my hands. I couldn't focus on anything except how close he was to me, and how I wanted him closer still.

Holy shit, is this really happening?

Tugging at his shirt, I lifted it over his chest, craving his skin on mine. Once it was off, I tossed it across the room. Edmund resumed kissing me, his fingers running along my spine. I startled when his fingers stopped at my bra strap.

Noticing my surprise, Edmund pulled back; breathing heavily, he met my gaze. "Is this okay? We can stop if you want."

Stopping wasn't an option. I wanted all of him.

Not trusting myself to speak, at least not coherently, I leaned into him and kissed him, my tongue swirling with his. A tremble coursed through him. His hands snapped my bra open, then went up to tangle in my hair, holding my mouth against his. His kisses became feverish and desperate.

Closer. I had to get closer.

Leaning me back on the bed, his body covered mine. The feel of him was intoxicating. Pressing himself up, he smiled cheekily at me. I raised my hands and pressed them against his smooth chest, running them down his torso, exploring his body. He closed his eyes and took a shaky breath.

I loved that my touch elicited such a reaction. It was a power I didn't realize I had until now.

Opening his eyes, he reciprocated the exploration, his fingers leaving a trail of goose bumps. "You're so beautiful."

With the palm of his hand, he followed the swell of my hips through my jeans and over my tummy. Bending over, he kissed the sensitive skin just below my belly button.

I couldn't breathe. I was dizzy with wanting him. My heart thundered in my chest. It felt on the verge of exploding.

God, I hope I'm doing this right.

Edmund pushed himself back up, inhaled deeply, and slowly blew the breath out. I leaned up on my elbow and, with one finger in his waistband, pulled him back down to me.

"Evie." His voiced sounded hoarse. He trembled as his body came back into full contact with mine.

He whispered my name as he slowly placed kisses down my body, places no one had seen until now. His fingers reached the button on my jeans and he flicked it open.

This was uncharted territory for me. *What is he expecting? Should I tell him?* I worried I wouldn't know what to do, that my inexperience would be painfully obvious.

"Wait." I stopped him.

He lifted his head and looked at me closely, breathing heavily. "Are you sure you're okay with this? You look nervous."

I laughed softly. "I'm very okay with this, but I-I just, I thought I should warn you."

"Warn me? About what?" His brows lowered in concern. I would have laughed if I wasn't feeling so embarrassed.

I looked everywhere but his eyes. "It's just that, I may not be very good at this."

"You're bloody marvelous so far; why on earth would you think that?" His face was close, and he sounded surprised.

I hesitated. "Because I've never done this before." I scrunched my eyes shut.

Edmund was silent a short moment. "Evie, that's nothing to be embarrassed about. Look at me, please."

When I opened my eyes, he held my face in his hands.

His voice raspy, he whispered, "I'm honored to be your first."

My last exam now over, I was catching a red eye late tonight. The walls of my room were bare as Suzy and Caroline helped me finish packing.

My brain kept skipping back to last night and to Edmund. This morning I awoke to an empty bed, no clue where he'd gone. *God, what was I thinking? Does he regret it?*

I saw him at our final, but we were forced to sit every other seat, so we didn't get a chance to speak. When he finished first, he left. I hadn't seen him since.

"I wish you'd stay the summer," Suzy said, latching the front of my trunk.

"A part of me wants to. But I need to go home, see my dad and Abby." *Plus, I'm not sure I can see Edmund again. Not after we . . .* "September isn't far and I'll probably be back next year."

"What do you mean by *probably*?" Caroline stopped mid-motion and turned to watch me. "You're coming back, right? You transferred here; you have to."

My shoulders shrugged. "I might transfer back to Seattle Pacific."

"I didn't realize you were even considering it." Suzy sat on my bed, a picture frame clutched in her hands.

"Does Edmund know?" Caroline scooted to the edge of the couch.

"No, I haven't said anything."

"I don't understand what there is to decide? Edmund's here and you're a duchess now; you *have* to come back." Suzy's eyes were wide.

"My life was so uncomplicated and drama-free in Seattle. I miss that." *And I just went and made things exponentially more complicated with Edmund.*

"Fine, forget Prince Charming, forget your title, come back for your friends." Caroline lobbed an angry ball of my clothes into my suitcase. "Complications are what keeps life exciting."

"Yeah? Well, I'm about to OD on excitement, if that's the case. Besides, right now, a break might be the best thing for Edmund and me."

"How so?" Suzy asked.

"It'll give me a chance to think, maybe help us sort things out." *Especially after last night.* I shook my head with a shrug. "I'm so in love with him I can barely see straight. I know a label shouldn't matter, but right now it does. What are we?" *Did sleeping together change anything?* If he were asked, would I still be just a friend?

"We've always thought of you as his girlfriend. Does that count?" Suzy wrapped another picture frame in bubble wrap.

I wish it did.

We stood outside a nearby pub. I tucked my brown corduroy jacket around me and flipped my hair over a shoulder, dreading the impending goodbyes. Especially Edmund's. Dinner had been tough. Arriving last and lugging all my travel bags, I'd chosen to sit across from Edmund instead of next to him. I could barely bring myself to look at him. Which he'd definitely picked up on.

"I can't believe you're really leaving." Suzy, tears running down her cheeks, wrapped me in a hug.

"You'd better come back next year, or I'll be flying to Seattle to drag your arse back." Caroline threw her arms around Suzy and me, all three of us now in tears. "You better keep in touch."

"I will, I promise." I stepped back, glancing at Edmund, who was signing an autograph, not paying attention to us. Just being around him brought back memories and made me nervous. *What does he think of me now?*

"Do you want us to take you to the airport?" Caroline continued.

"No, I was just going to grab a cab."

Suzy smiled. "We're coming with you."

I shrugged. "Let's move the party to the airport, then."

Marissa hugged me. "I'm meeting a friend for a last-minute study session. So, I'm gonna say bye." She gave me a serious look. "I'll see you in the fall."

"Good luck with your finals."

She hopped in the cab Caroline hailed for her.

"Hey, Marissa, wait," Preston called. He stopped and grabbed my hands. "I'd come to the airport, but I've got an early exam."

"No worries." I wrapped him in a hug.

"Fly safe and have a fun summer." He gave me one last tight squeeze and a kiss on the cheek.

"Bye, Preston." I sniffed, close to tears as he climbed in the cab with Marissa.

"I can't believe you're leaving." Edmund reached over and brushed my hair behind my ear, making me tremble. "Would you two mind giving us a moment?"

Suzy and Caroline nodded as Edmund and I climbed into his waiting Town Car.

His brows lowered and he grabbed my hands. "What's going on? You've barely looked at me all day."

I kept my gaze on my lap, nervous. "I woke up this morning and you were gone. I guess I assumed you regretted . . . everything."

"God, Evie, no." He squeezed my hands. "Last night was *the* best night of my life. I had a blasted final this morning. Trust me, nothing else could've pulled me from your bed."

Glancing up at him, I smiled, relief flooding my senses. "Really?"

"Really." He leaned forward and placed a lingering kiss on my lips. When he pulled back, his face looked confused.

"Wait, didn't you get my note?"

I shook my head. "I didn't see any note."

"I left it on your desk. On top of the stack of study notes."

Closing my eyes, I could guess what happened. I'd piled my notes there once I'd finished an exam. I didn't even think to look at them. "Caroline. She must've packed my desk up before I saw it."

"Ah." He placed another kiss on my forehead. "Speaking of Caroline, I'd like to know what she meant by you'd better come back?"

I sucked in a deep breath. "You heard that?"

Nodding, he said, "Kind of hard not to."

Breathing deeply, I looked into his blue eyes, focusing on the copper flecks, and bit my lip. "I might stay in Seattle in the fall. Enroll there again."

"What?" His face contorted with uncertainty.

"I-I haven't figured it out yet." I pulled my hands from his and studied my fingernails.

"I didn't realize this was up for negotiation. Were you even going to tell me?"

"I was . . . when I figured it out."

Edmund grew quiet and looked everywhere but at me. He opened his mouth several times just to close it again.

My vision blurred and I cleared my throat. "I should get to the airport."

Edmund nodded and reached to open the car door, then stopped. "So, this might be the last time I see you? How can I let you just walk away?"

"Edmund—"

Grabbing me, his mouth covered mine as his arms tightly pressed me against his chest. I gripped his shirt, a shiver coursing its way through me, settling low in my tummy. *Yes, this is what I want. What I need.*

My mouth willingly opened to him. One of his hands snaked up to coil in my long hair. The other splayed over my back. My arms curled around his neck as a moan escaped my throat.

"Evie," he whispered against my lips. "Please don't go." His mouth pressed against mine, stopping any reply.

If he continued kissing me like this, he could make me do anything.

"Ahem, sorry to interrupt, but we should probably get going." Suzy leaned into the car. I'd been so absorbed I hadn't heard the door open.

I pulled back, my brain clouded, and my heart completely torn in two.

"I'll be right there," I answered breathily.

Edmund looked gutted. "You really won't stay?"

"I can't," I whispered. "I need to be home, need to see my dad. And I never said I definitely wasn't coming back." I tried to smile, but knew it was shaky at best.

Suzy backed out of the car as Edmund clasped my upper arms. "Please?"

"Edmund, I can't." A tear trickled down my cheek and I felt my throat constrict. "I'll keep in touch, I promise."

I flew out of the car with a sob and dragged Suzy behind me. I had to get out of there, away from the pain in Edmund's eyes.

Chapter Twenty-Eight

Home

Random snorts and snores from passengers disturbed the peaceful silence of the darkened plane. We were supposed to be sleeping. Pushing on my overhead light, I rummaged through my bag, looking for gum. My fingers collided with Mom's letters. I pulled them out and set them on my lap, smiling. A familiar pang of loneliness twisted in my chest.

Untying the ribbon, I realized the final quest letter sat atop the stack.

I never read it.

I picked it up and slid my finger under the flap. Two folded pages slid out, one with my name on the front, the other with Dad's.

Darling Evangeline,

These letters were my attempt to gradually draw you into my world. To give you a mostly unbiased look at the Elliots and what the Duchess of Westminster is about. I couldn't bear the thought of this being thrust upon you with no knowledge.

Your grandmother was far from a perfect mother and most likely a completely absent grandmother, but as a duchess, she was exemplary.

After I met your father, the life of a duchess couldn't compete. It wasn't until I understood what love was that I knew what I wanted.

I refused to marry someone I could never love, despite how that would've pleased my mother. Instead, I gladly relinquished my claim to the family title.

I knew one day Clarice would come searching for you. She has few other options. You are her rightful heir. It's my job to prepare you, even if I'm not there.

The main thing I want you to know is this is your choice. Clarice can't force you to become a duchess.

You may wonder why you should take the title when I ran away from it. Truth is, I always expected to be the next duchess. I was excited about it, actually. When I told Mum about Henry she made it clear I'd have to choose. That if I left, returning wouldn't be an option.

My choice shocked her.

I never told your father about my family's title. I should have. At the time I was terrified he'd make the choice for me. Then over the years I tried to tell him, but after a while I failed to see the point. And now I'm sorry telling him has fallen upon your shoulders. Inside the envelope I've tucked a letter to give to him. Hopefully, it will help him understand.

Just know you don't have to make a choice. Be the duchess, marry whomever you like. A world of infinite possibilities awaits you.

Let your heart guide you and know that whatever you choose, your father and I will always love you regardless.

My heart will always be with you.

Love,
Mom
xoxo

Folding the letter, I smiled and wiped a tear off my cheek. I was the duchess she wanted to be. *For her,* that's why I ultimately took the title. *I'm glad I did.* It connected us.

The man in the seat beside me mumbled in his sleep. I glanced at him, tied up my letters, and slipped them back in my bag. Hitting the light, I was ensconced in darkness once more.

Leaning my head against my seat, I looked out the window. Moonlight illuminated the fluffy clouds. It may sound silly, but being up here, I imagined myself physically closer to her.

"I'll make you proud, Mom," I whispered. Kissing the pad of my thumb, I pressed it to the window. "Love you."

After two layovers and nearly nineteen hours traveling, I was home. I rushed through Sea-Tac Airport, eager to see Dad. Weaving through the other travelers, a pang of sadness hit me. I missed Oxford. I missed my friends. I missed my whole life there.

Edmund's face as he asked me to stay flashed before my eyes. My heart shattered, remembering what I'd done. I freaking ran from him. *What the hell is wrong with me?*

Slowing my pace, I tried to push Edmund from my mind. It was no use. Our night together kept tripping through and throwing me off balance. I stopped and leaned against a wall, taking a deep breath.

I'm back in the States, I'm home, I'm supposed to be happy, dammit.

I shook my head, inhaling deeply. Dad's first glimpse of me shouldn't be a teary-eyed, miserable Evie.

Pulling myself together, I made it through customs and in the distance spied the baggage claim. Dad was there, his back toward me, still wearing his suit from work. I walked faster, feeling brittle, as if I could break down at any moment.

He turned to scan the crowd and saw me. His face cracked into a smile and he headed for me.

"Dad." I ran and dropped my carry-on bags before I threw myself into his arms, squeezing my eyes shut.

"Evie, my girl." He chuckled and wrapped me in a hug, spinning me around. "Let me look at you." He held me at arm's length. "I'm so glad you're home. How were your flights?"

"Long. The last one was the worst; small plane, lots of turbulence." I shuddered. "I can't believe how much I missed you."

"I've missed you too." He ruffled my hair.

I blew out a long, tired breath. "Let's go home; I'm exhausted." I started for the baggage carousel, but Dad grabbed my hand and stopped me.

"Not quite. There's something I should tell you."

On the verge of tears, I was surprised Dad hadn't asked what's wrong. I looked exactly like I felt. Like crap.

Sighing, I asked, "Do we have to talk here? Can't we do this at home? I need to get out of this airport." I felt myself choke up. Could even hear it in my voice.

He shook his head, his eyes soft as he took in my fragile state. "No, we should deal with it now."

"Fine, lay it on me." I shook my head and slapped a smile on while attempting to blink back my tears.

Dad stepped to the side.

In a rush, the air was sucked from my lungs.

Edmund.

It was him. He was here. Standing in my Seattle.

"You aren't the only one who flew in today," Dad said quietly.

I walked over to Edmund, my heart slamming in my chest, my vision blurring as a tear trickled onto my cheek. "What are you doing here?"

Reaching up, Edmund wiped the tear away. "I wasn't about to let you walk out of my life not knowing if I'd ever see you again." He grabbed my hands and pressed his lips to the backs of them. His thumbs made circles where he'd just kissed, as if rubbing them in. "You *must* know." His eyes searched my face. "You really don't see it, do you? Evie, you make me happier than I have ever been. I love you. I want *you.* God! I'm so blasted in love with you."

I sucked in a sharp breath. *He loves me.*

Throwing myself into his arms, he pressed a kiss on my cheek, then slid his mouth to mine. On contact, I melted into him.

Right here, this is where I'm meant to be.

He held tight to me, as if afraid he might lose me. When he pulled back I looked into his eyes and whispered, "I love you too."

His smile took my breath away.

A year ago if you'd told me I'd fall in love with a prince and that he'd love me, I'd have called you crazy. Or that I'd be a duchess? Positively mental.

But somehow, here I am, living my very own fairytale and about to embark on a happily ever after with my prince charming.

But this isn't an ending. Oh no, it's just the beginning.

Mom was right, the world is full of infinite possibilities.

I'm living proof, *anything is possible.*

Happiness Is Right Where You Left It

Before I knew it, Edmund and I were back in England. Our summer in Seattle had swept past in a blur of sunset walks, exploring museums, watching movies while cuddling on the couch, and nights in Edmund's suite.

Glancing around my dorm room, I smiled. *This is definitely where I belong.*

It'd come as a bit of a shock to discover the life I'd left behind in Seattle didn't exist anymore. Dad had Clara, and Abby was so busy with school, work, and her new boyfriend that I barely saw her over summer break.

"You ready to go?" Caroline leaned in my open doorway and checked her watch.

Edmund, Marissa, and Preston were sharing an off-campus flat. I suspected Caroline and I would be spending a lot of time there together. Tonight, we'd been invited over to celebrate surviving the first week of school.

"Yup, let's go." I tucked my sapphire blue leather clutch under my arm and locked the door behind me.

Sitting in the cab, Caroline giggled. "You totally came back because of Edmund, but I don't care. Whatever it was that brought you back, I'm just glad it did."

"It wasn't just Edmund. I realized this is my home." I patted her knee. "Is Suze coming tonight?"

"That's the plan. I think she's bringing her professor. He's nervous about it. I guess he *actually* likes his job."

"I hope he comes; I'm dying to meet him."

Caroline smiled and put on a fresh coat of burgundy lipstick.

We rolled up to a fashionable townhouse. It reminded me of mine in London. *That's still so surreal.*

Caroline paid the driver, bounded up the front steps, and knocked. A man I didn't recognize opened the door as I caught up to her.

"Hello." He pushed his wire-rimmed glasses up on his nose.

I knew this was the right place, but I still double-checked the house numbers. "Hi?"

"I'm Leo." He offered his hand, which Caroline took first.

"Oh, you're Suzy's . . ." I faltered, unsure how to finish. "Friend?"

He smiled and shook my hand. He was as adorable as I thought he'd be. With slightly messy brown hair and a kind smile, he looked like someone who belonged with Suzy—sweet and unassuming.

"I'm Evie; this is Caroline."

"Nice to meet you both."

Edmund came over and pulled me in the door and into his arms, spinning me around. I squealed with delight and kissed him. Leo and Caroline vanished, giving us privacy. Kissing and whispering, we spent a few minutes sequestered in the entryway.

"Did you bring an overnight bag?"

I bit my bottom lip and shook my head. "I guess you'll have to come to my place."

"Deal." His eyes twinkled as he ushered me toward the back of the house where everyone had gathered.

Leo and Suzy stood apart, talking and smiling. The way he looked at her told me he was crazy about her. In the kitchen, Marissa and Caroline stood feeding each other. And Preston had spread out on the couch, watching a movie.

He so needs a girlfriend.

Looking up, Preston spotted me and hopped up to give me a quick hug. "How was your first week?"

"Can't complain. Yours?"

"I survived." He chuckled.

Squinting my eyes, I blurted, "Why didn't you bring a date tonight?"

Preston cleared his throat and glanced at the floor, his cheeks coloring. "The girl I'd like to bring is a little too far away."

"Really? So there *is* a someone?" I tried not to sound shocked.

"You could say that." He brushed it off. "I'm gonna grab a drink. You want anything?"

"We're good," Edmund replied.

I turned to Edmund. "Did you know about this girl?"

He nodded. "He met her in Scotland. I don't know much more than that." He leaned closer, his lips brushing my hair. "I'm just relieved he's moved on from you."

I looked at him and rolled my eyes. "Please, his attention wasn't on me for long."

"You'd be surprised." One of Edmund's eyebrows arched.

By the end of the evening, Suzy and Leo finally relaxed enough to cuddle on the couch, cautiously. Meaning, their legs touched.

Caroline and Marissa had retired for the evening.

"You ready to head to your place?" Edmund came up behind me and kissed the side of my neck as Preston and I cleared the table and straightened the kitchen.

"I am. Why don't we walk back? It's so nice out."

He nodded. "I'll be right back." Edmund ran upstairs to grab his backpack and, I assumed, to stuff in the essentials. "Night all," he called as he returned to my side and grasped my hand.

"Good night!" chorused through the house.

"Let's cut through the park," Edmund suggested. Security in tow, we veered around an ivy hedge into a public garden.

Lampposts lit our way, guiding us toward the small creek trickling through. A warm breeze lifted my hair. I loved late summer nights like this. I stepped onto the wooden bridge and stopped, looking up to admire the stars.

"I have something for you," Edmund said.

"Really?" I turned, thinking he wanted to kiss me.

"I came across this the other day; it made me think of you. I want you to have it." From his pocket, Edmund pulled out a small navy leather case and handed it to me.

"Oh." I took a tiny step back. This was unexpected. My heart fluttered and my eyes darted up to his. A smile filled his face as I flipped up the lid.

I gasped. A glittering necklace stared up at me from a bed of white satin. My fingertips ran over a large, cushion-cut blue topaz: my birthstone. Wreathed around it were baguette-cut diamonds. I'd never held something so sparkly or so beautiful— or, I suspected, so real—before.

"Edmund," I whispered. "It's beautiful." I covered my mouth with my hand.

"It was my grandmother's favorite necklace; she wore it all the time. Blue topaz was her birthstone, too."

I glanced up at him and shook my head. "This is too much. I can't." I closed the lid and tried to hand it back. "It's way too special; it wouldn't be right. This should stay in your family."

"You are far more special to me than any necklace or bauble. I want to share a piece of my grandmother with you. She would've

adored you," he whispered as he slipped the necklace from its case. Taking both ends of the chain in his hands, he leaned in and brushed my hair aside. Reaching behind me, he clasped it. Once it was secure, he placed a kiss on the side of my neck. "It suits you; I want you to have it. And who's to say I'm *not* keeping it in the family?"

My eyes watered. *Did he just say what I think he did?* I clasped the pendant between my fingertips.

"I love you so much." I stood on my tiptoes and kissed him.

"I'm glad you like it."

I chuckled. "I don't like it, I love it. How could I not?"

Edmund captured my lips in another kiss, this one more demanding. His fingers twined in my hair and he breathlessly broke his lips from mine. "Let's get to your room."

"Smashing idea." I smiled.

Edmund pulled me to his side and we walked down the path, our arms around each other. I was right where I should be. And more importantly, thanks to Mom's quests taking me halfway around the world, I'd found exactly where I *wanted* to be. *Home.*

The End